# TEN STEPS TO HAPPINESS

Daisy Waugh is a journalist and author. She lives in London and has two magnificent children.

DAISY WAUGH

# TEN STEPS TO
# HAPPINESS

(in a Safe and Healthy World)

HarperCollins*Publishers*

HarperCollins*Publishers*
77–85 Fulham Palace Road,
Hammersmith, London W6 8JB

www.**fire**and**water**.com

A Paperback Original 2003
1 3 5 7 9 8 6 4 2

Copyright © Daisy Waugh 2003

Daisy Waugh asserts the moral right to
be identified as the author of this work

A catalogue record for this book
is available from the British Library

ISBN 0 00 711905 4

Typeset in Giovanni by Palimpsest Book Production Limited,
Polmont, Stirlingshire

Printed and bound in Great Britain by
Clays Limited, St Ives plc

For Peter de Sales La Terrière
with love

# Acknowledgements

Hammersmith and Fulham Council, though I bitterly resent its parking fines, was incredibly helpful in the research of this book and I am very grateful – most especially to Environmental Health Officer Claire Godfrey, who sent me so much useful literature, answered hundreds of questions and, most generously, let me accompany her on several of her inspection tours. She was intelligent, friendly, elegant and utterly sane. So Claire, if you read this, please don't be offended.

Many, many thanks also to Dr Lauren Turner and Dr Arabella Onslow. Also to Kristy Jell and Jamie Donald, Pat Van Hoey Smith and her colleagues at Somerset County Council, Jamie Hibbert, Layland Branfield, Terry O'Leary of the London Fire and Emergency Planning Authority, Bob Bacon of the British Hospitality Association, Imogen Edwards-Jones, Charles Campion, Patrick James, Anthony Harwood and Tanith Carey, Ian Cook, Glyn and Kate Howells, the HSE (Health and Safety Executive) for its prodigal supply of 'free' information sheets, Maxine Hitchcock, Fiona McIntosh, Esther Taylor, Martin Palmer, James Prichard and Jane Harris.

And special thanks to Lynne Drew, Clare Alexander and of course to my magnificent husband, Peter.

Since writing *The New You Survival Kit*, in which the imaginary village of Fiddleford features in a small way, I have discovered that in Dorset there is already a village called Fiddleford. I only hope it's as lovely as the Fiddleford of my imagination, which is not in Dorset but much further from London, near an imaginary town called Lamsbury, in a distant and imaginary county which I purposely haven't named.

## MISSION STATEMENT

### (i) To acquire, facilitate and maintain:

- an anxiety- and stress-free, healthful being-state in no less than 10 (ten) self-existent increments, the causal effect of which shall enable and release feelings of increased personal confidence, thereby leading to dynamic rebranding and repackaging of integrated learned responses to all living experiences.

# YES!!

**because HAPPINESS *is* achievable!**

AUTHOR'S NOTE: TO MAXIMISE EFFECTIVENESS AND ENJOYMENT OF THIS SIMPLE, STEP-BY-STEP PROGRAMME PARTICIPANTS ARE FIRST INVITED TO . . .

# • . . . CONJECTURISE AN OPTIMAL CONTEXT

**February 2001**

Imagine a moment of perfect happiness with no past and no future and no thoughts of time ebbing away. With no thoughts of anything. No conscious thought at all. An instant of perfect happiness. Soft breeze. Soft sea. True love. True laughter. Giant turtles. And so on. These moments come once in a while to the very, very lucky. Of course they don't usually last for long.

Jo Smiley and Charlie Maxwell McDonald, on the fourth day of their honeymoon, were lying in the moonlight on a small, empty, private beach in Mexico, only recently disturbed from their canoodling by the sound of a giant turtle dragging its hefty weight across the sand towards them. Its progress was slow and they watched it for ages before Charlie said – whispered, quite seriously, as if it were some new discovery:

'It's *definitely* coming towards us.'

Jo started giggling because they'd been watching intently all this time. There had never been any question where it was headed.

5

'Why? What's so funny?' he murmured, turning to look at her, and then because he loved her, and he loved her laughter, starting to laugh himself.

The turtle stopped still. Silence.

'Oh. Now we've frightened it,' said Jo.

'Or it thinks it's frightened us. Either way we should set its mind at rest.'

Slowly they stood up and tiptoed back to their hut. It was a magnificent hut. Booking into this simple-looking corner of Paradise had been the most extravagant thing Charlie had ever done. He had imagined that his elegant, metropolitan wife, who until recently had been thriving in the luxurious world of Public Relations, would have been disappointed with anything less.

But he underestimated how much she loved him. Jo Smiley knew all about creature comforts, as fine-looking, highly effective, well-connected thirty-one-year-old London PR women are prone to. Jo had spent a lot of time and clients' money in some of the smartest restaurants and hotels in the world. But that was all in the past now. And anyway it wasn't the point. She would have been happy with Charlie anywhere. *Anywhere*. To have found a companion like Charlie; unworldly, unpretentious, tall, dark, funny, wise, kind and handsome (of course) was without doubt the greatest luxury of all.

In fact when Jo looked at Charlie and imagined the bucolic life which lay ahead of them she felt light-headed with hope for the future. The house they would be living in was beautiful; crumbling and uncomfortable and an insatiable swallower of cash, but it was lovely, and destined shortly to be lovelier still. When they returned to England she and Charlie were going to set to work restoring it. She and Charlie were going to build a dream-place together. Not only that, they were going to make it pay.

So when they weren't watching tortoises or doing all the other things which enhanced their perfect happiness, they were talking about the future of Fiddleford Manor. It had been home to Charlie's family for over two hundred years and now it was theirs and to keep the roof from caving in and everything else from falling apart, they were turning the house into a business. They were going to open the place up as a refuge for anyone in hiding from an angry public, or a baying and bullying press.

Jo envisaged a stream of tearful popstars, politicians and football managers knocking at the Manor door. She envisaged comforting them in a newly refurbished kitchen. With green tea, and Cristal champagne (if they wanted). And home-made flapjacks, perhaps. She envisaged Fiddleford Manor becoming a part of modern mythology, a perfect haven where no media was admitted and where suffering celebrities had to plead to be allowed in.

'I was thinking, Charlie – don't you think,' she said some time later, as they wallowed in the beach hut's circular sunken bath, 'we could have a sort of meditation room. With very, very quiet spiritual music playing. And candles. A sort of multi-denominational-non-faith-specific *chapel* effect. Because people are going to be feeling very troubled when they first arrive to stay with us. They might appreciate a nice, quiet place to sit and think . . .'

'It's an idea,' Charlie said tactfully. 'If that's what you want. But the bedrooms are pretty big, remember. If they want peace and quiet they could just stay in their rooms—'

'And do you agree, Charlie,' said Jo, who hadn't been listening, whose mind had already moved on, 'I was thinking maybe we could *ban* anyone who's been in *Big Brother*. On principle. Do you think? Or do you think that's a bit mean and snobbish?'

'Big brother,' repeated Charlie vaguely. *'In* big brother . . .'

'The telly programme.'

'The *telly* programme . . .' It didn't ring any bells. 'Anyway, we're supposed to be open to anyone, if they need us. And if we can fit them in. That's the whole point.'

'Quite right. We'll just have to hope and pray they never realise they need us. I had another idea, though. Lovely idea. We could wire the house so it's all on the same sound system. With speakers in every single room – can you imagine? So you've got music which is really beautiful – upbeat-but-ethereal – and it's playing everywhere! In the kitchen, the bathrooms, the hall. Everywhere. All over the house. Wouldn't that be amazing?'

'So *upbeat* ethereal in the multi-faith-non-specific chapel?' he said, smiling lazily. 'But with the volume turned very, very low?'

*'Non*-faith-specific,' she corrected. 'You think it's a stupid idea.' She didn't mind. She had a thousand new ideas for the refuge every day, and so did he. Some of them were practical – they were going to have to build a couple more bathrooms. Most of them were pretty stupid. 'I think we should employ a pilates instructor, don't you? Live-in. Nobody will want to go to a retreat which doesn't do yoga and pilates, however much trouble they're in.'

'Grey McShane didn't seem to mind.'

'Grey's different. I love him, but he's a lunatic. And an alcoholic. *And* he came to stay when it was still a house and he wasn't paying.'

8

'He's paying now.'

'No, but he wasn't then. Anyway he's a friend, he doesn't count . . . By the way I don't suppose he mentioned anything to *you* about moving out did he, before we left?'

'Not exactly, no. I think he and Dad are both assuming they're going to stay on and help run the refuge, since it was partly their idea. Dad says he'll move into the cottage, but I'd be surprised . . .'

'Well.' Jo shrugged. Grey wasn't a problem. She felt less enthusiastic about sharing a house with her intractable father-in-law, who didn't like her and never would make any attempt to hide it. But he was old and lonely. He'd lived at Fiddleford all his life. And Charlie, who loved him, was all the family he had left. So he thought she was – whatever he did think. She didn't care. She thought he was a fascist buffoon. They squabbled virtually every time they spoke, but it was harmless enough. Sometimes she wondered if they both didn't even enjoy it. Either way she certainly wasn't going to force him out. 'It doesn't matter, does it?' she said. 'It's not like the house isn't big enough.'

'Grey wants to pay to put high voltage electric fencing all around the park.'

She smiled. 'Can't blame him after what they put him through.' She sighed. 'Poor sod. I think we should find him a girlfriend.'

'And *I* think,' Charlie laughed, slowly leaning across the bath towards her, 'with his track record he's more than capable of finding one for himself . . .'

And they lapsed into silence, and through the opened windows the breeze softened, the turtles frolicked, and any thoughts of the past and the future slowly ebbed away . . .

9

**Accident** – an unplanned, uncontrolled event with the potential to cause injury, damage or other loss.

**Control** or **control measure** – an item or action designed to remove a hazard or reduce the risk from it.

**Reportable accident** – one that must be reported to the appropriate enforcement authority.

*Health and Safety First Principles Workbook, Chartered Institute of Environmental Health*

(i)

# • UTILISE A SAFETY-FIRST ENVIRONMENT

**Spring 2001**

Fiddleford Manor lay deep beneath snow. The boiler was broken, the house was freezing, the roof was leaking and there was a policeman at the bottom of the drive. Jo and Charlie had returned from their Mexican honeymoon only three weeks earlier, besotted, euphoric, absolutely one hundred per cent in love. And yet, as she looked out at the frozen landscape and the heavy, grey, endless sky, she thought for the first time of the perspex desk she had left in Soho, and of the low-fat, high-concept working lunch she would have been enjoying at exactly this moment six months ago, and briefly, treacherously, found herself wondering if she might have been better off staying in London, where mass cullings never interrupted the running of things, and where there was always emergency hot water at the gym.

A ludicrous thought, of course. And wrong, too. Jo loved her new life. She loved her new husband – of course. And she loved her old house.

It would have been difficult not to. Fiddleford Manor,

built from the warm red local stone nearly three hundred years ago – vast, elegant and mostly held together by ivy – nestled magnificently inside its own landscaped park and, beyond that, a small and unspoilt and entirely unprofitable agricultural estate. There was a rose garden and a small lake with an old rowing boat to one side of the house, and a decrepit Victorian stable yard with its own broken clock tower on the other; at the front the long, wide lawns stretched past one towering cedar tree and the occasional jungle-like rhododendron all the way to the river bank. The house was a mile from the local village, where there was a church and a school and a small shop, four miles from the market town of Lamsbury and thirty-seven miles from the nearest train station, in the neighbouring county of Devon.

But right now Devon, like everywhere else, was out of bounds. The whole world was out of bounds. Ever since the man from Trading Standards had managed to struggle up the drive, with his appalling lilac-coloured office shirt, his appalling 'Form A', and his disinfected Wellingtons, it had been against the law for anyone to come on to or off the estate without a licence. And what with everything else that was going on, the entire countryside and every bureaucrat related to it in tailspin, no one had seen fit to grant a licence to the plumber. So the inhabitants of Fiddleford, Jo, Charlie, their difficult friend Grey McShane, and Charlie's difficult father the General, huddled together in the kitchen, shivering and waiting.

They had been waiting for three days now. Or five days if you counted from the first telephone call, which was when everything really started changing. It came as they were finishing dinner. The General, who was meant – though he still showed no signs of it – to be in the process of moving into a large cottage at the end of the drive, had said, 'Who the bloody Hell calls at this hour?' and Charlie had gone off to find out. He came back into the dining room twenty minutes later, looking very bleak.

'MAFF,' he said simply.

Nobody spoke.

'They've found a case of foot and mouth at Tom Shattock's place. They're sending a man round here in the morning.'

His father groaned.

'But, listen, you never know.' It sounded very hollow. 'We might be fine . . . We might be absolutely fine.'

'Poor old Shattock,' murmured the General. 'And it's definite is it? Confirmed case?'

Charlie nodded. 'Plus there's another one suspected. It's definite all right.'

The morning after that, while a Ministry vet inspected their cattle, Charlie led the lilac-coloured Standards man into the library. He'd wanted to know the exact whereabouts of every livestock animal on the estate: for 'future reference', he said; 'in the event of evidence leading us to suspect . . .' But they both knew what that meant. Charlie had been as helpful as he could. Or as he could bear to be.

He listed everything. Every single one of their 542 sheep, including the pregnant ewes, the three-day-old lambs, the seventeen rare and precious Dorset Horns. He told the man about his prize-winning dairy herd, and about his magnificent Jersey bull. He even mentioned his beloved twin sister Georgie's billy goat which since her shocking death (in a riding accident a year and a half ago) had been

15

bought a nanny companion and allowed to roam freely among the animals.

'And that's it?' said the lilac man, clicking the top of his stainless steel pen and slipping it neatly into his lilac pocket. 'Nothing else? No pigs?'

'No.'

'No new calves unaccounted for?'

'No. None I haven't mentioned.'

Lilac man offered a measly smile: 'No nasty surprises lurking in forgotten corners anywhere? It's a sizable estate.'

Charlie averted his eyes. He was a rotten liar, and he hated lying, but there were two animals he'd left out, whose existence at that particular moment was causing his body to break out in a cold sweat. Caroline and Jasonette, an ancient couple of Highland cows, had been wandering the park at Fiddleford ever since he and his twin sister were ten. They had been delivered, all those years ago, as a birthday surprise from their mother: twin calves, one for each of her twins. He and Georgina used to spend hours with them during the holidays, lounging around on their hairy backs, taking them on picnics (or taking picnics on them). They pinned photographs of their cows on their bedroom walls at school.

Once, when the twins were still small, and the cows were still calves and the sun was always shining and his twin and their mother were still alive, someone had left the front door open and both animals had been discovered looking bewildered, side by side in the middle of the hall. Their mother (the General had been away at the time, or it never would have happened) hadn't yelled about the valuable paintings or the boring Japanese urn on the side table. She'd behaved as if everything was completely normal, as

16

if the two little calves were making a perfectly ordinary social call.

She opened the door to the drawing room, since it was 'nearly drinks time', and invited the calves to come in. They followed her, the way calves do. The children had fetched bowls of milk from the kitchen, and the five of them had stood about beneath the portraits of disapproving soldiers, while Mrs Maxwell McDonald conducted a jolly conversation with all of them, exactly as if she had been entertaining the local vicar. Charlie and Georgie thought it was the most topsy-turvy thing they'd ever seen. They thought they would die from laughing. And the calves had looked so sweet and confused in the middle of that big drawing room, and their mother had looked so happy. It was one of the last memories they had of her before she fell ill. She must have died less than a year later . . .

Charlie looked out of the library window over the frozen hills to where the village lay, and the church, whose tower he could see, and the churchyard where his mother and sister lay side by side . . . He looked back at the lilac-coloured penpusher, with his measly lilac-coloured grin.

'Nasty surprises?' he said coolly. 'At Fiddleford? Certainly not.'

The Ministry vet checked in with Jo and Charlie at the end of the same day. He'd not completed his inspection yet, he said, and he would be back first thing in the morning to finish off.

'No signs yet, though,' he said. 'So fingers crossed.'

It gave them false hope. They all four drank too much that night. And then in the morning the vet returned

17

and within minutes he'd found one of the heifers was limping.

She could have trodden on a sharp stone. More than likely, she had trodden on a sharp stone. Or one of the other cows might have kicked her. Or she'd woken up feeling stiff. It could have been any number of things. But the people from the Ministry weren't willing to take the risk. Later that night came the official confirmation. There would be no need to take further tests. The limp was evidence enough. Death warrants had been signed and the slaughtermen were booked for Wednesday morning.

Since then, time for everyone at Fiddleford had been passing abnormally slowly. Jo wandered the house with her notebook, making obsessive and pointless notes about facilities which might be required for her future paying guests. Grey and the General, for lack of tabloid newspapers to argue over (their favourite – almost their only – pastime for several months now), were reduced to watching housewives' television. Charlie, meanwhile, dealt with the animals, the farm workers, and the people from MAFF.

On Monday evening he telephoned the Ministry to inform them that the heifer's limp had disappeared. On Tuesday evening he called again to inform them there were still no signs of infection among any of the other animals. But it was too late. That night the last of the animals were herded together into outhouses. The pyre was already built, and the sheep crushes and the cattle stocks lay waiting.

The snow turned to sleet that evening, and a cruel wind blew. Grey McShane, in a futile attempt to lighten everyone's spirits, had lit a fire in the dining room. There was no food in the house, since the garden was covered in three feet of snow, and nobody was allowed out to go shopping. But Grey found an ancient tin of spaghetti at the back of the larder, which he plopped into a saucepan and burnt and then, with absurd fanfare, carried through to the dining room.

He doled out a plateful to Jo, who looked at it for several minutes and then suddenly leapt from her chair and ran out of the room. Charlie found her vomiting over the kitchen sink.

'Are you all right?' he said.

'I'm fine. Completely fine. You go back in.'

'Was it the spaghetti, do you think?'

She laughed.

'Oh Christ, Jo, I'm so sorry. This must be awful for you.'

'It's fine. *Please*. Never mind me. I'm fine . . . I'm fine.'

'We could get a licence and you could go and stay in London until it was over.'

'Certainly not!' She made an effort to smile, but the smile turned into a retch. 'Oh, God—' She retched again. 'I think I'll go upstairs.'

Jo ran to her bedroom and only just reached the basin in time. She stood there for a while, recovering, thinking, examining the splashes of vomit at her lovely, Mexican-tanned feet. She straightened up, wiped her mouth and, before she could change her mind yet again, headed over to the wardrobe and pulled out the testing kit which had been languishing there, driving her crazy, since the day before the MAFF people first called.

Afterwards she didn't quite know what to do. Call her mother? No. Anyway she was away in El Salvador, taking artistic holiday snaps. Burst in on Charlie – and Grey and the General – in that freezing cold dining room? Definitely not. Have a bath?

There was no hot water for a bath. She decided to go straight to bed. She took off her uncomfortable urban clothes (skintight jeans @ £125, stripy cashmere jersey with pointless zip and hood), which were so incredibly ineffective in her new rural life, and replaced them with a pair of pyjamas and every jersey she could find in Charlie's cupboard.

She lay awake for what felt like hours after that, trying to persuade herself it was real, trying to feel what she was meant to feel – fulfilled and magical and womanly and blessed, trying not to feel terrified of how her life, which until she met Charlie had always been so painstakingly well structured, seemed so quickly to be slipping out of her control. But then somehow she must have fallen asleep because she woke with a start at about three o'clock to discover that Charlie still hadn't joined her.

Out on the icy landing she could find no sign of him either. The house was quiet. The vast, stone-floored entrance hall beneath her was shrouded in black. She bent over the banister and thought she saw a faint crack of light coming from beyond the back lobby, and then suddenly, from the same direction, she heard the muffled sound of something large crashing to the ground.

'. . . Charlie?'

The house was old – especially the back part, the part where the noise was coming from. Among her many strengths (her warmth, her determination, her well maintained contacts book and, though she felt far from beautiful that night, her delicate elfin good looks), Jo was

20

a practical woman, not remotely given to superstitious anxieties. But she was terrified.

'. . . *Charlie?*'

No response, just a distant shuffling, followed by a long, low moan.

'. . . *Charlie!*'

Slowly, carefully, in almost total darkness, she followed the sound as far as the back lobby, where she paused for a moment. She could hear breathing very clearly now: heavy, quick-fire, phlegmy breathing, like a sleeping giant. The back lobby led on to the kitchen, and beyond that to the pantry and the boot room, and from there to the stairs which went down to the cellars. The thin stream of light was coming from the cellars, somewhere Jo and her notebook had not bothered to venture before.

Tentatively, she walked down the steps and found herself in a large, dank room cluttered with what looked like pieces of rotting furniture. There was a room on either side of her, both of them in darkness, and in front of her, a miserable, decaying corridor. She could hear the noises coming from beyond it: the breathing, someone hammering and then Charlie, 'It's OK, girl. It's OK. Take it easy. Just a bit of noise. I'll be done in a sec.'

Which was when she finally saw them. Dwarfing the corridor and the small room at the end of it, dwarfing Charlie: two old Highland cows, covered in cobwebs and flakes of rotting paint, puffing after their strange exertions.

Charlie looked up. 'Jo!' he said. 'It's— How are you? I thought you were asleep.'

'What the fuck are you doing?' she asked.

'What? Me? Nothing.'

21

'*Nothing?*'

'Shh! You'll frighten the girls.'

'The *girls?*' Gingerly, to ensure that she wasn't dreaming, she edged forward and put out a finger to touch one of them. It responded with a friendly grunt and by wiping its damp nose on the sleeve of her outer jersey. She snatched her hand away quickly. 'Charlie, they're not girls, they're cows. What are they doing in the cellar?'

'Jo . . . You're wonderful.'

'*What?*'

'I'm just saying—' He hesitated. 'This has nothing to do with you.'

'Are you *hiding* them?'

'Please. Mind your own business.'

'What if they're infected?'

'They're not infected. They've been nowhere near any other farm animals for almost twenty-five years. But I'm going to let them work out their quarantine down here, just to be sure.'

'Don't be ridiculous, Charlie. We've got to get these cows back in the shed where they belong—'

'They're not going anywhere.'

'Apart from anything else it's not— I mean they're probably not going to make it through the winter *anyway*. It's not worth it.' Charlie glared at her and, without another word, turned back to his hammering. He was trying to fix a plank over a large air vent, but every time he hit the nail, chunks of wall fell out. She watched him for a while. 'I'm sorry. I don't mean to be—' She paused to think of the right word, but all she could come up with was 'realistic'. She decided not to fill the gap.

'You must be freezing,' he said over his shoulder.

'I'm fine, Charlie, my darling. That's not really the point.'

'I know it isn't.' He turned back to face her. 'The point is I've got to get this place soundproofed before morning. So please. Seriously. I love you and everything. But either give me a hand, or – go away.'

She looked at the old cows, so gentle and decrepit, their heads and necks still bobbing rhythmically from the trouble of getting down the cellar stairs, flakes of paint the size of saucers hanging off their enormous horns. She looked at Charlie, so utterly in earnest. A year ago, in her more black-and-white days, she might easily, at this point, have decided to bring in the police. That night she didn't know what to do. The cows couldn't do any harm, working out their quarantine down here in the cellar, and the idea of getting them out again, and then tomorrow of watching Charlie lining them up for the stocks . . .

'By the way, Charlie,' Jo said sulkily about a minute later, sounding absurdly, self-consciously casual. They were squeezed between the cows and the decaying wall, trying together to fix the soundproofing plank without causing the whole rotten cellar to disintegrate. 'I'm pregnant. *Already*. OK?' (She was embarrassed; it was embarrassingly quick.) 'I only mention it because we'd better not get caught. I mean I'm definitely not going to prison over this.'

The extermination process was a long and horrible one, beginning before dawn had properly broken, and not ending until dusk on the following day. First to be slaughtered was the dairy herd. It took seven men five hours to dispatch them. Les, the Fiddleford farm hand, would set

23

each one on her journey, steering her the hundred-odd yards through the snow, down the steep path, to the makeshift stall where Charlie stood ready to slip her head into a brace. She would be injected with sedative and then led from the stocks to the land in front of the pyre, as close as possible to the body of the cow which had preceded her, where she would be shot in the head.

Nobody spoke much. The animals rolled in, the animals rolled out, the bodies piled up. The Ministry people had seen it all before. They'd been doing it every day for weeks, which isn't to suggest that they were enjoying themselves. But it was a job with an hourly rate. It wasn't their twin sister's billy goat who was waiting in the yard to have its brain scrambled.

Grey McShane shuffled out to the killing fields just before noon, by which time the slaughterer's regulation white body suits were soaked in blood. He should have been wearing one himself. One had been left by the back door for him. But Grey was not fond of orders.

In fact he was wearing a Prada suit which had lost its buttons and a pair of the General's old gumboots. He was carrying a bottle of gin, as he always did, and his big black coat was dragging in the mud behind him. One of the Ministry men hurried across the field to intercept him.

'It's strictly no access without the suit,' he said, inadvertently wiping the blood from his cuff across his nose and forehead. 'I'm sorry, sir. Someone should have told you. The clothes will have to be burnt now.'

'What clothes?'

'The er— suit. Everything. Sorry. Regulations.'

24

'Aye,' muttered Grey distractedly, walking politely around him.

Having offered Charlie his help, and been greatly relieved when it was rejected, Grey had intended to play as supportive a role as he could in the proceedings, but from inside the house, as far away from the smell of blood as was supportively possible. Looking at the carnage, the rows of bodies, the white-suited men with their disinfectant sprays and bloodstains, the sound of the gun, he was finding it very hard to stay focused. He wished he could turn back, but a crisis was developing and he needed Charlie's help. He took a deep swig at the gin to stop himself from vomiting. He looked back at the Ministry man. 'Where is he, then?'

'Who?'

'Where's Charlie?'

'Charlie?'

'Charlie,' he said coldly, 'is the man whose animals you're in the process of exterminatin'. Charlie Maxwell McDonald.' Grey glanced disconsolately around the field. 'Where the fuck is he?'

'He's round the corner, by the stocks. But you really can't— I must insist—'

Grey, thirty-eight years old that summer, had been quite famous once, when he was thirty-seven. Like his friend Jo, he was a refugee from London, from the successful people's party circuit, but unlike Jo, who'd thrived in it for ten years or more before she pressed the ejector button, Grey McShane had lasted only a matter of weeks. An enormous, miraculously handsome Scottish ex-jailbird, alcoholic and former tramp, he was 'discovered' by a handful of fashionable opinion makers, drunkenly reciting his own poetry outside a well-known theatre in Islington. Not long afterwards, Phonix Records had hitched itself onto the McShane bandwagon and offered him an unheard of £1 million contract to make an album of his poetry. The marketing people proclaimed him a genius, a voice for a disenfranchised generation, a living embodiment of a modern generation's pain. And Grey was one of the few people who had never believed them. Anyway the contract was withdrawn soon afterwards, when Grey was wrongly denounced as a paedophile, at which point (for about a week) he became the nation's most hated figure, hounded and jeered at on the front of every newspaper. Nobody was surprised when, a week or so after that, the geniuses at Phonix suddenly came to the conclusion that Grey wasn't a genius after all.

That was back in October. He'd been hiding out with his friends at Fiddleford ever since, the living inspiration for Charlie and Jo's new business venture, a lonely, private figure who insisted on paying over the odds for his board and lodging, and who so far displayed no signs of ever planning to leave. He was bad-tempered, lazy, reckless, argumentative, funny, brave and, when he thought someone deserved it, heroically loyal. The General adored him. Charlie and Jo, both several years his junior, often suggested that he find somewhere else to live, but they no longer expected it and in fact they would have been quite sorry to see him go. He had been instrumental in bringing the two of them together, and now, as he picked his way through the carcasses, swallowing his own bile and dodging the bossy men in suits, he was about to fight for their interests once again.

'Ah. There you are, Charlie,' he said. 'At last. How's it goin'?'

'Hi Grey,' muttered Charlie, without looking up. There was a cow's head lodged between his forearms. He was watching intently while a vet emptied his syringe into the vein beneath her tail. A moment later Charlie released the cow and stood back, patting its fat, healthy rump for the last time as it was ushered away. Grey leant towards Charlie. 'Something's come up,' he whispered. 'You're needed at the house.'

'Is it Jo?'

'Excuse me,' interrupted the vet, 'but you need to be wearing one of the suits down here. Someone should have told you.'

'I know that already,' said Grey helpfully. 'I've come to fetch Charlie.' He looked back at the space where Charlie had been standing. '. . . Charlie?'

Grey didn't catch up with him until they reached the boot room door. 'It's nothing to do with Jo, you silly sod,' he panted irritably. 'Calm down. It's yer bloody cows.'

'Cows? What cows?'

'Och, for God's sake! You woke the whole bloody house last night. What bloody cows do you think?'

Just then, from almost directly beneath them, came an unmistakable, ground-shaking bellow. Charlie removed his cap and tugged with embarrassment at his dark hair. 'Oh. Those cows,' he said feebly. 'Has anyone else heard, do you think?'

Grey chuckled. 'The General and me have bin ignorin' it all morning, shouting at each other to pass the marmalade, pretending there's always cows bellyaching through the kitchen floor at us. I swear they've been making the fuckin' windows rattle . . . I don't know about Jo, though. I haven't seen her.' Grey looked as tactful as he could, but he, like Charlie, had known Jo in the olden days, when she was as priggish as all her fashionable friends. Ex-friends. She was much more laid-back recently, but there were times when she still reverted – especially when she was under pressure.

'Oh. No. Don't worry about Jo. She helped me,' said Charlie. He looked at Grey and smiled slightly. 'Jo's fine. Has anyone else heard?'

'I don't think so, no. Mrs Webber's not in today. I checked. Anyway she's totally deaf. Have you noticed? She can't hear a bloody word.'

'What about Les?'

'I don't know.'

'Mr Tarr?'

'I don't know.'

'Have any of the MAFF people used the lavatory?'

'Fuck, I don't know. What do you think? I've been standing guard here all mornin'? If they had they would have said something. So I suppose not.'

There came another earth-shattering groan from beneath them. 'Aye,' said Grey matter-of-factly. 'It's happenin' about every couple a' minutes. It's pretty constant. Sometimes they just keep goin' on. Did you not think about the soundproofing? What were you bloody doing down there all night?'

Neither of them had the faintest idea how many sleeping pills each cow needed but since Grey had only twenty left, they gave ten to each. They ground them into bowls of warm milk and Charlie took them down to the cellar while Grey and Jo – whom they'd found wandering the boot room with her notebook – kept guard and each other company at the back door.

The cows looked resentful, bewildered and slightly mad when Charlie found them. They were covered in sweat and a thick layer of ceiling plaster, which rained onto them every time their vast horns knocked against any of the walls. But they drank the milk without any trouble and Charlie stayed with them talking, reminiscing. They seemed to draw comfort from the familiar sound of his voice.

After a while Jo grew worried that the MAFF people would be missing him, and decided to go down and fetch him out. She found him sitting on one of the straw bales they had carried down together the previous night. He was leaning his long legs against the rump of one of the animals, holding his dark head in his hands, deep in thought. He looked so sad it stopped her in her tracks. She watched him for a moment, unsure how to break the silence. She felt like an intruder.

'Which one was yours, Charlie?'

He looked up slowly, with a faint smile of welcome. 'This one,' he said, nodding at his feet. 'Jasonette. At least, I wanted to call her Jason. But Georgie said . . . you know . . . Jason was a boy's name . . .' He fell silent.

'Jasonette . . .' Jo smiled. 'You know you should probably get back out there, Charlie,' she added gently. 'They'll be wondering where you are.'

'I know.' He didn't move. 'I just— it sounds ridiculous, but I don't much want to be there when they kill . . . I should never have told them about the bloody goat.'

'You had to. He's been living with the other animals. If they were infected—'

'Which they bloody well aren't.'

'Yes, but for all you knew he was infected, too.'

'He could have been down here now . . .'

Jo went to sit on the bale beside him. She put an arm around him and they sat together for several minutes without speaking, watching as the animals' eyelids grew heavy. Charlie was lost in his grieving, and Jo could do nothing for him except sit with him and wait. She had never known Charlie's sister but he spoke about her so often she sometimes forgot they'd never actually met. Strong-minded, bold, friendly and incredibly hearty, Georgina Maxwell McDonald would have been the sort of girl Jo disliked on sight not so long ago. Now, living in a house with three men, and already far less troubled than she used to be by what passed for urban hip, Jo wished that she and Georgina could have been friends. Sometimes (which she kept to herself because she knew it was absurd) Jo even found herself missing her. At that moment, sitting beside Georgina's mourning twin and feeling hopelessly inept, hopelessly impotent, Jo didn't care how absurd it seemed. She missed her sister-in-law, or the sister-in-law she imagined, more than she had ever missed anyone, alive or dead.

'I'm so sorry,' she burst out. 'It must be so awful for you. I wish I could . . .' and to her dismay she started crying.

'Hey,' he said, laughing slightly and giving her shoulders a squeeze. 'Hey . . .'

'I'm so sorry.'

'Oh, I know you are, Jo . . . thank you . . .'

And they fell silent again, neither noticed for how long.

Suddenly Grey (whose natural impatience had been kept in admirable check until then) yanked them rudely back to the moment.

'Jesus fuckin' hell, I'm freezin' my arse off out here! Are they not asleep yet? I can't hear a soddin' sound!'

The cows slept all that afternoon and all night and most of the following morning. By the time they started getting restless again it was lunchtime and most of the work was already done. But there were still half a dozen Ministry men hanging around and the pyre was yet to be lit. Charlie, Grey and Jo met up in the cellar to decide what they should do next. They had run out of sleeping pills and the cows had rejected the litre of vodka mixed with milk and golden syrup. Jo produced a small bottle of Rescue Remedy and was arguing about how to get the drops onto the animals' tongues when Jasonette's right horn sent the bottle flying.

'Well, fuck that,' said Grey. 'That's fucked that then, hasn't it?' He made the animals jump.

'Will you stop shouting,' snapped Charlie.

'Charlie, calm down. He's only trying to help.'

'Well. He's not succeeding. He's scaring the girls.'

'Och, sod off.'

'Yeah, Charlie,' said Jo. 'Actually I second that.'

The humans were growing as tetchy as the animals, and the animals were growing tetchier and noisier with every minute. Nobody noticed the General until he was standing right beside them.

'EXCUSE ME!' They all jumped. 'Sorry to butt in,' he said dryly, 'but we may have a small problem. The fellow from Trading Standards has just called. He's been in touch with the BCMS, whatever that may be. Or the BC something else. Anyway he seems to think there may be a couple of beasts up here which we haven't accounted for . . . I told him it was nonsense, of course, but I'm afraid he's like a dog with a bone. He's on his way over.'

When he arrived the four inhabitants of Fiddleford were standing in a line at the end of the drive waiting for him. The plan, in as much as they'd had time to form one, was first and foremost to keep him away from the house. It was decided that the General, as soon as things looked dangerous, would discombobulate by feigning some sort of health attack; Jo, who didn't like long walks, would rush him into the house and then Charlie and Grey, with an air of repressed panic and polite martyrdom, would insist on pressing on with the business, leading him on a circuitous route to the furthest end of the estate. When the man was looking exhausted, blue with cold, faint with boredom and regret at ever having returned to Fiddleford, they would direct his attention to a mound, a little hillock, a snow drift, anything which looked appropriate, and tell him they *thought* (though they couldn't be certain what with the snow, and after so much time had passed) it was the place where the cows had been buried eleven years earlier.

It was a ludicrous plan and it didn't work. Obviously. Because the first thing the man wanted to do, after expressing wholly unfelt regret for disturbing them once again, was to go to the lavatory.

'Lav's blocked,' said the General, squaring his shoulders, refusing to break the line. 'Sorry about that. Pipes are frozen. Have to go behind a tree . . . I think— Charlie, didn't you bring a trowel with you, just in case the fellow came up with something like this?'

'Certainly did,' said Charlie, producing one from his back pocket.

'Oh goodness, not to worry.' Mr Coleridge gazed longingly between their heads at the handsome building behind them. 'Isn't there, perhaps, a functioning toilet I could use upstairs?'

'No toilets,' said Charlie. 'Sorry.'

'Ah well, never mind. I shall just have to store it up . . .' He rubbed his soft white hands together and shivered. 'Perhaps a cup of tea then? I won't take up too much of your time. It's just a simple matter to clear up, as you know. I'm sure it's nothing. A minor oversight.'

'Tea's run out,' said Jo. 'Anyway it's a diuretic. It'll make you worse. Why don't you let Charlie and Grey quickly take you off to where the poor old cows are buried? That way we won't be wasting your time – and goodness knows you must be busy. And then if you get caught short along the way—'

Coleridge frowned. He didn't like to be outside for any longer than he needed to be and he had absolutely no intention of spending his afternoon trudging through the snow in search of illegally buried animals. 'This probably isn't the time to mention it,' he said, 'and of course I realise the Act doesn't, strictly speaking, apply to me. But you should be aware that you are in fact legally obligated to provide workers with a functioning toilet as well, of course, as the usual facilities for making hot beverages. Under the Health and Safety at Work Act. 1974. I only mention it because I wonder how the others are managing. Or perhaps you have provided alternative arrangements . . .'

Jo opened her mouth to say something appropriately soothing, but the General didn't give her a chance to speak.

33

He had yet to learn what a powerfully efficient ally he had in his annoying new daughter-in-law, so at the mention of unfulfilled legal obligations, he panicked.

'Aaarrrggh!' he cried, clutching his heart melodramatically and staggering forwards.

Immediately and with surprising elegance, Mr Coleridge lunged to catch him.

'Quickly!' he shouted, gripping the General's shoulders. 'Don't just stand there! Let's get him inside the house!'

The General struggled ineffectively for escape, but the man from Trading Standards was not to be put off. Transferring the General into one tight arm, he used the other to loosen his patient's tie.

'Get your hands off me, you filthy bugger!' shouted the General. '. . . *Help!* Someone! . . . *Charlie!* Get this bugger off me!'

Mr Coleridge's own father-in-law had died from a heart attack right in front of him only two years earlier, and it had been horrible. Whatever the General chose to call him he would do everything he could not to repeat the experience. Amid loud protestations from all four of them, Mr Coleridge lifted the General off his feet and carried him back into the house. Short of knocking the man unconscious, which was more or less out of the question, there wasn't much they could do to stop him.

'He needs,' puffed the lilac hero, after he'd gently laid the General onto the drawing-room sofa, 'a cup of hot, sweet tea. Don't you think?'

'I'm perfectly bloody well all right,' spluttered the General, puce with rage. 'Bit of wind, that's all. And if you touch me again, you officious little bugger, I'll have you up for assault. Is that clear?'

Lilac Man nodded phlegmatically. 'I tell you what, though,' he looked playfully across to Jo, 'I could use a nice cup of tea myself!'

Just then, from the back of the house, came the unmistakable rumble they had all been dreading. Charlie, Jo, Grey and the General froze. They looked across at Coleridge in trepidation. They waited . . .

'Mrs— Maxwell McDonald?' wheedled Coleridge doggedly. 'Or failing that a coffee would be super.'

The rumble continued. Was he deaf?

'Smiley,' said Jo quickly. 'The name is still Smiley. In fact. And *of course* you could have tea, if we had any. But we don't.' She paused. The cows were in full voice now, and in unison. It seemed to her that they were getting louder every second. 'But why are you asking me as opposed to anyone else? We're all as capable of making cups of tea as each other. Or we would be. If there was any tea. Which as I say there isn't . . . Isn't that right, Charlie?'

'Mmm? Oh, absolutely. The thing about tea . . .'

Slowly, at last, the man from Trading Standards held up a finger and frowned. 'Shhh,' he said. 'What's . . . that . . . ?'

Charlie clapped his hands together and stood up. 'So,' he shouted. 'Who has sugar? Dad, I know you do. I know you do, Grey. You don't, do you, Jo. And I don't either. So the single remaining mystery, on the sugar front, is you, Mr Coleridge. Mr Coleridge, are you a sugar man?'

'Shhh!'

'Do you have sugar, Mr Coleridge?'

'Shhh! Please. Be quiet—' Still with one finger aloft, he headed into the hall. Charlie followed him.

'I hate to be rude,' said Charlie, padding unhappily

35

after him, 'but the back of the house really is out of bounds. I thought I explained. We can't just have people trespassing . . . Mr Coleridge? Please! Where do you think you're going?'

Mr Coleridge broke into a jog. As Jo had done two nights previously, he followed the by now thunderous noise through the back hall, past the boot room to the cellar door, where he paused and turned victoriously towards Charlie.

'I have reason to believe— ' he said smugly.

'What? Reason to believe what?' snapped Charlie. The cows lowed again, more quietly this time, as if they were settling down at last, now that it was too late, and Charlie looked at him with hopeless desperation. 'Mr Coleridge,' he said quietly. 'Please. Why are you doing this?'

'For reasons of health and safety—'

'But they're in quarantine down there! They couldn't be healthier or safer!'

'We're not talking about the health and safety of your animals, Mr Maxwell McDonald. We're talking about the health and safety of the community at large. For which, at this moment in time, I am currently responsible.'

'They've had no contact with any livestock for over twenty years, Mr Coleridge. And they're in quarantine. Please . . . What harm can they do down there? Can't we at least test them? Can't we *test* them first? And if they're carrying the disease— Which they aren't . . .'

'My job, as you know, is simply to make a note of all livestock on the premises, and that is what I have come here to do—'

'But what harm are they doing? What harm can they possibly do?'

36

'For reasons of health and safety—'

'This has nothing to do with health and safety! You know as well as I do the cows are no threat to anyone down there.'

'For reasons of health and safety,' he said steadfastly, 'I must ask you to open that door.'

'Not me,' said Charlie. 'Open it yourself. But watch out. They've been known to attack strangers.'

Coleridge hesitated for a second. Highland cows are always gentle, and Charlie's were the most gentle of all. But Coleridge didn't know that. He knew only that they were hefty, and horned and very hairy . . . He considered retreating to fetch reinforcements, but then they might hide the cows somewhere else, somewhere he might never find them. He couldn't risk it. Plus he had the law on his side, and a delicious, intoxicating sense of his own efficiency. Mr Coleridge garnered all his courage, thought briefly of whom he might sue should anything go wrong, took the few steps to the cellar door and opened it.

The animals had somehow managed to break out of their makeshift stable at the end of the corridor and were standing in the middle of the main room, surrounded by broken bottles and in a large pool of what at first glance looked like blood but was in fact some of the General's best wine. They greeted Coleridge with a long, low wail of pitiful bewilderment.

Coleridge quickly summoned the vets, the slaughtermen and two of the pyre operators who could be spared, now that the fire was lit. They all looked on (or stood guard) while Charlie coaxed the animals up the cellar stairs again.

'I am *sorry*,' said Mr Coleridge as they passed him – and

in his own humdrum way he meant it. 'I'm sure you will understand, once the heat of the moment is passed, so to speak. I'm only doing my job. Please don't run away with the impression that I'm enjoying this.'

Charlie shrugged. 'At least if you were enjoying it,' he said, 'there would be some point to the exercise.'

He led them through the back yard, across the yard beyond, to the steep path which led to the bottom field. Grey, the General and Jo walked silently beside him, and, like a gaggle of official mourners, the law enforcers followed close behind. It was dark by then, and their slow journey was lit by the snow's reflection of the flames from the distant pyre. As the three old friends shuffled along, the one leading the others to their execution, the animals kept up their mournful wails of protest, and Charlie chattered to them incessantly. They were his childhood companions, his link with the past. In their gentle, affectionate souls he felt that a small part of his mother and his sister were living yet, and he felt that his mother and sister were watching him on this long slow walk, and that with every step he took, he was forsaking them.

The cows seemed to have no sense of what was about to befall them until they came to the point, over the brow of a small upward slope, where for the first time the smell of roasting flesh hit their nostrils, and the full, loathsome scale of the burning pyre and the great pile of carcasses which lay illuminated at its base became clear for all to see.

After that the cows wouldn't move. They were transfixed. Nothing Charlie, or Grey or Jo or the General, or the pyre builders, or the slaughtermen, or the vets said or did could make them take another step. After a while Mr Daniels, the burly senior slaughterman, made a point of looking at his watch. 'We can't stand about 'ere fur ever,' he said. 'We shall have to kill 'em as they stand.'

'No,' said Charlie.

'But they ain't movin' nowhere, Mr Maxwell McDonald. We shall be 'ere all night.'

'You're not killing them here,' said Charlie. 'You're not. They need . . .' He cast around for something, anything, to delay the moment. 'They need to be tranquillised first.'

'With respect,' said one of the vets, 'you're only prolonging the process. They don't need to be transquillised. As you can see they're quite calm. They need—'

'Don't tell me what they need,' said Charlie. 'Don't fucking tell *me* what they need.' He rested his head on Jasonette's shoulders and all the humans fell silent, looking at him.

Mr Daniels nodded at his assistant and stepped forward, his bolt gun at the ready. The two of them walked around the side of the animals and came to a halt at their heads.

'Sedate them,' barked the General suddenly. 'Why don't you sedate them?' Something in his voice made Jo look across at him. There were tears rolling down his face.

'The longer we stand here,' the senior vet tried his best to sound as patient as he wished he could feel, after so much killing, 'the more alarmed they're going to become. Go on, Mr Daniels. Please. Continue. Get it done.'

Mr Daniels held up his gun and Jasonette stood there, waiting, offering him her large furry temple. 'We'll be doin' 'em a favour, you know,' he muttered disapprovingly. 'Old beasts like this. They're better off dead.'

Charlie leapt at him. Before he had time to think, before anyone had time to stop him. Charlie had never in his adult life hit a single soul, but there was a *crack* as his fist struck the slaughterman's jaw. Mr Daniels lurched backwards, blinked in surprise, and immediately lurched forwards again to wreak his revenge. And then Jo, until that point strangely anaesthetised by the horror, sprung suddenly to life. Head down and yelling, she lunged for Mr Daniels' burly chest.

'No!' cried Charlie, trying to catch her before she got hurt. 'No, Jo, don't!'

Daniels looked from one to the other in confusion. It distracted him for a second, long enough for Grey, 6'4", fearless and frightening without even trying to be, to step up between them.

'*Leave it,*' he snarled, glowering down at Daniels. '*Leave it.*'

They eyeballed each other. Daniels hesitated. 'They're only a couple of fuckin' cows,' he said, retreating with a surly shuffle. And with that, and with Charlie and Jo both restrained by the pyre builders, and the animals standing alone, helpless but not entirely oblivious, he took his gun, took aim and fired.

Bang.

Bang.

They were almost dead. The assistant slaughterer bent over the bodies and inserted his serrated rod into the bullet holes, twisted. With a final jerk, a final grunting, hiccupping moan, Caroline and Jasonette departed.

'As a gesture of goodwill,' Mr Coleridge said, 'I shan't be making a detailed report about the incidents surrounding this case. Suffice to say, Mr Maxwell McDonald, that all livestock on the Fiddleford estate has now been duly recorded.'

# FIRE SIGNS

Since 24 December 1998 the older, text-only 'fire exit' signs should have been supplemented or replaced with pictogram signs. Fire safety signs complying with BS 5499 Part 1:1990 already contain a pictogram and do not need changing.

*Safety signs in the catering industry. Health and Safety Executive Catering Information Sheet No 16*

# • SECURE TIME-BOUND PROGRAMME OF IMPLEMENTATION

## Autumn 2001

They had spent the Ministry's compensation money and a lot more besides rebuilding the park's crumbling walls, and they'd refurbished the two-hundred-year-old gates at the bottom of the front drive so they could be operated by remote control.

'That'll keep the buggers at bay,' said the General, standing in front of them with his clicking machine, opening and closing them until they broke. (It took two weeks and £950 plus VAT to get them mended.) 'They won't be able to get at us now! Ha!' Nobody was certain if he was referring to unscrupulous news reporters or to the whole human race. It didn't matter. Either way he was quite right. They'd laid barbed wire on top of the twelve-foot walls. Unwelcome visitors to Fiddleford would need to work hard to find a way in.

A lot had changed since the foot and mouth purge and the estate, if you could still call it that, was less than a tenth the size it had been a year ago. Charlie, like so many other farmers, had realised that if they were to survive at all, there needed to be some radical rethinking, and as a result he'd done many things at Fiddleford which he'd always hoped to postpone until after his father died. He decided to restock only a fraction of the animals he had lost in the cull, and now all but sixty acres of the land was sold, and there were only two cottages remaining; one which Mrs Webber, the old housekeeper, had been promised for life, and the other, at the bottom of the drive, which was still awaiting the arrival of the General. Mrs Webber, sixty-four last summer, now only worked in the mornings, which meant Les Chedzoy was the single full-time employee left. He was useless at his job – at almost everything he did – and not even very pleasant, but he'd been born in a cottage on the estate and he was exceptionally stupid. Much too stupid, Charlie believed, to survive in a world beyond Fiddleford. He lived in the village now, in a small house which, on his retirement twenty-two years ago, the General had given to his father.

In all, after the sale and including the MAFF compensation cheque, Charlie and Jo had raised just enough money for the park walls and the gate, to build one extra bathroom and to do all the most urgent external repairs. Jo had needed to fight to be allowed to spend anything on the inside of the house. (Any highfaluting dreams of kitchen refurbishments and so on had been very quickly disbanded). But she had been to IKEA and bought ten new duvets and duvet covers, which had cheered everyone up, and finally, after Les claimed to have a fear of heights, lugged her increasingly bulbous belly onto a stepladder and repainted most of the upstairs rooms herself. And then that was it. All the money was gone.

The end result was a generally sturdy old house with a mended boiler (but no pilates teacher; no chapel-effect-chill-out-room; certainly no gym in the junk-filled stables), and a phenomenal, unimaginable amount of paperwork. On his solicitor's advice Charlie was in the process of applying for a myriad of licences and government permits, all apparently necessary if Fiddleford was to operate legally in its new form.

And while they waited . . . and waited . . . for government officials to hand out all the licences they insist on inventing, Charlie, Grey and the General had been trying to persuade Jo that they should press ahead and open the refuge anyway. Jo was adamant that they should not. But she too began to lose confidence in the system when, after four and a half months of silence, two letters arrived from the local planning office on the same day. The first, rejecting outright an application, already withdrawn, in writing, twice, to convert the old stables into a gym. The second, saying it had 'temporarily mislaid' all documents relating to that same application, and requesting that the application be 'resubmitted' at once.

Fiddleford desperately needed an income. Jo, seven months pregnant now, understood that as well as any of them. She understood it even better the day Charlie returned from the local animal feed merchant with an empty trailer, having had every credit card rejected.

'I think I can persuade them to extend the overdraft a little bit,' he said drearily, sitting at the unrefurbished kitchen table, his head in his hands. 'But after that . . . This is serious. We can't just talk about it anymore. We've *got* to get some bloody guests.'

That afternoon he and Jo went on a final recce of the house to convince each other once and for all that it was ready. They didn't choose to comment on the damp patches already beginning to show through Jo's paintwork. Nor on how most of the landing rugs had worn, in patches, right through to the wood. Nor on the numerous paint splodges which had been left by Jo all over the floor and furniture, nor on the frayed and faded state of all the sofas, armchairs, curtains . . . nor on the fact that the windows in the bedrooms all rattled and leaked.

By the time they reached the end of the tour neither had managed to speak for several minutes. They paused on the upstairs landing, glanced nervously at each other.

'It's not quite what we'd envisaged, is it?' she said at last.

'It's not perfect. Yet. But it will be!'

'*Yes. It will be*. As soon as the money starts coming in.'

'That's just what I was going to say.'

'Anyway *I* like it,' she said. '*I* think it's *better* than perfect. In its own way. It's got character . . .' They both smiled half-heartedly. 'And if people *don't* like it they can fuck off – I mean— No. I don't mean that, obviously. I mean—' Jo wasn't sure what she meant. But the reality of sharing their home with a lot of grumbling, dissatisfied strangers suddenly seemed rather more real and a great deal less enticing than it had this morning. '. . . Anyway,' she finished lamely, 'they're all going to be very happy here. I'm sure.'

'Dead bloody right, they will be! And if they aren't, I quite agree, they can just fuck right off again.'

'It's exactly what they would do, I suppose,' she said glumly.

'Right. *And see if we care!*' They both started laughing. 'Now then. I've got exactly . . .' He emptied his trouser pockets. '. . . £11.87 . . . Altogether . . . Oh. How much have you got?'

'I've got £25. But it's meant to last us until Friday. They won't let us get any more out until the end of the week.'

'Fine. *Excellent.* I think we should drive out to Lamsbury and buy ourselves a bottle of champagne.'

'Charlie, we can't.'

'Of course we can. We've got to *celebrate.* With or without the bloody licences. Fiddleford Manor Retreat is now officially open for guests. So let's hope they come soon or we shan't be able to buy the greedy little sods any breakfast.'

It was Messy Monroe, though she didn't realise it yet, who was destined to be Fiddleford's first illegal guest. Which is strange because until a fortnight or so before she arrived most of the country had forgotten she ever existed. One of a stream of wide-eyed girls with nice bellybuttons who flit across our television screens, she'd had a stint presenting *Top of the Pops* about seven years ago. In December 1995 she was voted TV's Hottest Totty by one of the men's magazines and she spent the following eighteen months or so capitalising on it, endorsing all sorts of things from Breast Awareness Week to easi-grip toothbrushes. She was given a holiday show to present, which meant everyone got to see her in her bathers, and then five years ago, just when life couldn't have been looking any better, she

49

made the mistake of falling in love with a pretentious and impoverished novelist.

This one, who was small and softly spoken and who used unnecessarily long words to hide the fact that he was never actually saying anything, made her head spin with an irresistible mixture of lust and mental confusion. He could have chosen to ruin any number of beautiful women's lives, and in fact he had (and continues to do so). That winter, the winter of 1996, he just happened to pick on Messy.

At the time Messy was a young twenty-five, and in a funny way slightly frightened by her easy success. She had emerged onto the scene three years earlier, from a life of dreary and impoverished oblivion, the daughter of a father she had never met, and a mother who worked in personnel at a shirt factory in Middlesbrough. She'd been surviving in an idea-free zone ever since, surrounded by the sort of spoilt and happening crew who find it embarrassing to use long words at all, let alone use them to say anything confusing, and she hadn't realised it until the writer came along, but she was bored. She was wilting with boredom – and guilt and bewilderment. Because she was living, after all, the very life that a lot of women have been encouraged to fantasise about.

Enter the little writer, putting on an excellent show of being interested in her mind. They spent almost a year together, just long enough for him to destroy what there ever really was of her confidence. In a series of desperate bids to impress him, she applied to read a degree course in Philosophy (and was rejected). She resigned from the holiday show, refused to cooperate with a *Hello!* magazine

TV Totty special, and sacked her agent. But the little novelist remained unimpressed. Nothing she did, or didn't do, could escape his soft-voiced disdain. In September 1997, just six weeks before he was due to desert her, Messy produced the only decent thing that ever came out of the relationship, a daughter called Chloe.

She and Chloe went to live in a small cottage in Oxfordshire, where the British public very quickly forgot about her. She looked after her daughter, educated herself to a level where she would never again find herself intimidated by chippy little novelists, and ate. She was fifteen stone, lonely, broke, and Chloe had just turned three when she finally felt desperate enough to start rebuilding her life again.

Messy did the only thing she could think of doing under her restricted circumstances. While her daughter was away at nursery school she wrote a book about *being fat*, and about what she claimed to have identified as the 'fat/thin hate divide'. And because she was quite clever and because the book, however silly, was often funny and very frank, and of course because she herself had once been so famous and thin, Messy's book caught people's attention. *The Secret Revolution: Fatties Fight Back* was given an undue amount of publicity, almost all of it negative.

Which brings us pretty much up to date. *Fatties* had been out for just one week and it was infuriating everyone. Thin people, obviously, because for the first time ever they were under open attack, and fat people because – well, for a myriad of reasons. After all the subject isn't an easy one, and Messy should never have used the word FATTIES in the title if she wasn't prepared for a rough ride.

*Messy Monroe may be finding it hard, now she's just like every other female, worrying 'does my bum look big in this?'* read one of a hundred readers' letters running in publications around the country that week, *but maybe it's just a problem she has, adjusting to not being a 'star' anymore. I'm 'fat', as she calls it, and believe me I KNOW I'm fabulous, and I've got lots of skinny friends who accept me as I am. So Messy, all I can say to you is, try looking out and seeing the love in this world next time, instead of harping on about fat versus thin!!!*

Messy, having hidden away for four years, was now suddenly giving interviews galore, and she hated it. She hated being on show, but the wretched Fatty theme had spiralled into the unofficial Light Relief Topic of the Week, and it was out of her control – or so she felt. The whole thing culminated in an invitation to appear alongside three Very Important Men on the panel of *Question Time*.

In fact she acquitted herself quite well at first. She came up with something suitably anodyne when they asked her about the effect of September 11th on other terrorist groups, and again when they asked her (as if she knew) about the likelihood of biological warfare on Britain. It was only towards the end, when the questions turned from world war to people's weight, that she ran into trouble.

'I for one am very slender,' announced a sensible-looking woman about three rows from the front, 'but I have many, many dear friends who are on the larger side—'

'They're *fat*,' snapped Messy. 'If you mean they're fat, then for Heaven's sake say so.'

'Rubbish!' somebody shouted back. Messy rolled her eyes impatiently.

'Doesn't the panel think,' the very slender woman

continued, 'that we have enough hate divisions in this world already, without people like Messy Monroe falsely inventing any more?'

The entire audience, fat and thin, broke into hearty applause. They were angry and frightened, after so long discussing a possible World War Three, and they needed to vent their frustration on an easy target. Messy, with all the adrenaline that was pumping through her, was only fuzzily aware of the audience mood. She was more acutely aware of her own terror, and of the possibility that at any moment she could simply lose her nerve. So she over-compensated and answered the question without any of the conciliatory ramble which served her more experienced panellists so well: 'Firstly, and most obviously,' she said, much too aggressively, 'these divisions are not "invented". You and your friends may not want to acknowledge them, but that doesn't mean they don't exist. My fat friends and I could refuse to acknowledge the WTC attacks. A fat lot of use that would be!' She paused. It was meant to be a joke. Not an especially funny one, obviously, but not necessarily deserving of the cruel 'Ver-y Funn-y' yelled out from the back of the auditorium, which made everyone laugh. She pressed on. 'You can't heal a rift— You can't heal *any sort* of rift without first identifying the causes. And that's what my book is doing. Trying to point out that fat and thin people, and especially women, have a deep and very understandable mistrust of one another—'

'RUBBISH!' somebody shouted again.

Messy ignored it, and the burst of applause which followed. 'Which is *why*,' she continued, 'there has been such a strong reaction to my use of the word FATTIES in the title. If people weren't so jittery about us they wouldn't take such exception to the word that describes us. Obviously. It's the same reason we can't say "coloured" or "negro" or "spastic" or "dwarf" . . .'

She hesitated, waiting for the jeers to die down. 'And to illustrate that—' she said, and faltered. '. . . To illustrate that,' she began again. Messy had been facing hostility on radio phone-in shows all week, but this was different. Looking around at the angry faces in front of her, and the smug unhelpful expressions of her Very Important fellow guests, she realised she had forgotten what she was going to say. Completely. She tried another tack: 'For example, I would like to know how many fatties here tonight . . . How many *fatties* in the audience—' What was she meant to say next? She had no idea. 'How many fatties . . .' She couldn't remember. She couldn't remember any words at all. All she could do was repeat herself. And every time she repeated herself, she repeated the word 'fatty', and every time she said 'fatty' the audience grew more enraged.

It reached a point where one of her Very Important fellow panellists decided to step in.

The eternally marvellous Maurice Morrison, twice married and divorced and also, as it happened, a furtive (but busy) preferrer of teenage boys; multi-millionaire entrepreneur, ex-Marlborough pupil and the government's brand new Minister for Kindness; slim, attractive, *concerned*, with a full head of salty blond hair and an Armani-clad well-exercised torso, held up his suntanned, elegantly masculine hand and called calmly for hush.

'OK, look, come on, guys,' he said, 'I think we should appreciate that Messy is entitled to her opinion, and since she's come on the show to *tell* us about it, we should at least have the courtesy to listen, yeah? Even if we don't agree.

Becuz, basically— For *me*, that's one of the beautiful things about this country. It's one of the things we're fighting for right now, over in Kabul! Becuz – here in Britain, OK – we can stand up and say "Listen, guys. You may not agree with me, but *this is actually an issue I believe in!*"'

By God, it brought the house down.

Messy glowered at him as he peeped across, smiling with encouragement and warmth and a lovely little smattering of diffidence. She didn't need Maurice Morrison – the last thing she needed was patronising, good-looking Maurice Morrison trawling for admirers off the back of her humiliation. She was furious. Gradually the cheers faded to silence and everyone waited to hear how she would respond.

She could have said so many things. If she'd been even an eighth as efficient at crowd control as Mr Morrison was, she could have turned the whole situation to her advantage. But she wasn't. She had barely emerged from four years in hiding, she was still battered by a broken heart and the cruel transformation in her looks and general fortune, and the lights were beaming down on her and making her very hot. The whole world, or so it felt, was looking on. She said: 'Get lost, you phony little creep.'

And that was the end of Messy. Really, she was lucky she wasn't lynched.

The performance boosted her book sales, but it also set her up as a national target for mockery and general abuse. Over the next two days a lot of inane and cruel things were written about her. One paper found a nutritionist to express revulsion at a picture of sweet, chubby little Chloe sucking on a lollipop. Another paper dedicated a whole page to what they imagined Messy Monroe needed to eat each day in order to maintain her great bulk. Several papers ran Before and After photographs, alongside pseudo serious articles about the stresses of early fame/sex appeal/faded stardom/single motherhood . . . It was pretty standard stuff, the usual newspaper fodder. It certainly wasn't an enormous story, what with everything else that was going on.

But it was big enough to catch the eyes of the tabloid scanners at Fiddleford Manor.

'There's a bloody great cow here,' said Grey McShane, slowly lifting his large feet off the kitchen table and laying his paper down in front of him, 'who lost her rag on the telly a couple o' nights ago. Have you seen the size of her?'

'Yes, I noticed her,' mumbled the General, without looking up. Dressed smartly, as always, in a tweed jacket and old regiment tie, he was sitting in his preferred position for this time in the mid-morning, bolt upright in the worn leather armchair beside the Aga, and surrounded by a sea of downmarket newspapers and magazines. 'I thought she was rather comely.'

'No!' Grey examined the photograph more closely, this time trying to overlook her most obvious weakness. And it was true, she had beautiful long dark shiny hair . . . and an attractive mouth which curled up slightly at the edges . . . and round, intelligent, bright blue eyes . . . 'But she's a bloody whale!'

'Modern girls are too thin, McShane. I thought we'd agreed on that.'

'Well I know . . . But there's a limit.'

Just then Jo came in, waddling efficiently as she tended to these days, now that she was tense and working again, with her large but very neat seven-and-a-half-month bump in front of her and her notorious contacts book resting open in her hands. 'Oh good,' she said. 'Are you discussing Messy Monroe? That's just who I wanted to talk about.'

'Aye. Apparently she really hates thin people.'

'She actually did a couple of P.A.s for us a few years ago. Ha! When she was thin herself. And she was great. Very professional . . . Because there was that phase when an M.M. P.A. pretty much guaranteed a show in the red tops, wasn't there? She could charge whatever she liked . . . Do you remember?' Grey and the General looked at each other in weary incomprehension, as they often did when Jo started talking shop. 'Anyway it doesn't matter,' she continued blithely. 'The point is somehow or other I've got her number. And that's what counts. I think we should invite her to come down.'

'Jesus Christ!' bellowed Grey. 'Have you seen the size of her? She won't fit through the front door!'

'Well. Short of inviting Osama Bin Laden to stay with us—'

'Don't be disgusting,' snapped the General.

'. . . she's about the only person left anybody can be bothered to hate anymore.'

'I don't hate her,' said the General mildly. 'As a matter of fact I think she looks delightful . . . In a *largish* sort of way.'

'Well, good. Because I'm about to persuade her to come and see us. She's going to be our first celebrity refugee. What do you think about that?'

Grey sat back with amusement to observe the General's

reaction to this new autocratic management style. He was amazed, actually, that Jo had managed to prevent herself from adopting it from the beginning. The house had been unofficially ready to receive people for a fortnight now and so far the 'Guest Selection Board Meetings', as Jo, back in full professional mode, now insisted on calling the Fiddleford Four's rather goofy and extremely argumentative confabs, had not been a great success. There had been five meetings altogether, each one angrily and prematurely disbanded because three of the four board members could never agree. On anything. At the last meeting even Charlie, the most tolerant of men, had walked out before the end.

'What's that?' said the General stiffly. 'The adorable little fat lady? Invited *here*? Don't you think we should have some sort of conference about this before you take the law into your own hands?'

Grey McShane chuckled.

'The meetings,' said Jo, using her most reasonable voice (also unfortunately the one most guaranteed to infuriate her father-in-law) 'don't seem to be getting us anywhere. And the fact is – the fact *is* – they're not going to increase our overdraft again. Unless we do something pretty soon, we are seriously going to have to start selling pieces of furniture—'

'I'm aware of that,' interrupted the General haughtily and then, uncertain how to continue the argument in the face of such appalling news, repeated himself, before turning lamely towards Grey for help.

Grey shrugged. 'She's right, you know. These meetings are a bloody waste o' time.'

'Fine,' he snapped. 'Fine. Have it your own way. Of

course I know you will anyway. Don't consult *me*. After all it's no longer my house . . .'

'Och, belt up,' said Grey good-naturedly. The General pretended not to hear. He picked up his newspaper, opened it at a random page, and managed, apparently, to be instantly engrossed.

Jo and her father-in-law's relationship had not grown any easier over the past months, in spite of their shared trauma at the hands of the government slaughtermen, their pleasure at the coming baby, and even their shared love of Charlie. Jo had employed all her best, most charming tactics to try to win him round but to no avail. She and the General had argued the very first time they met, and it seemed they were incapable of doing anything else.

Jo tended to lay undue emphasis on the retired General's utterly irrelevant political opinions (which were always unfashionable and occasionally, it has to be said, quite unpleasant). She took offence to almost every opinion he had. The General simply took offence to Jo. Which was unfair because she had enormous warmth and kindness, and occasionally, when her fashionable opinions allowed it, and she was feeling brave enough, she was even capable of being quite funny. But she was too modern, too bossy, too equal, too clever. Altogether too many things that a fading General would be bound to find alarming.

And now she was living in his house, or rather he was living in hers. She was imposing ridiculous new telephone systems on him, and inviting people he didn't know to come and stay. Because although the dream of opening a refuge had at least partly been his, the reality of having paying strangers in the house was of course quite different. More so for him than for any of them. And if sharing his old home with a kind but bossy daughter-in-law was difficult, then sharing it with incomprehensible new telephone 'units' and a lot of ghastly, self-pitying 'celebrities' was likely to be more than even the most open-minded of Generals, could be expected to stand.

Jo was by no means oblivious to these complications and not, in spite of his hostility, completely unsympathetic to them either. But it didn't alter the fact that she intended to get her way. She hesitated, feeling unsure exactly how to proceed. 'So that's agreed then, is it?' she said, to the back of his newspaper. He ignored her. 'Um . . . General? [He had never asked her to call him James] . . . You quite like the idea of having Messy down here? To stay? . . . I mean she's only small fry, I know—'

'*Small?*' bellowed Grey.

'—but it's a start, isn't it? I don't think we should try to charge her too much, do you? We should probably see what sort of a deal we can drum up with one of the mags. Try to squeeze them for a bit of cash, don't you think? While we cut our teeth, sort of thing.' She knew they weren't really listening, and they knew that she was only pretending to consult them. They didn't bother to reply. 'Anyway,' she said, sounding determinedly upbeat. 'Ha! Here I am, counting my chickens. She may not even want to come!' And with that Jo hurried out of the room.

'Officious little minx,' mumbled the General quickly, while she was still in earshot.

'Aye,' muttered Grey. 'But she'll be the saving of this place. Saving of all of us I should think. We're bloody lucky she puts up with having us around.'

Once again, the General didn't feel tempted to respond.

\*     \*     \*

60

Messy Monroe had given up answering the telephone by the time Jo summoned the courage to put in her first call. With all the hacks and their editors, and the PR people and the publishers, she and Chloe had lived the last couple of days to a backdrop of answer machine babble. It just so happened that while Jo (having heard nothing and feeling increasingly desperate) was leaving her seventh unanswered message in two hours on Messy's machine, Messy was alone in the room, and her brain was lying idle. Which meant the odd snippet of welcome information kept seeping through.

'. . . keep calling you and I know what a tremendous amount of stress you must be under . . . worked with a lot of people in your position . . . even at the rough end of it myself recently . . . beautiful media-free sanctuary . . . isolated old manor house . . . lovely walks . . . Chloe to play . . . very *very* comfortable and *guaranteed reporter-free* . . .'

As Jo spoke there was another knock on Messy's front door. Another creepy reporter, she assumed, carrying a bunch of flowers and pretending to be her friend. (She was wrong in fact. The creepy flowers were from Jo.) Anyway it was the last straw. She lunged for the telephone.

'Hello?'

'Hello!' Jo couldn't disguise her relief. She started laughing. *Messy had taken her call. She would come and stay. She would bring money with her. Everything was going to be OK.* 'Goodness! Ha ha. *Goodness!* Messy! Oh! Are you there?'

'What? Of course I am!'

'Of course you are. Of course you are.' Jo took a deep breath. 'No, I meant to say *are you OK?*'

'What? I have to tell you, you probably think I'm loaded,

but I spent it all. I spent everything. That's the main reason I wrote the book. So you're not going to be interested in me anyway.'

Which took Jo by surprise. She had imagined someone much fiercer, but Messy sounded terrified. Poor thing. The realisation gave Jo's confidence a welcome boost, and within seconds the slick PR-girl spiel was slipping off her tongue as if she'd never taken a break from using it.

Messy's financial status didn't matter, Jo said. She explained – and it was one of the few things the Fiddleford Four had all agreed on – that guests' rates depended on their ability to pay, and on the income she could draw (and split down the middle) from any exclusive interview deals she arranged. 'I've been a senior partner [only a minor exaggeration] in one of the top public relations firms in London for over ten years. In fact we've met. We actually worked together on a couple of P.A.s a few years ago . . . But perhaps you don't remember.'

'Oh really?' said Messy, trying politely to muster some enthusiasm but still sounding miserable, as she always did when people reminded her of her past. 'Which ones?'

'Anyway we can talk about that when you get down here,' said Jo, realising it wasn't helping. 'Messy, I expect the last thing you want to think about right now is giving any more interviews—'

'Ha! You're right there.'

'Exactly. And you see the point of your staying here would be twofold. Partly, just to get a break from the madness, so to speak . . .'

Messy laughed grudgingly. She knew she was being manipulated, possibly even slightly patronised. But for once she didn't care. She was so tired of making decisions for herself. They were always the wrong ones. And Jo seemed to know exactly what to say and do. She was making Messy feel better than she had in days.

'—And partly so I can help you turn this publicity around; launch what I always call a damage-limitation counterattack.' Messy laughed again. 'Any interviews you do decide to give would be very, very carefully handled. I can negotiate the deal, ensure we have copy approval, sit in on the interview. And so on. I hate to blow my own trumpet, Messy, but I do have a great deal of experience in this area.'

'I bloody well hope you do. So who else have you had to stay down there?'

'One of the most essential components of this sanctuary,' said Jo (she had prepared this one earlier), 'is *secrecy*. Obviously . . .'

'Yes. I suppose so.'

'So though there's nothing I'd love to do more than to reel off a long list of names, I can't. I just can't. Basically, Messy, all I can say is – if you're not happy with the service we provide then don't pay us! Simple as that! This operation has got to work on trust. That's very important. We've got to trust you and you've got to trust us . . .'

'Hm . . .' said Messy, pretending she wasn't already convinced.

'We can send a car to come and pick you up right away. We could be there in three or four hours . . .'

'Hm . . .'

'And we've just bought a donkey, which might entertain Chloe.'

*     *     *

63

The car from Fiddleford arrived at Messy's door seven and a half hours later. Les, the farm hand, had forgotten to take a map and, for reasons known only to himself, had rejected the offer of Charlie and Jo's more comfortable car and taken instead the old Land Rover, which was filthy and could never go above forty miles an hour. He'd also, poor fellow, managed to get lost four times on the same stretch of motorway before finally taking the right exit.

Messy gabbled jovially as she and Chloe clambered into the Land Rover, fighting their way between horses' head collars, bits of bind-a-twine, stray potatoes gone to seed, and piles of empty paper sacks. 'I hope,' she said, 'that the state of this car isn't any sort of indicator of what's to come!' The truth was, after such a long wait, she was relieved to see any car at all. 'You know I hadn't even taken a number for Fiddlefrom. Fiddleforth. I was beginning to wonder if the whole conversation hadn't been a dream!'

Les looked at her morosely for a while, only faintly noticing that she had been talking, and certainly not expecting to make a response. Suddenly his face lit up. 'Well I never!' he said. 'But you're that fat lady off of the TELLY!'

'Of course I am. Who did you think I was?'

'I SAW YOU ON TELLY!'

'Did you watch *Question Time?*'

'A few nights back, it was. I don't know *why*. A bit like one o' them quizzie things.'

She'd been without any adult company, brooding solidly, ever since the BBC car had dropped her back at the cottage, and now here was a friendly face. Well, a face. It was all she needed. She couldn't stop herself. 'Didn't you think Morrison was a creep? Or have I lost perspective on this? I mean – honestly, Les. Tell me honestly. Was I being paranoid? Was he exploiting my situation? . . . I felt so incredibly *patronised* . . .'

Les gazed at her long and hard before slowly turning away to start the engine. In the four hours it took to return to Fiddleford he didn't speak another word. Chloe fell asleep.

It was eleven o'clock by the time they arrived.

'I'm so sorry,' said Jo nervously, rushing out of the house to greet her. 'You must be exhausted. Les wasn't – Les, why didn't you call? You left the map behind. We've been worried to death.'

'I don't like maps.'

'For Heaven's sake!' Until she came to Fiddleford Jo hadn't really believed such stupid people actually existed. She sighed with the usual mixture of boredom and exasperation that overcame her when dealing with Les's 'working' methods. 'Les, you can't *not like* maps. There's nothing *not* to *like* about them.' She sighed again, and was preparing (professional as always) to deliver an easy-to-understand discourse on the subject, when Grey, Charlie and the General came wandering out to join them. 'Oh look, here are the others,' she said with relief. 'This is Grey . . . Grey, this is Messy. And Chloe . . . Who's actually asleep, poor little mite . . .'

Grey shook Messy's free hand without a great deal of interest but then seemed to reconsider, and bent down to scrutinise her more closely. 'Oh!' he said, pleasantly surprised. 'You look much better than you do in the pictures.'

'Depends which pictures,' Messy muttered grumpily,

but she blushed. It was the nearest thing she'd had to a compliment for a long time. 'They tend to choose the ugly ones.' She looked up at him with a smile. 'You're not so bad-looking yourself.'

'Aye,' he said, relinquishing her hand, gazing at her curiously. 'It's been said.'

'And, er – Messy, this is my husband, Charlie.'

'Hello, Messy. Welcome to Fiddleford,' said Charlie. 'You're our first guest, as I expect Jo explained. So I hope you won't be too disappointed if things don't run perfectly straight away—'

'And this,' said Jo quickly, 'is my father-in-law, General Maxwell McDonald.'

'Crikey,' said Messy doubtfully.

The General stepped smartly forward, determined to present a good face, however he might have been feeling. 'But most people just call me General,' he said, bowing slightly to avoid eye contact. 'Well come in, come in, for Heaven's sake. Somebody get the child to bed and then perhaps Miss Monroe would like a drink?'

They walked together into the hall. Messy looked up at the large gilt chandelier hanging from the ceiling, and then at the magnificent mahogany staircase sweeping up to the landing thirty-five feet above her head.

'Crikey,' she said again.

Weighed down by the child and still enormous, even in these vast surroundings, Messy looked very ill at ease standing there. It reminded Jo of the first time she came to Fiddleford, when in spite of all her kneejerk disapproval (of inherited wealth and environmentally unsound houses) this hall had still intimidated her. 'I know it's large,' she whispered apologetically, 'but we don't actually heat the rooms we don't use. And of course,' (she lied, entirely unnecessarily. But she was nervous) 'we grow all our own vegetables.'

Messy, who always imagined people were patronising her, buried her face in her daughter's cheek and pretended not to hear.

'Chloe's in the smaller room, next door to you,' said Charlie as they climbed the stairs together. 'And there's a bathroom up at the end. On the left. I'm sorry,' he turned back to look at her, 'Jo says it's absolutely unheard of not to have adjoining bathrooms when you go to hotels these days, but then Fiddleford isn't exactly a hotel. So I hope you can forgive us.'

'I must admit,' said Messy, puffing slightly, not quite keeping up, 'it's beautiful. Of course. But it isn't exactly what I expected.'

'Oh dear.' He paused in front of her bedroom door, put down the three large suitcases he had been carrying. 'What exactly has Jo been telling you?'

Months ago, before they were married, his and Jo's relationship had nearly ended because of her unnerving inability to distinguish fact from fiction. Charlie knew (to his cost) that when she was working, and she set her sights on something, she was capable of telling any number of lies in order to bring it about. He had watched her in amazement. She lied so automatically sometimes, she didn't even seem to notice she was doing it.

'She told me it was a refuge for celebrities.'

'Oh!' He sounded relieved. 'Well it is. Or it will be. But not just for celebrities. Obviously. That would be very unfair. It's for anyone who's being attacked, really.

For anyone who doesn't stand a chance to stick up for themselves because whatever they try to do or say it gets drowned out by a sort of mass jeering, or sneering, or general bullying. If that makes any sense. Which I'm sure it does to you, Messy. After your last week.'

'You don't need to feel sorry for me,' she said curtly.

'No, no. Of course not.'

'Am I the only guest you're feeling sorry for at the moment? Or is the tall guy, Grey—'

'Grey? Oh no. Grey lives here.'

'He looks very familiar. What's his second name?'

'McShane. Grey McShane. You may remember—'

'The *sex offender*?'

'Well, he isn't actually—'

'You've asked me and Chloe to stay here with a *sex offender* in the house?'

'You shouldn't –' Charlie made an effort to smile – 'believe everything you read in the press.'

'He was *convicted*. I remember reading about it. He went to prison.'

Charlie shrugged. 'He has a bad reputation. But that's the whole point of this place. Who did you think you were going to find here?' He opened her bedroom door, switched on the light and quickly slid the suitcases inside. He didn't want to have this conversation. Grey was innocent. If she wanted any more details, she would have to prise them from him – and good luck to her. Because Grey didn't much like talking about it either. 'We'll be up for another half an hour or so, if you want to come down and have a drink,' he said, backing towards the stairs. 'You'll meet Grey. And perhaps you can decide for yourself.'

\* \* \*

68

When she first walked into the room, still carrying her daughter, she was so pleasantly overwhelmed – by the size, the general impression of worn elegance and welcoming, cosy grandeur – she let out an involuntary gasp.

Against the far corner, almost reaching the ceiling and upholstered in the same faded pink flowers as the walls, was a four-poster bed so high off the ground it came with its own set of steps. Jo had put a large bunch of pink and white roses on the table beside the bed, and the room smelled delicious, she noticed: of smoky, polished wood and fresh flowers. There were thick, pale blue velvet curtains already drawn across the two large windows, and to the left of the windows, fifteen or twenty feet from the end of the bed, was an armchair with a little footstool, and in front of the footstool, lit in her honour, a flickering fire crackling in the grate. It was lovely. Like a film set. She didn't notice the paint splodges, or the damp patch above the bed. It was the loveliest room she had ever seen.

The next-door room, where Chloe was meant to be sleeping, was smaller and more homely than hers, with a two-poster instead of a four, and a large old-fashioned doll's house in the window bay. 'Hey-ho, Chloe,' Messy whispered. 'It's not so bad here, is it?' . . . The little girl slept on. But she would be beside herself when she woke up. She would never want to leave.

After putting the child to bed, changing her own clothes, unpacking their suitcases and finally running out of excuses to delay the moment any longer, Messy braced herself and headed downstairs.

She found everyone in the library, listening with varying

degrees of inattention while Jo illustrated some point by reading out loud from a book about natural childbirth. She was sitting in the lotus position, looking flexible, Messy noticed, and exceptionally luminous.

'"Pregnancy,"' Jo read, '"can be a magical time. Many women feel sensuous, harmonious and naturally creative . . . These are—" Listen to this, OK, everyone. "These are all primitive expressions of fertility . . ."' That's what I'm saying, of course. Women are by necessity more in touch with their fundamental life rhythms. Because we have to be. There simply isn't any choice . . .'

The General, scowling over a copy of *Heat* magazine, sat in his usual upright position but with a finger stuck into each ear. Grey McShane lay flat out on a sofa with his eyes closed and a tumbler of gin balanced on his chest. He was smirking. And Charlie was leaning on the mantelpiece, gazing forlornly into the fire.

'Sounds fantastic,' he said vaguely, 'I think you're probably right. But Jo, come on, be fair. This isn't exactly Dad's favourite subject. Or Grey's, I don't suppose. Perhaps we could—'

'I don't see why not,' said Jo indignantly. 'I really don't see why pregnancy has to be such a taboo subject.'

'Excuse me,' murmured Grey, still with his eyes closed, 'but taboo is not the fuckin' word. You've read that soddin' book to us every night for a week. It's been givin' me nightmares.'

'Well, you shouldn't be so squeamish.'

'Och, bollocks!' said Grey. 'I don't read you books about what it feels like to have a crap—'

'That is not *remotely* the same thing—'

Messy, who for the last minute had been standing

awkwardly in the doorway wondering how to announce herself, suddenly burst out laughing.

'Ah, there you are,' said Jo, clambering to her feet. 'At last! Come on in. Have you got everything you need? Is the room comfortable?'

'Absolutely,' said Messy. 'It's the prettiest room I've ever stayed in. Everything's lovely.'

'Is that correct?' She heard Grey chuckling complacently. 'That's not what you were sayin' to Charlie, so I hear.'

'Oh.' She looked embarrassed.

'Aye . . . Is it for yourself or the wee daughter that you're worryin', Messy?'

'No. Neither,' she said, blushing furiously. 'I wasn't thinking anything of the kind. Don't be disgusting. Can I have a drink?'

''Cause, darlin', you really needn't worry on either account.'

'You can be as rude as you like,' she snapped, 'but the fact is you're a convicted sex offender and I had no idea when I agreed to come here—' She nodded at the vast space where Grey was lounging, watching her insouciantly through his long dark lashes. 'I had no idea we'd be staying here . . .' He smiled at her, an incredibly intimate smile, full of mischief and good humour. She lost her thread. For such a famously evil pervert, she thought, he was amazingly, really *amazingly* attractive. '. . . With a convicted sex offender,' she finished weakly.

'Ha!' said Grey. 'And I had no idea that anyone could be so bloody fat!' He laughed, a low rumble at his own wit, and waited lazily for Jo to step in and smooth things over.

But she didn't. She'd been doing her breathing exercises when Charlie reported Messy's concern about Grey's difficult history, and now she was thunderstruck. All this

71

preparation, all the money they had spent, all the telephone calls, the clever little plans ... and this most obvious of problems had never even occurred to her. Grey McShane, however innocent, was going to frighten away all her guests. 'Grey's a nice man, Messy,' she said half-heartedly. 'You shouldn't believe everything you read in the press.'

'That's what I told her,' said Charlie.

'After all this *is* meant to be a sanctuary for—'

'*The universally condemned.*' Grey lingered enjoyably on the words.

'—The victims of media abuse,' corrected Jo. 'You're going to get all sorts. You're hardly likely to be meeting Snow White. And I think, you know, that we all have to respect that. As I said to you on the phone, this thing isn't going to work if we can't trust each other. We've invited you into our home with a lot of *trust*, OK? And I think it's only fair for you to trust us in return . . .'

The General groaned quietly to himself.

'Och, Messy. *Relax*, for Christ's sake!' said Grey. 'Do you think these fine people would allow me near this place if I was as wicked as people say I am? Have a drink! Sit that great big fat arse o' yours on the chair over there, if it'll take the weight. And if it's not collapsed in a minute or two I'll reward you wi' a nice big glass of gin.'

'Ha ha ha!' spluttered the General. 'I mean as a matter of fact,' he added hurriedly, to camouflage the snort of naughty amusement with which he had greeted Grey's rude and feeble joke, 'you really look quite – petite – in the flesh.'

'Absolutely,' Jo lied blatantly. Charlie cleared his throat. 'Well, maybe not petite, but then you're so lovely and tall. *Anyway!* Ha!' She patted her bump. 'I mean who am I to talk!'

Messy wavered. They looked so relaxed by the soft light of the fire. And she'd been so lonely for so very long. 'I'll have some whisky then,' she said with a wan smile. She had no idea where she was, and she was already feeling slightly confused as to why she had ever agreed to come. But there was something about the place, about this peculiar mismatch of people, which made her feel less lonely and more relaxed than she had for a long time.

'Good on you,' said Grey. 'And good luck to you, my chubby darlin'. By tomorrow morning you'll never want to leave our little Eden ever again.'

## ACCIDENT REDUCTION

There are large numbers of non-fatal accidents in and around gardens. These involve mainly those under 65, and 60% of the victims are men. The question of falls in the context of the garden will be difficult to reduce. It will be difficult to reduce cuts and abrasions except where specific activities are involved. The use of protective gloves while gardening may help.

*From GARDEN SAFETY, Home Safety Network, UK Department of Trade and Industry's website on home safety*

(iii)

# • PRIORITISE END-PRODUCT-RELATED GOALS

The following morning Charlie had yet another early meeting with his solicitor, so he left before anyone else was up. Afterwards he was ambling down Lamsbury High Street back towards his car, worrying about this and that. Worrying mostly, on this occasion, about the council's announcement that it needed to inspect the Fiddleford water supply (from a private spring. They might choose to declare it illegal), when he was startled by the nearby sound of shattering glass. He looked up to see the greengrocer's shop window had been smashed and the obvious culprit – a feeble-looking red-headed boy barely in his teens – belting away from the scene of the crime, hurtling blindly along the pavement towards him. Instinctively Charlie stretched out an arm and grabbed him.

'Fuck you. Leave me a-fuckin'-lone,' shouted the boy, in a rich West Country accent. He was twisting helplessly. 'Bloody . . . *fucker*! I'll fuckin'—'

It soon became clear that everybody in Lamsbury knew the boy by name. A crowd very quickly gathered to gloat at his captivity – something, Charlie got the impression, they had been wanting for a long time.

He was standing there holding the boy, wondering what to do next and actually feeling slightly uncomfortable about his role in the proceedings, when a middle-aged man – one of many already mustered around the action – dashed right through the crowd and skidded to a halt in front of them. '*Now* we've got you,' the man panted happily. 'And no law here neither.' At which, and to Charlie's astonishment, he delivered a fast, efficient thump to the middle of the boy's face.

The crowd gave a spontaneous cheer.

'Hey!' said Charlie. 'He's half your size. What the bloody hell do you think you're doing?'

'He's a pain in our backsides and he knows it. Don't you, Colin Fairwell?'

Next thing Charlie knew, a man from the vandalised greengrocer's shop had stepped forward to thump the boy again, and once again Lamsbury High Street was voicing its approval.

'Do that one more time,' said Charlie, 'and I'm letting him go.'

'Anyway I don't fuckin' care,' said Colin Fairwell, smiling defiantly from behind a large bubble of blood. 'I don't fuckin' care about none of you.' The bubble popped, leaving a scarlet spray across his cheeks and forehead.

'You're not allowed down this street, you little bugger. Next time we see you down here, we're going to belt you 'til there's not a breath in your puny, pathetic little body, do you hear?' The man from the greengrocer's thumped him yet again.

'Oh no,' said Charlie sadly, reluctantly doing as he'd

promised and letting the boy go. 'Really. You can't do that.'

In a flash, before anyone had even thought of recapturing him, the boy had ducked under Charlie's arm and run for it. They could all hear him laughing as he disappeared around the corner of Market Street, but nobody bothered to go after him. They knew from experience they wouldn't catch him. Colin Fairwell looked pale and feeble, but he ran very fast.

'Silly sod!' shouted a woman with low-slung bosoms. She pulled a can of baked beans out of her shopping trolley and flung it haphazardly after him. But he was long gone. A few people watched as the tin plopped onto the pavement and rolled slowly into the gutter but most of them had already started to wander away. Colin Fairwell's destructive and apparently motiveless outbursts were a fairly regular feature on Lamsbury High Street. It was his entrapment which had caused so much excitement. By the time the police arrived only Charlie and the greengrocer were left.

'It's that bloody Colin Fairwell again,' said the green-grocer, absently wiping some of Colin's blood from his thumb knuckle. 'When're you goin' to lock that bugger up and throw away the key?'

The policeman shook his head sympathetically. The boy was a bane on the existence of the entire town. He was forever wandering alone into the shops, randomly knocking over displays and smashing things, and then running away. Nobody knew why he did it.

'Attention, I shouldn't wonder,' said the policeman amiably. ''Is mum's a nutter, in't she, David? In 'n' out o' the nut'ouse, poor ol' thing. And God knows where 'is dad is.'

'Bein' frank with you, Carl, I'm not one of these ones 'oo cares too much *why* someone's doin' somethin'.'

'I know you aren't, David.'

'I'm more interested in gettin' the little buggers to stop. He should be scared, walking down here. But he's not, Carl. That's what's so strange. The more we 'ave a go at 'im the worse he seems to get. And we all do, mind. We all 'ave a go.'

'I know you do, David. I know.'

'We don't put up with 'im down 'ere. Anyone catches sightin' on 'im, we're after 'im. We 'ad Margaret throwin' her beans at 'im this afternoon.' David shook his head in bewilderment. 'But he just gets worse . . .'

The boy was cowering behind the van next to Charlie's car when he next encountered him. His face and clothes were covered in blood and across his cheeks his tear tracks were outlined in red. He was sitting on his haunches, scribbling with a stone on the tarmac around his feet and he looked so small, huddled up like that, Charlie wouldn't have noticed him if it hadn't been for the muttering.

'Colin Fairwell?' said Charlie, looming over him. 'We meet again.'

Colin Fairwell's head shot up. 'How d'you know my name?'

'Everybody knows your name,' said Charlie. 'Everybody in Lamsbury. You heard them. They want to lock you up and throw away the key.'

The boy turned back to the marks he was making on the tarmac. 'So why d'you let me go then?'

'I didn't like the way they were bashing you.'

'Did you like the way I was bashing the shop window?'

'Don't be silly.' Charlie hesitated. He wasn't sure what to do next. What he wanted to do was to go back to Fiddleford and set to work on a ruse to keep the water inspectors at bay. He wanted to talk to Mr Gunner about the fishing licences, and, more urgently, he needed to talk to Jo (preferably without Grey or the General present) about how quickly she could rope in more paying guests. But the boy looked so pathetic crouching there: wretched and friendless and bloodstained. With a mother in the nuthouse. And a streetful of angry shopkeepers waiting to beat him up if he ventured out of the car park again. Charlie couldn't quite bring himself to walk away.

'Look, er—' he said irritably, making a point of examining his watch. 'D'you want a lift somewhere? I'm going out towards Fiddleford, if you know where that is . . . I can drop you off at your – mother's. Place. Or something. Is she there? I can drop you off at home if you want. Where do you live?'

'No thanks,' Colin said drearily.

'What're you going to do then?'

The boy shrugged.

'Well, come on, buck up,' said Charlie. 'What're you going to do? You can't sit here muttering to yourself all afternoon. And you certainly can't go back out that way . . .' He indicated the car park's only exit, which led directly onto the High Street. 'Shall I drop you off at school, perhaps?'

The boy laughed suddenly, a blast of genuine mirth which took Charlie by surprise. 'I'm better on Lamsbury

High Street, thank you very much,' he said. 'But you can take me down Fiddleford if you like.'

'I don't like. That's not what I was offering.'

'I used to love Fiddleford,' he said wistfully.

Bloody hell. Nobody wanted this little thug hanging around in the village. But it was a small village, and Charlie loved it too. He couldn't help being curious. 'Really? What do you know about Fiddleford?'

'Nothing,' Colin said automatically.

'OK. Fine . . . Look. Perhaps you should take that nose to a doctor.'

'My nan used to live in Fiddleford.'

'How about the surgery, Colin?' asked Charlie hopefully. 'I could drop you there.'

'If you're comin' from Lamsbury, right? She used to live in the place with the little, little door, two up from the old post office. On the left. D'you know? It's got a tiny, tiny door. About—' The boy, all sullenness, defiance and misery suddenly eradicated by the memory of the tiny door, was even moved to stand up to demonstrate. 'So high,' he said, indicating with his bloodstained hand an unfeasible two feet off the ground.

Charlie laughed. He knew the house Colin meant and the door was small but not that small. In fact until a couple of years ago, when Charlie first took over management of the estate, his family had owned it. Charlie sold it soon after the old woman died. He tried to remember her name and was ashamed when he realised he couldn't. Anyway, it now belonged to a couple of weekenders from London, who were almost never there.

'D'you know it?' said Colin enthusiastically. 'Will you drive me there?'

Charlie shook his head. He didn't want the boy in Fiddleford. What would he possibly find to do there, except cause trouble? 'There aren't any doors that small in Fiddleford,' he said unhelpfully. 'Look—' Again, he hesitated. 'I'm sorry, Colin, I've got to go. So if I can't drive you anywhere in Lamsbury. If I can't drive you home . . .' He smiled unhappily and started walking towards his car. 'Don't go smashing any more shop windows now, will you?'

Placidly, the boy sat down again, apparently unperturbed by Charlie's unwillingness to pass the time with him, quite accustomed to this and any other form of rebuff. It occurred to Charlie that this was probably the first conversation the boy had had all day . . . Christ, all week . . . Oh dear God, probably since his grandmother had died . . . Charlie was beginning to hate himself for trying to walk away . . . 'I mean,' he said suddenly, turning back, sounding very abrupt, 'what're you going to do next? Don't just *sit down!* For Christ's sake, Colin Fairwell, I've got enough on my plate. Please! *Pull yourself together!*'

Colin looked at him in astonishment. 'You what? What're you getting like that for? I only told you about the door. I don't know why you can't remember it. It's right there. Right in the middle of the village.'

'Well, of course I—' But he was determined not to allow his good nature to get the better of him, as it almost always did. 'Of course I remember the house,' he snapped. 'I'm just saying—'

Suddenly there came a cry from the opposite end of the car park: 'There 'e is!'

They looked up to see a group of adolescent boys in school uniform standing about fifty yards away, all pointing at Colin. 'Oi, you!' they shouted, breaking into a run. 'Colin Fairwell, you poof. Come 'ere! We got unfinished business with you!'

Charlie thought they hadn't seen him. 'Not to worry,' he shouted. 'I've got him! The – er – the police are on their way!' The boys came to a rapid halt, looked at each other and quickly huddled into a muttering bunch. Charlie, somewhat surprised by his own effect, turned back towards Colin with a reassuring smile.

'Oh, fuck,' said Colin, looking terrified, staring wide-eyed over Charlie's shoulder. 'For fuck's sake get out the way! They're gonna—' He pointed; Charlie looked up in time to see a lighted bottle flying through the air. '*Duck*, you idiot!' shouted Colin. 'It's one o' their petrol thingies . . .'

It hit the tarmac several yards in front of them. 'Bloody hell!' said Charlie.

'*Run!*' said Colin. 'They'll kill us! I'm not jokin'! They'll fuckin' kill us!'

A second bottle came hurtling over the car rooftops towards them. This time it landed so close the flames whipped over Colin's trainers. 'Get in my car,' Charlie shouted. 'Behind the van. The Land Rover. It's unlocked.'

Colin didn't wait to be asked twice, and by the time Charlie had made it to his own seat, the boys had the Land Rover surrounded. Charlie started the engine. He waited for the boys to clear out of the way, but when one of them produced a third – unlit – petrol bomb, he reversed anyway, sending them flying in all directions. And as he sped away they shouted at him, full of indignation: 'Nutter! Crazy bastard! Fuckin' *roadhog*! You shouldn't be allowed on the road!'

Charlie and Colin drove for several minutes without saying a word, both of them too shaken to speak. Eventually Colin broke the silence. 'I'm bloody glad you started driving when you did,' he said quietly. 'They would a' had us, you know.' He and Charlie smiled at each other and then slowly, as the horror and relief began to settle, they started laughing, and once they'd started they found they couldn't stop.

Which is how Colin Fairwell first tipped up at Fiddleford. The second official visitor to the refuge, and one who would certainly never be able to pay his way.

Jo was on the telephone to *Hello!* magazine when Charlie and Colin arrived home, so she didn't see them come in. The General, as usual, was working his way through the papers; it was something he did with more intensity than ever since the bombing of Afghanistan had started, much to Grey's irritation. And Grey (on whom the bombing had wrought quite the opposite effect; he'd given up most newspapers in boredom and disgust, and had taken up cooking increasingly elaborate meals for everyone instead) had just put some bacon on. He had spent the morning feeling uncharacteristically restless, unable to get any decent conversation out of the General, and was hoping that the distant smell of a late breakfast might finally lure the fat new guest and her daughter out of their beds.

Whether it was the bacon or not, at the moment it was ready the fat new guest, her daughter, Charlie and Colin all walked into the kitchen at once.

'Ah!' Grey cried triumphantly. 'So you're alive are you, Messy Monroe? I was beginning to wonder if the bed had collapsed and you were lyin' up there concussed, or somethin' . . .'

'Ha ha,' said Messy mildly. 'You needn't have worried. The bed and I both survived the night very well, thank you.'

'I'm doin' some eggs, darlin',' he said, turning back to the stove. 'Ducks' eggs. Very rich and quite disgustin'. Unless you eat 'em in tiny wee mouthfuls. With the bacon, o' course. An' a little bit of fried bread. How many do you want?'

'Anyone seen Jo?' said Charlie, glancing nervously around the room.

Chloe said, 'Why's that boy got blood on his face?'

But nobody paid any attention to either of them. Messy absently stroked the back of Chloe's head, as she always did when her daughter was within stroking distance. She said, 'No eggs for me, thank you, and just one for Chloe . . . I had no idea it was so late. We didn't wake up, did we, Chloe? Either of us. Must be something to do with the West Country air.'

'Has anyone seen Jo?' Charlie said again.

'Excuse me for bein' rude,' said Colin loudly – surprisingly loudly for someone so small, who hadn't yet been introduced – 'but can *I* 'ave some o' those nice rich eggs?'

Which was when the adults finally noticed he was in the room.

'Good God!' said the General, looking up from his paper at last. 'Charlie, did that pasty fellow come in with you?'

Poor little pasty Colin. Their first impressions could not have been less favourable. He looked terrible. The blood on his face had turned crusty and black against his dead white face. There were deep rings beneath his pale eyes and on the top left side of his head, his red hair had flopped apart to reveal a long bald strip of scalp with an angry-looking scar running across the middle of it.

''Course you can,' said Charlie. 'Grey? There's enough for Colin, isn't there? Everyone, this is Colin by the way. His grandmother used to live in Forge Cottage . . .' But nobody heard the last bit, because he was already leaving the room.

'One impression you're probably not receiving from the cuttings, Alyson, is how *attractive* Messy actually is. Think – Catherine Zeta-Jones, if you like. Only a bit – larger. But she's actually fabulous-looking. Better-looking than Catherine in a way because of course she's got those amazing Elizabeth Taylor eyes . . . The point is, Alyson, you and I know how negative the media's projection of the size-plus group is. And of course I can't speak for you, but it's certainly something *I* feel very uncomfortable about. *For them.* For the Size-Plus Group . . . Well exactly. It's dreadful, isn't it? And here is an opportunity to turn that around! To put someone size-plus but fabulous – with a lovely, darling little daughter . . .'

Though you could never have guessed it from her enthusiastic, professional tone, or from the smile she gave to Charlie when he first found her, hard at work in the back office, Jo, at that moment, was suffering from a major confidence crisis. *Perhaps*, she was thinking, *she had misjudged Messy's news value? Perhaps nobody would be interested in her? And if she had misjudged Messy's news value, what was to stop her from misjudging the next person's? And the next? Until Fiddleford was forced into bankruptcy. And the*

*General would have to go and live in a home and she and Charlie and their family would have to—* 'Mm, yes Alyson – can I stop you there? Because I do, I agree with you one hundred per cent. But the fact is Messy's hit a nerve, hasn't she? Like it or not. I think – larger – people do carry around a lot of negative feelings. I think there *is* a lot of anger out there. Now what I'm saying to you, Alyson, is that here we have Messy Monroe and she's a very acceptable face of that— anger, for want of a better word. Everybody knows who she is . . . Messy's bringing a message of HOPE to all your size-plus readers . . . She's telling people that you CAN be size-plus and, you know, write a book about it.'

But Alyson wasn't biting. It was obvious Jo was wasting her time. Worse than that, she realised, she was teetering on the verge of sounding desperate. Quickly, coolly and with her customary good grace, she extricated herself from the conversation, hung up, looked across at Charlie and grimaced.

'Shit,' she said. 'That pretty much leaves us with *Too True!* And they don't pay much . . . Mind you, they're very downmarket. They've probably got fat readers galore.'

'That would be the size-double-plus group, would it?' Charlie said, but he'd only been half listening. He had picked up a handful of invoices from the desk and was learning for the first time the full cost of Jo's ludicrous new telephone system (which, as well as costing a fortune, required that each house member carry a personalised 'telephone unit' with them at all times). 'Have we paid this bill?' he said. 'Because if not I think we should send the whole thing back. Dad refuses to use his and so does Grey, and I think I've lost mine . . . I had no idea it was so expensive.'

She leant across the desk, less simple than it used to be

with the bump in front, and snatched the invoices away from him. 'The system works,' she said stubbornly. 'We've just got to persuade the others to cooperate. In a house this size we've got to have some sort of procedure to stop calls going astray.'

Charlie laughed.

'It's not funny, Charlie. *It's perfectly possible* . . . It just needs a bit of focus on everyone's part.'

'Right,' he said amenably, suddenly realising how tired she looked and not wanting to make things any more difficult for her than he was already about to: 'I've got two pieces of news; one's good and one's bad. Which do you want first?'

'The bad.'

He told her the good news first. 'You'll be delighted to hear,' he said, 'that Fiddleford Manor is now officially registered with Lamsbury District Council as an Accredited Food Premises.'

'Crikey,' she chuckled, 'what the Hell does that mean?'

Charlie shrugged. 'I don't think it means anything much. You have to fill in the form . . . But apparently they're not allowed to refuse you.'

So that was the good news. The bad news, of course, was Colin.

Jo tried; she wanted to feel as generous as Charlie did. But she was tired and pregnant and terrified about their lack of cash. She was furious.

The thought of eating while Grey leant against the Aga and watched, and no doubt kept up a running commentary on the life expectancy of whatever chair she was sitting on, had done something highly unusual to Messy's appetite.

So unusual, in fact, that when she sat down without duck's egg or bacon or anything more than a cup of black coffee Chloe stared at her in silent, fearful astonishment. She was much more startled by her mother's lack of breakfast than by Colin's tale of battery in Lamsbury that morning. She had never seen her mother refuse food before.

'Come on, Chloe, eat up,' Messy said tetchily, when eventually Colin paused for breath. 'What are you looking like that for?'

'Are you dying, Mummy?' the little girl whispered.

Grey cackled happily. 'Your mummy thinks she's come to stay in a fat farm,' he said.

'A *fat farm!* Oh. Ha ha. I know what that is,' jabbered Colin, spraying the table with blobs of fried egg. The excitement of having an audience polite enough not to thump him was making Colin very unwilling to shut up.

'Hey!' snapped Grey. 'Eat that egg in bloody great gobfuls and you'll never look at a duck's egg again. Not without vomiting.'

'But this ain't a fat farm, though, is it?' Colin said, adjusting his fork-load obligingly. 'Can't be. With you givin' us eggs with all the cholesterol in. And then all the fat in the fryin' that's terrible fer your arteries. No, Messy. If you don't mind my sayin', this ain't no fat farm. You come to *completely* the wrong place.'

'Where d'you learn all that crap?' said Grey.

'It's jus' a borin' ol' house in fact. A big 'un. But jus' a borin' ol' house anyway. It belongs to that fellow over there readin' the newspaper. I know 'cos he's been 'ere since I was visitin' my nan. In fac' proba'ly,' he added, 'proba'ly even longer . . .'

'This place,' interrupted Grey, 'is not just a boring old

house, Colin. If I can get a bloody word in edgeways. *This place*, you little sod, is about the only piece of Paradise you get when the rest o' the world has told you to go to Hell.'

'Oh,' said Colin, looking blank. 'So it's not a fat farm then, is it?'

'It's not a fat farm, no. That was a joke. But it is – this beautiful place is more than just a house. It's a hiding place. And a business. A *commercial enterprise*, if you know what that is. D'you know what that is?'

'That's right,' said Colin mildly. His attention was beginning to wander.

'And the point is if you can't pay for the bit o' peace you get comin' here – and Colin, God knows how long you'll be staying but don't go tellin' me *you'll* be puttin' much in the fuckin' pot – you have to ask yourself how you're gonna make yourself useful in other ways.'

'What's that then? Puttin' what in the pots?'

'You too, Chloe. Your mother may be coughin' up a bit. Actually I don't believe she is, but that's another matter. *You* certainly aren't. So you've got to think what you can do. D'ya understand, Chloe? The General there's scourin' the papers – an' as you can see,' he added irritably, 'it's a bloody full-time job . . . I'm doin' the cookin', OK? And bloody well, I might add, though nobody around here appreciates it. Messy Monroe's addin' a bit of glamour—'

'Ha!' said Messy, blushing ferociously once again. 'That's a funny one.'

Grey pretended not to notice. 'The point is, Chloe – Colin, are you listenin' to me?' (They nodded politely.) 'Whether you're payin' or no, it's a haven. A little oasis. A bloody godsend. And you're all responsible. We are *all responsible* for keepin' it that way. For keepin' the bastards—'

'Easy does it,' said Messy. 'She's only four.'

'—the bars— the ba— the fuckin' *baddies* at bay.'

'What baddies?' said Chloe.

'Robbers and things,' said Messy evasively. 'All sorts of baddies.'

'Aye,' said Grey. 'And the reporters who were writin' cheeky things abou' you and your mother . . . Animal slaughterers, too. And other people. People carrying little black suitcases. Or brown ones—'

'People wearin' blazers with St George's on 'em,' added Colin enthusiastically.

'Anyone, really,' said Grey, 'whose only purpose in comin' all the way up that drive is to make trouble for any of us.'

'Oh,' said Chloe solemnly and fell silent to think about it. 'So you think we should set some traps?'

'Aye, we should,' said Grey. 'Excellent idea.'

'And mines,' said Colin.

'Another excellent idea!' said Grey.

'I mean *explosive* mines.'

'Absolutely,' said Grey impassively. 'But you have to know how to build 'em.'

Colin turned a shade paler – hardly possible, but he managed it. 'Explosions aren't funny, you know.'

'Ah! And there's me thinkin' *you* were jokin'!'

'But we could do somethin',' he added. 'Maybe so they land in a whole load o' cowpats. On their heads. Or somethin' . . .'

Chloe started giggling. Which made Colin giggle. The way she was looking at him actually made him feel like his chest would burst. Colin had never felt so respected in his life.

It was Messy who suggested that, rather than go outside, which was Colin and Chloe's preferred option, they look up how to make booby traps on the internet. By the time Charlie and Jo had finished arguing and come to find them they were all in the library, jostling each other for space in front of Charlie's computer, and Colin was giggling again, because Messy had put in 'booby trap', and a bra firm had come up.

'Oh, I get it!' Colin was saying. 'D'you get it? *Booby* trap! It's a booby *trap*! Chloe, d'you know what boobies are?'

'Hello, hello!' said Jo, smiling brightly but feeling very tense. 'What's the big joke?'

'There's a bra firm!' said Colin, sniggering uncontrollably. 'We put in booby trap. And a *bra firm* come up!'

'Here we are,' said Grey. 'This is more like it. Listen to this, Colin. Chloe. Everyone. Listen to this. "*In the absence of explosive materials the enemy may resort to non-explosive booby-trap techniques. These may include punji stakes, spiked mud balls, bear traps and scorpion-filled boxes. As a rule, these traps in themselves are not lethal or completely destructive, and as a result may be accompanied by ambushes . . .*" Doesn't mention cowpats . . . Still.'

'You must be Colin,' said Jo patiently. 'I'm Jo. I hear they were giving you a rough time in Lamsbury this morning?'

Colin nodded, still chortling about boobies, not yet quite capable of speech. Jo watched a string of spit dribble from the side of his mouth and land in a little puddle on his bloodstained sweatshirt. This, she thought sadly, was not what she'd had in mind when the idea of a celebrity sanctuary had first been discussed.

'Where's your mother, Colin. Your mum?' (Jo corrected

herself.) 'Your mum'll be worried not to have heard from you. Don't you think you should call?'

'No,' he said simply, wiping his eyes. Jo's mention of his mother had sucked all the life out of the joke. 'My mum's never worried.'

'Where is she? Is she—' Jo hesitated, uncertain how to proceed, but very keen to be tactful, 'in the hospital?'

'Nope.'

'Is she at home?'

'Nope.'

'So . . . where is she?'

Colin shrugged. 'Dunno, do I? Gone on one of 'er walkarounds, I shouldn't doubt . . .' Sagely, without a hint of self-pity, he shook his head. 'They do 'er no ends o' good.'

'And . . .' Jo struggled unhappily against the surge of warmth for him which was seeping through, in grave danger of clouding her professional judgement, '. . . When do you expect her back?'

'That's up to 'er, innit?'

'Well – Colin. I don't want to be rude and – you know – you're obviously very brave. But *somebody* must be responsible for you . . .'

'Me,' he said. 'Jus' only me.'

'He's a fuckin' prodigy,' muttered Grey. 'Takes most people a lifetime to work that out.'

'Do you have a social worker?'

'No.'

'Well. For Christ's sake, Colin—' It burst out before she could stop herself. And as she said it she knew that the battle was lost. 'You know perfectly well you can't stay here!'

He looked at her with the same calm surprise with which he'd looked at Charlie when Charlie had snapped at him back at the car park. 'What're you gettin' so het up about?' he said gently. 'I'm only passin' through. Jus' lookin' at the computer here.'

'I'm sorry. Sorry, Colin. I didn't mean to shout.'

'Of course the question remains,' said Grey, 'if you're only passing through, where exactly are you passing through *to*?'

Colin scowled at him. 'What am I, a clerrvoyan— thinge-mejig? How'm I s'posed to know the answer to a bloody stupid question like that?'

'Well—' said Jo. 'Most people do.'

'Is that right?' he said confidently. 'I don't think so.'

'Are you any good with horses?' Charlie asked suddenly.

Colin shrugged.

'Or chickens?'

'How do I know?'

'Gardening? Chopping wood?'

'For Christ's sake, he's a child!' snapped Jo. 'And this isn't a fucking poor house. He's not chopping wood! He should be at school.'

Charlie thought of the uncommonly disagreeable St George's boys he and Colin had encountered that morning. 'I hardly think so,' he said. 'Anyway there are plenty of old books in the nursery if he wants to learn something. But if he's going to stay at Fiddleford, he's got to make himself useful just like everyone else.' He turned to Colin, who was standing there as alert, suddenly, as a hunted animal, his pale face rigid with attention and hope. 'I suggest,' said Charlie coolly, 'and obviously assuming Jo's all right about it—'

'Oh God,' she sighed, gave Colin a grudging smile. 'Well of course I bloody well am.'

'—that you stay here,' Charlie continued, 'at least until you can work out where you want to go afterwards.' The width – the amazing width – of Colin's answering grin made the dried blood on his cheeks crack and fall in little flakes onto the floor. 'And in the meantime, is there really no one we should call? I bet you're on some sort of list. People usually are. Somewhere. Shouldn't we at least telephone the school?'

'I haven't been there fer weeks. It'll only remind 'em. Anyway I reckon they're pleased to see the back o' me.'

'Or – Jo's already mentioned social workers . . .'

'Oh! Ho ho! They used to come round, but they haven't been round fer months!' He grinned. ''Cos they can never catch up wi' me! I'm too fast. You saw 'ow I went this mornin'!'

'I did,' said Charlie coldly. It was a timely reminder of how the two of them had met. 'And by the way, Colin, if I hear the sound of breaking glass – breaking anything – I don't even care if you're responsible for it – you're out. Out. Is that clear?'

'Yes, sir,' Colin said solemnly. 'Yes, it is clear. I shan't break nothin' at all. I shall only be useful round about.'

Grey laughed, a deep appreciative rumble.

'How old are you?' continued Charlie.

'Seventeen.'

'Don't lie.'

'Fifteen.'

Charlie stared at him.

'Fifteen. I am! I just look ever so young . . . all right, fourteen . . . Fourteen?'

'You're not fourteen,' said Jo.

'I'd say about eleven,' said Messy.

'That's very close,' said Chloe. 'Because I actually know how old he is, don't I, Colin?'

'Don't tell 'em!' said Colin.

'Och for God's sake! You're behaving like the fuckin' Gestapo. What does it bloody matter?' Grey looked down at Colin, smiling gratefully up at him. The boy was not an appealing sight, even to Grey, who had never rated a tidy appearance as highly as other people did. 'Mind you,' he said, wrinkling his handsome Roman nose, 'I don't give a bugger how old he is, but I think he'd do well to take a bath.'

For a week or so after that everything at Fiddleford worked like clockwork. Even the General showed signs of mellowing. He didn't participate much. He sat quietly by the Aga in the kitchen, muttering to himself about the disappointing state of the world, but he was slowly discovering that the fresh injection of life into his old home was not entirely unpleasant after all. In fact he'd recently gone to the trouble of identifying two potential new recruits: a British tennis player called Nigel, currently ranked 87th in the world and accused by Davis Cup officials of match-fixing (of purposely dropping a national match for his own financial gain); and an obscure young Royal cousin called Anatollatia, who'd been set up and recorded by a Sunday newspaper negotiating an £85,000 fee to participate in a 'nude photo-shoot' for a magazine which didn't exist.

And though he still didn't like her much, it would have been impossible for anyone to remain unmoved by Jo's industry. Charlie pleaded with her to slow down but it seemed that she couldn't. After so many years in London, fighting to keep her place at the top of the game, she didn't know how else to approach life. She was a perfectionist, and she couldn't help it. Relaxing (except on honeymoon) never had been Jo's greatest talent. And she had recently taken to doing thirty minutes of meditation and yoga every morning, specifically to improve on that.

She worked hard at her pregnancy just as she worked hard at everything. She drove to London once a week for her ante-natal classes. She avoided alcohol, cigarette smoke, caffeine, tea, soft cheeses, blue cheeses, cured ham, raw meat, raw fish, shellfish, soft boiled eggs, non-organic dairy products, hot baths, cold medicines, hair dye, heavy weights, steam rooms, mobile telephones, computer screens, loud noises, sudden movements, negative feelings and foot massages. She drank a herbal tea to help prepare for labour and another for inner calm. She took a first aid course, examined the league tables for the local state primaries ... She also repainted the boot room, the pantry and the back hall. She negotiated a highly satisfactory Messy exclusive with *Too True!* magazine. And she found telephone numbers for Nigel the tennis player and for Anatollatia in her contacts book ... And she was very happy. As happy as a highly strung workaholic is ever capable of being.

Meanwhile Grey cooked up ever more exquisite dinners; Charlie filled in interminable forms for interminable government departments and even managed to escape his desk for long enough to mend the fences in the top two fields; Colin vandalised nothing at all, and he and Chloe laid the foundations for a new business venture.

Charlie had introduced the children to what was left of

the Fiddleford animals – not very much any more: the donkey, his twin sister's retired hunter, two pigs, a dozen dairy cows, fifty sheep, five peculiarly aggressive geese, and the chickens, whom Les insisted were in a permanent state of shock as a result of the murderous MAFF visits and were consequently no longer capable of laying eggs.

'You got thirty-six chickens,' Grey said. 'That should be near on thirty eggs, which leaves at least two dozen eggs for the village shop every day. Not a fortune, I grant you. But it's a bloody start, isn't it? Get the chickens laying – Les's a lazy bugger, I'll bet they only need a feedin'. And you can put some money back in the pot!'

With the help of Messy – and later the General, who always found diagrams irresistible – Colin drew intricate, colour-and-date-coded maps of the hens' living area, making marks wherever he or Chloe suspected there would soon be a stash of eggs. The two of them could think and talk of little else.

Messy took a little longer to fall under the Fiddleford spell. It was only when she discovered the walled garden, on the same day that the dreaded team from *Too True!* were due to see her, that she really began to get the point of the place. That morning she was trying to make notes for a possible *Fatty Revolution* sequel. But combined with her terror of the forthcoming interview, the delicious cooking smells wafting up to her bedroom (a continual reminder not just of her nervous love-sick hunger but of its handsome and inscrutable cause) made concentration impossible. After about an hour she gave up and took herself for a walk around the park.

Normally Messy hated walking, but on that day she

ambled along very happily: through the ornamental wood to the side of the chicken runs, past the moss-covered tennis court and the croquet lawn riddled with molehills, through an archway of overgrown laurel bushes, to a high stone wall covered in ivy, and an old door which opened only after she'd kicked it several times. Behind it she discovered a garden – smothered in weeds and clearly long since neglected, but which took her breath away.

A straight path ran down the middle of the garden, lined by perfectly spaced rose bushes, all of them eight or ten feet tall and contorted through lack of pruning. Behind the rose bushes there were apple trees with linking branches, planted in perfect parallel lines, and each emerging from a thick carpet of rotting fruit. As she wandered in awe from corner wall to far corner she tried to imagine what the place must have been like in its prime, when all the vegetables and house flowers flourished in meticulous, regimented lines, and the raspberry cage hadn't collapsed, and the glass in the greenhouse hadn't been broken, and the beds weren't overcome by nettles and grass. It must have been perfect once: elegant, functional, busy, required, and it struck Messy, neglected and overgrown herself, as unbearably, extraordinarily romantic. She looked around her, but there was no one there. Nothing. Only waste and chaos and tantalising promises of splendour. Without pausing to consider anything, least of all the enormity of the task ahead, Messy, who had never gardened in her life before, never even considered it, found a fork at the back of the broken greenhouse, and started digging.

'*Excellent!*' bellowed the General, his eyes shining, his face ruddy with joy. 'Right-i-ho. Thank you very much. And do drop in if you're ever in the neighbourhood, won't you? Absolutely! We're always here! Otherwise we must look out for each other at the old Pearly Gates, what? Ha ha ha. That's right! Shan't be long now!' He said goodbye very merrily, pressed a random series of buttons on his infernal 'telephone unit', slipped the receiver into his jacket pocket and headed back out to the hall.

'Charlie! . . . Charlie!'

He found his son in the library (in his gumboots because he was still hoping to put in a few hours on the farm), waylaid as always by paperwork; on this occasion by the application form for a Certificate of Safety Approval from the Lamsbury District Fire and Emergency Planning Authority.

'Charlie!' whispered the General. He closed the door behind him and looked furtively around the room. 'Where are the ladies? Are they out?'

'Hi, Dad. Do you think we've got any "explosive or highly flammable materials stored or used in or under the premises"?'

'What?'

'They want to know the "*maximum quantity* . . . the *maximum quantity* liable to be *exposed* at any one time".' Charlie scrunched his hair and scowled at the form in front of him. 'But what do they mean? What quantity? Exposed to what?'

'I don't know, Charlie. And nor do I care. *Where are the ladies?*'

Charlie sighed in despair. 'Makes no bloody sense at all. I'll put a "6". See if that keeps them quiet . . . Sorry, Dad. If you're looking for Messy, she's out in the walled garden being photographed for a magazine.'

'Oh yes. Of course. *Too True!* Excellent. Excellent

magazine.' He checked the room for a second time. 'What about Jo?'

'They're together.' Charlie looked at his father more closely. 'What's up? Are you all right?'

'I think,' said the General decisively, walking with great gusto to the front of Charlie's desk, *we've got the Big One*. I've been talking to an old chap—' He chuckled. 'I think he was surprised to discover I was still alive as a matter of fact. However, in other respects he's a man very much in the know . . . And the good news is, he's going to put in a good word. But it is rather difficult. With Messy, of course . . .'

'What's difficult? What are you talking about?'

'Mmm? For Heaven's sake, Charlie, concentrate! Don't you read the papers?'

'Not much. You know I don't.'

'Dear fellow, does the name *Maurice Morrison* mean nothing to you?'

# HOW TO WASH YOUR HANDS

Always use a wash hand basin provided exclusively for this purpose. Use comfortably hot water and soap. Liquid soap is best because a bar of soap may carry bacteria left by the last person who used it. Use a nail brush to clean your nails after handling raw foods or going to the toilet. Rinse your hands before drying them. There are several methods available for drying your hands including disposable paper towels and clean roller towels. Never dry your hands on a tea towel, service cloth or protective clothing; you could cause contamination.

*Food Safety First Principles Workbook, for the Basic Food Hygiene Course. Published on behalf of the Chartered Institute of Environmental Health*

(iv)

# • SUPPORT AND DEVELOP
# APPROPRIATE PROCEDURES

The eternally marvellous Maurice Morrison was experienced enough in the business of his own popularity to be feeling very frightened that morning. He'd seen it happen to colleagues: men who had previously seemed unassailable. One day they find themselves undermined by some silly, unfortunate, *wholly unrelated* little incident. And the next thing they know their whole damn life begins to unravel. A whiff of vulnerability and suddenly all the worms in the woodwork feel empowered to come out and play. Maurice Morrison's marvellous existence was riddled with worms. Rotten with them. He needed to be careful.

Not, of course, that what had happened was in any way his fault. It wasn't. And the fact that he was being blamed, although inevitable, was also extremely unfair. In fact the more he thought about it the more indignant it made him. After all, wasn't he still, teeny-tiny secrets and all, just as he had been yesterday: one of the most media-friendly multi-millionaires in the country? Wasn't he still, as he had been the last time he looked, the Labour Government's only appointed Minister for Kindness? Wasn't he as unceasingly generous to charity? And as persistently well-mannered? And as likely to come to the rescue when unattractive lady panellists were out of their depth on influential television shows? And wasn't he still, in spite of everything, the creator of fulfilling employment for many, many thousands of grateful personnel? Yes, dammit! Yes, he bloody well was!

Yet here he found himself, cowering in the bright white corner of his West London office (which, in lighter moments, he liked to call his 'Zone-of-Zones', because of course he had many offices; the top floor of his head office here in Notting Hill just happened to be his favourite). He was too afraid to answer his own telephone, too afraid to look out of his own window, too afraid to get into his own private elevator and walk out into his own steel-and-marble ground-floor reception hall. Too afraid to think straight. Which was very rare.

What had happened yesterday was a tragedy. Of course. There was no other word for it. And he had released a statement saying exactly that. Extending heartfelt – *heartfelt* – sympathy. And it was heartfelt. But, honestly – he glanced resentfully at the headline in that day's first edition *Evening Standard* – if the reporters had only bothered to look at this thing in the perspective of his lifetime's, of Maurice Morrison's whole *lifetime's* achievements, they would be forced to agree – everyone would be forced to agree – that he was being outrageously shoddily treated.

Because apart from anything else Maurice Morrison believed passionately in health-and-safety-in-the-workplace. (Passionately enough, the PM himself had once humorously remarked, that when he talked about it, as he often did, he could say it – health-and-safety-in-the-workplace – so quickly it sounded like a single word.) Not only that, sitting on his desk at his office in Westminster there were documents awaiting his signature which actively supported the implementation of many more health-and-safety-in-the-workplace regulations, specifically for unkindly treated persons in the sixteen- to eighteen-year age group. Until this moment his myriad of magnificent companies had safety records which were impeccable. Unimpeachable. His employees benefited from some of the most rigorous safety directives of any employees in the land.

Meanwhile, needless to say, in other parts of the country, in companies not owned by him, terrible work-related accidents were happening every day. He knew because he had the statistics here in front of him. And did any of those make the front page of the *Evening Standard*? They did not.

He sighed with frustration, momentarily forgetting that of course by far the most serious infringement recorded that day, and the single reason the Minister for Kindness was cowering, so alone and angry, in his Zone-of-Zones, had occurred at an airy wine bar in Fulham which was part of a chain of airy wine bars, which was part of an empire, which belonged to— Him. Seventeen-year-old Albanian busboy and illegal immigrant, Gjykata Drejtohet, had been employed at Simply Organic for only a week when the accident had happened. At about 8.30 p.m. and for an hourly rate of £1.20 less than the lawful minimum, Gjykata had been carrying the remains of two large salads and a half-eaten portion of potato skinz back towards the kitchen when he tripped on an *uneven floor surface*, stumbled into an open beer hatch by the side of the bar and cracked his head on a metal ladder. Sixteen hours later he was still unconscious and the newshounds were keeping a vigil outside the hospital where he lay.

Maurice felt terrible. Of course he did. He had a young son of his own: Rufus, aged twenty-three. Maurice had already tried to imagine, twice, how he would feel if Rufus had fallen down a manhole and on a metal ladder at his place of work. But he couldn't do it. Rufus, who was actually in the middle of a postgraduate course at Yale, tended to look where he was going. But that wasn't the point.

The point was Gjykata Drijitohit. *Drejtohet*. Gjykata Drejtohet, who had been an outstanding busboy, according to the wine bar staff: bubbly and willing, hardworking – and very, very good at English for someone who had only emerged from the tunnel (it now bloody well transpired) about three weeks earlier. The point *was*, it was a tragedy. And the other point was, it wasn't Maurice Morrison's fault.

With another heavy sigh, he picked himself up from his cowering place, and risked a tiny peep through the Zone-of-Zone's slatted blinds. It was teeming with people down there, all of them journalists, no doubt. Two bloody great satellite vans had joined the throng since he last looked. He should have stayed at home, bided his time, worked out a strategy. Except reporters were lurking for him there, as well. Even, if the housekeeper was to be believed, at his irritatingly remote castle half an hour north of Inverness. There was absolutely no escape.

As he stood there in the semi-darkness, in his bright white office, with all the slatted blinds pulled closed, he felt more tempted to cry than he had since the day his mother died, fifteen years ago. Where was his family now, when he needed them? Where were his friends? Rufus was at Yale of course, and his daughter and two ex-wives no longer spoke to him. But what about the *friends*? The people he trusted and the people who trusted him? He tried to conjure a face – the face of that sort of friend, where trust flowed freely between them, to-and-fro, to-and-fro . . . Maurice Morrison felt a blast of icy loneliness. Because not a single face came to mind.

It was just at that moment, that rare moment of fear in his frantic, successful life, that the call came from General Maxwell McDonald. With an animal-like whimper and without pausing for a moment's thought, Maurice Morrison leapt onto the telephone.

As soon as the General learnt the astonishing news that Morrison had accepted his invitation, he whisked himself off to his dressing room for a sprucing, returning to the library twenty minutes later with his thick grey hair flattened against his head, and wearing a regiment tie with a stripe which indicated the great significance of the occasion.

'Charlie?' he said. 'It's confirmed! I'm on my way to fetch him right now. We've devised a plan to get the hounds off the scent, so to speak, and I'm to pick him up at . . .' The General paused, took a precautionary look around the room, and finished his sentence in a whisper – '*I shall tell you later*. Tell Jo . . . *Tell Jo* – ha ha! She *will* be surprised, won't she? Tell Jo he's going to need . . . a lot of towels and things. Soap. Bath bubbles and so forth.'

*     *     *

Jo was a pragmatic woman and Maurice Morrison was a catch beyond the reaches of even her contacts book, a catch beyond her wildest dreams. In fact he made her own little victories with Nigel the tennis player (due at Fiddleford the following morning) and Princess Anatollatia the would-be stripper (due in time for dinner) look paltry. So she took the news of the General's coup with her usual professional good grace. What did it matter, so long as they all paid? 'Well done to him,' she said. 'Now then,' as ever getting straight to the crux of the matter, 'someone's got to break the news to Messy.'

'Well – Grey,' said Charlie casually, 'I would have thought. Wouldn't you?'

'Grey?'

'Crikey!' He laughed. 'Don't tell me you haven't noticed?'

She was amazed – and slightly irritated, though she couldn't have explained quite why, but it made her feel overlooked somehow and pregnant and insignificant and unattractive.

'Jo, you're incredible! It's completely bloody obvious!'

'No, it isn't,' she said. 'Not remotely. I mean I don't mean to be horrible but—' She grimaced. 'Charlie, she's *very large.*'

'Not as large as she was last week,' Charlie said simply. 'Anyway she's not that large.'

'Yes, she is,' snapped Jo, before she could stop herself.

Charlie looked at her. 'No, she isn't.'

'Yes, she bloody well is.'

'Jo,' he said. 'What's the matter with you?'

They found Grey in the kitchen crouching over the minute ingredients of a sauce to accompany that night's *paupiettes* of salmon. The kitchen, as usual when Grey

110

was working, looked like a bomb site. There were dirty saucepans, vegetable peel and half-empty packages on every surface and all over the floor.

'Ah, Grey. There you are,' said Charlie, weaving his way through the mess. 'The, er – Oh! What are you cooking there? Looks delicious.'

'I suppose you're wantin' me to tell Messy the news about Morrison,' Grey said, without bothering to look up.

'Ah-ha! You're a step ahead of me again. But since you mention it . . .'

'Do your own dirty work.'

'He's quite right,' said Jo. 'Why the Hell should Grey do it? One of us should do it.'

'Anyway,' Grey continued blithely, 'Messy won't be leavin' here in a hurry. Have you not seen how much blubber she's lost recently?' He laughed. 'Would you leave a place that was doin' that to you?' But then suddenly he slapped his knife onto the kitchen table. '. . . Fuck it. I don't want her gettin' upset. I'll go and talk to her.' He strode out of the room.

Charlie looked across at Jo. 'See what I mean?' he said.

But she looked strangely unamused. 'See what you mean, *what*?' she snapped. 'I suppose you think she's pretty fabulous too, do you, Charlie?'

'Me?'

'I know you do, anyway. I'm not stupid.'

'I don't think she's *"fabulous"*,' he said irritably.

'Why not?'

'What? Oh, come on, Jo. Of course— I mean— She's not exactly hideous. Obviously. What's all this crap about?'

'It's not *crap*,' she said vehemently – the more so because she was suddenly terrified she was going to cry. She knew how unreasonable she sounded but she couldn't help it. It was only a reflection of how utterly, uncontrollably unreasonable she felt. 'Don't be so fucking patronising.' She glared at Charlie – who was reeling slightly, stunned by her onslaught – and walked silently back to the attic.

Grey rarely ventured out of the house, except to fetch ingredients in Lamsbury, so Messy took it as a great compliment that he should have walked all the way to her garden – or what she increasingly considered to be her garden since nobody else ever went near it. And he looked magnificent, she thought: unkempt and gigantic in his big black coat, striding purposefully towards her, his shaggy dark hair blustering this way and that, his dark eyes fixed on her . . .

He drew up beside her and paused, his hands in his trouser pockets, half a smile on his lips, so much warmth and humour in his brown eyes. 'Hi there, Beau'iful,' he said at last.

'Oh, yes,' she said, 'very funny.'

He glanced vaguely around the garden, which in spite of all her work was still chaotic.

'It's lookin' . . . better . . . up here . . .'

'It is, isn't it?' she said enthusiastically and then laughed. 'I mean – this little corner, anyway.'

'Aye. The rest of it's a mess . . . But you never know, darlin',' he added, 'maybe they'll let you stay long enough to turn the whole place around. You could stay here for ever. Like me.'

'Ahh,' she said wistfully. 'Wouldn't that be nice?'

'But I pay, you know,' he said suddenly – surprisingly – because he didn't often feel the urge to justify himself.

'I pay every week. And I work, too. Aye. I'd be ashamed otherwise.'

'And I pay too,' said Messy defensively. 'I've nothing to be ashamed about. Those stupid magazine people this morning paid us—'

'Och I know, Messy. I know that. That's not what I meant.'

'Everyone seems to think I've got so much money.'

'Aye. You keep sayin'.'

'But I spent it all . . . Well, didn't you? I mean when you were famous and it was just *pouring in*? Didn't you spend it all?'

He laughed. 'I've got a bi' o' money tucked away.' He nodded, more to himself than to Messy. In fact he had nearly a quarter of a million gathering interest in his bank account. After the scandal broke, his record company had been keen to disassociate themselves from him as quickly as possible. Rather than face the publicity of a possible court case, they had allowed Grey to keep hold of all of his initial advance. 'Don't you go worryin' abou' me.'

'I wasn't. I was just asking.'

'I know you were, darlin'. I know you were.'

He gazed down at her angry face – her perpetually angry, suspicious face. She was beautiful. In London, where he'd seduced at least forty per cent of all the passably attractive women who crossed his path, Grey had found it easy, not to say automatic, to know how to delight them. But Messy was altogether more difficult. She was absurdly insecure, always bristling, always on the cusp of taking offence. And yet he couldn't help liking her: her frankness, her humour, her intelligence – but above all the aura of peaceful loneliness which surrounded her. It was that

113

which made him wonder – made him occasionally dare to wonder – if he hadn't at last found a kindred spirit, a solitary soul just a little bit like his own.

'Anyway,' he said eventually, suddenly noticing that he'd been staring at her for ages and that she was beginning to blush. Again. 'I came to give you some bad news. Have you seen the papers today?'

'I gave up reading them weeks ago.'

'Your friend from the telly show – Mr Morrison – he's run into a bit o' trouble.'

'Good.'

'Aye. Except he's scurryin' down here to join the party. So to speak. He's on his way here now. The General's gone to get him. Do you mind?'

'Mind?' she laughed. 'Of course not! How intriguing . . . Why, what's he done?'

'He's been murderin' his employees, I think. If you believe what the papers say.'

'Oh dear,' she said gleefully. 'Poor Mr Morrison!'


His chauffeur's brilliant success in sending the journalists off his trail, followed by the long and peaceful journey with the General, had quickly restored Maurice Morrison to his usual effervescent form. By the time his host was demonstrating the efficacy of his new remote control gates, any doleful thoughts regarding the unfortunate busboy had long since left his head. Not only that, since he'd been in the General's car he had received a telephone call from the Big Man Himself, offering thoughtful condolences and assuring him that his position in government was not in imminent danger, at least. It had been gently suggested that if he lay low for a few days, and turned up (assuming the family would have him) at the boy's hospital the following Friday, with flowers etcetera, then all would almost certainly be forgiven.

'What marvellous gates!' babbled Morrison to the General, with an accent much truer to his roots than the one he'd chosen for *Question Time*. 'Did they cost a fortune to restore? I bet they did. D'you know, James, I know a fantastic chap in – well, just outside Guildford as a matter of fact – who does the most tremendous restoration jobs on exactly things like this. Absolutely marvellous. I must give you his number when I'm back in town. Ahhh! Look at that cedar tree in the moonlight . . . and . . . is that a clock tower? . . . Goodness! A stable yard! Victorian if I'm not mistaken . . . how fascinating. Tremendous! Lucky you! D'you know I've been looking for a decent house in this part of the world . . . But they're so hard to come by . . . OH I SAY!! Look! . . . Queen Anne? Well, of course it is. I suppose it's been in the family for centuries . . .'

Maurice Morrison had kept up a pretty consistent monologue since Leigh Delamere service station, when he had waved adieu to his chauffeur and climbed furtively into the General's car. And that was quite a long time ago. Not that the General minded. He preferred to listen than to talk, or just to tune out and think his own thoughts. He found Morrison's company rather soothing. Quite like being with a girl, in fact. Except of course Morrison was a Minister in Her Majesty's Government – and one, the General couldn't help noticing, with exceptionally good manners.

'Here we are . . . oops,' the General said vaguely, yanking on the handbrake and skidding slightly on the gravel.

'Welcome to Fiddleford . . . The house where I was born . . . Home to Maxwell McDonalds since 1801.'

'Fabulous!' said Morrison. 'And very well driven, if I may say.'

Jo and Messy had independently decided to make a bit of an effort for Maurice Morrison's arrival. At about seven o'clock, just as he was drawing up outside, they both suddenly noticed little marks on their clothing, and went upstairs to change.

'Happy coincidence,' Grey drawled.

Charlie smiled. 'Is he supposed to be very attractive, this man? I didn't realise.'

'Aye, he is. He's a lady-killer.' Grey took a gulp of his gin. 'Good-lookin' . . . Charming . . . Powerful . . .'

They were in the drawing room at the time, lounging peacefully on opposite sofas, staring into the fire and waiting for the evening to begin. Anatollatia (the stripping princess) had called, sounding very self-pitying, to say she probably wouldn't make it in time for dinner after all, but Grey's feast was all prepared and an extra place had been laid up for her in the dining room just in case. Charlie and Grey felt very tranquil as they waited, idly contemplating the magnetism of their future guest. It would be their last tranquil moment for some time, because, outside, the whirlwind of energy which was Magnetic Morrison was just then erupting through the front door—

'OH! I SAY!' His voice echoed through the hall and into the drawing room. 'But this house is a hidden *treasure*! Have you had a lot of filming done here?'

'. . . And he's extremely rich o' course. But you know that,' muttered Grey. 'And very, *very* sincere. That's what gets to the ladies. Every time.'

'Shh!' Charlie laughed, climbing unenthusiastically to his feet. 'Shut up. He's coming through.'

The door flew open, and the boy-preferring lady-killer burst in. 'Hullo! Hullo! Charles? Sorry to barge in on you like this.' He grasped Charlie's hand with both of his. 'I'm Maurice. Maurice Morrison. May I congratulate you, Charles, on having such a beautiful house? And may I thank you, also, for coming to my aid at a time of such great *personal* adversity.'

'See wa' I mean?' muttered Grey.

Charlie's face cracked. 'I hope . . .' said Charlie. But Maurice's look of sincere attention was making it very hard for him to stop grinning. 'I hope everything works out,' he said feebly. 'Glad you made it anyway. And I'm sorry about the boy. You must feel terrible.'

'Indeed I do,' said Maurice mournfully. 'Of course, as I explained in my statement this afternoon, which you may already have heard, it was, and continues to be, very much against our company policy to have our cellar hatches open at any time while customers are on the premises and I am, in conjunction with local environmental health officers, in the process of inquiring about that oversight. The manager assures me that under normal circumstances the hatch is not only closed but *padlocked*. So we can only wonder, you see . . . I mean the mystery remains *who* unlocked the hatch, *who* opened it— *who* left it open—'

'And why the fuckin' busboy wasn't looking where he was going,' snapped Grey. 'This isn't a press conference by the way.'

'Oh, I think that's a little harsh,' said Maurice, a touch of frost passing over his sun-kissed face as he turned to scrutinise Grey – disconcertingly handsome, Maurice

117

noticed, and still lounging rather annoyingly on the sofa at the far end of the room. 'Hullo, by the way. I'm Maurice. Morrison. How do you do?'

'Grey McShane,' said Grey. 'How do ye do? I'm so sorry to hear of your troubles, Mr Morrison.'

A little frown. Confusion. 'Grey McShane . . . I must say that's a very familiar name. Have we met? I foolishly can't remember.'

'No,' said Grey.

'Ohhhh . . . So?'

But no further explanation was forthcoming. They were saved from what looked set to be an awkward and quite hostile moment by the arrival of the General, at which point Grey slowly pulled himself up from the sofa and offered to get anyone a drink.

'Oh Grey, you are kind,' said Morrison, smiling automatically, his mind still rushing . . . Grey McShane . . . *McShane . . . Grey* McShane . . . Where the Hell had he heard that name before? Worst case scenario, and he hadn't managed to discover the truth tonight, he would telephone his secretary in the morning and get her to find out. 'I'll have a glass of white wine if I could. That would be lovely.'

And then Messy came in and he experienced a spasm of pure panic. A million thoughts spun through his head, first and foremost, that it was a setup.

. . . But she actually looked much better than she had a couple of weeks ago, he couldn't help registering. She'd lost weight. In fact she looked – she looked bloody fantastic. In a fat sort of way. But that wasn't the point. The point was, he was a fool. Under normal circumstances Morrison didn't commit himself to anything without first ordering abundant and usually quite unnecessary research. But now here he was, utterly unprotected, in a house – beautiful, admittedly – with a doddery, and possibly even slightly insane, General who incidentally drove like a bloody maniac, a bitch from Hell who'd insulted him on live television, a very tall and threatening-looking Scotsman whose name was disturbingly familiar, and God only knew what other odd bods still wandering the corners of this great pile, waiting to pounce on him at unpleasant moments . . .

'Well I never!' he said, smiling broadly. 'If it isn't my very own nemesis, Messy Monroe! What a – stunning – surprise. How *are* you? And what on earth are you doing *here*?'

'Same as you,' said Messy, returning his smile just as she hadn't intended, because he was shaking her hand so nicely, and looking with such confiding humour into her newly made-up eyes. 'Hiding out. This is Chloe, my daughter. Chloe, my darling, this is Mr Morrison, who made your mum look a bit of a twit on the telly the other day. And this is Colin. Colin, come and say hello. Colin and Chloe have recently become very obsessed by chickens.'

In a swift and graceful *whoosh* Morrison concertina-ed himself down, so that his and Chloe's heads were on a perfect level. 'Hello, hello,' he said, 'are you a fairy princess? I bet you are!'

'Do you know if it's nearly supper?'

'What's that?'

She turned to Messy. 'Is it nearly supper, Mum?'

'Oh! So you have supper with the adults, do you? Isn't that lovely?' He straightened up to look at the mother. 'Very European. After all they're only kiddies for such a short time, aren't they? Blink and you've missed it!' His mind flicked back to when his own children were growing up. He tried to remember them – in paddling pools, sand pits and so forth. On holidays. On the beach. But at that time, as always, he'd been doing a lot more than blinking when he missed it all. He'd been building an empire. 'No, but seriously,' he moved quickly on, 'what I *really* wanted to talk to you about was your book—'

'Oh God,' said Messy. 'Not that again.'

'No! No! Not a bit of it. It was actually terribly remiss of me, but I must admit I didn't have the time to look at your marvellous book before we went on air all those weeks ago – and Messy, please, accept my apologies for stepping in when I did. The last thing on earth I wanted was to upset you. And I realise, with benefit of hindsight – ha! what a wonderful thing that is – that I did step in, rather, with my size ten boots. And of course you were handling what must have been a very *difficult* situation, very efficiently – and courageously, if I may say – without any help from me!'

'Yes, well,' said Messy, melting pathetically, the way people always did in the face of Mr Morrison's energy and charm, 'I was so nervous, that was the problem. I'm sorry. I was very rude.'

'Not a bit! *Not a bit!* But the point is I took a *quick* peek at the book after the show and it occurs to me that your publicity people have been doing you quite a disservice. Because you're actually making some *very important* points. Fascinating points. And funnily enough I've been meaning to contact you, because I thought perhaps – if you were willing and I've no doubt you're incredibly busy, but if you can find a moment in your schedule—'

Messy smiled.

'Ha ha, yes. So easy to say, isn't it? But, er, what are you up to at the moment?'

'I'm supposed to be writing another book, but I can't think of anything to write.'

'Mmm.' He nodded sympathetically. The word *hopeless* flashed through his mind. 'Well, while you're uncertain about that, why don't you come along and give a few talks to some of our more vulnerable youngsters? Get them into discussion, encourage them to have *a really good think* about the issues you've raised in the book. Because of course I don't need to tell you, body image among young people today . . .'

Grey wandered up. 'What're you two witterin' on about?' he said.

'Ah, Mr McShane. I was just suggesting to Messy—'

'Oh, hello, Grey. Maurice has just had an interesting – *terrifying*, actually – but really a very good idea—'

'Oh, aye?'

'Because, you know, Maurice, it's still something I feel very angry about.'

'Well, ha ha—' They laughed. 'Messy! Ha ha! Goodness! So I opined! The mind wanders inexorably back to a certain television show! Ha ha ha!'

'It's dinner time, by the way,' said Grey. 'So whenever you're ready.'

At Grey's instigation, Charlie seated Maurice and Messy at opposite ends of the long dining-room table. He put Maurice between Colin and Jo and needless to say, within minutes, he had worked his magic on both of them. He chatted enthusiastically, revealing an ideal balance of knowledge and curiosity in both chicken care and foetal gestation. He questioned Colin about the aggressive nature of bantam cocks – 'I've always been fascinated by bantams, haven't you?' He questioned Jo about the nature of her heightened emotional and creative state, about her swollen breasts, vivid dreams, and difficulty in sleeping. They discussed the inferior treatment of pregnant women in western societies, as opposed to those in less developed cultures, where childbirth, they both agreed, was not 'swept under the carpet'. Maurice Morrison looked interested and concerned, and pretended not to be revolted by the thought of Jo's placenta coated in olive oil and pepper. 'Apparently they're chock-a-block with nutrients,' he said. 'Well exactly,' said Jo. And it transpired they were as appalled as each other by Britain's record on teen pregnancy. 'We have to ask ourselves *why*,' implored Jo. '*Why* isn't the message hitting home? Where, exactly, are we going *wrong*?' 'Well exactly,' said Morrison.

Charlie looked across at them from the far end of the table, communicating with such enthusiasm and skill, and was reminded of Jo as he'd first met her, shining, as she always could, in the company of handsome, important men. He sighed.

'Don't you worry about it, Charlie,' bellowed Grey, from about half a metre away. 'They're only talking bollocks.'

'Oh I know that. I just wish I could join in.'

'Thank God you can't,' he said. 'Enough bloody chatter around this table already . . . By the way,' he turned towards Messy, 'Messy . . . Hey, *Messy!*' But she was staring at Morrison again – marvelling, she couldn't help it, at his ability to talk to people, torn between suspicion and envy, wishing, if the brutal truth be told, that she and Jo could swap places, just for a little bit . . . 'MESSY!' bellowed Grey.

She jumped. 'Colin thought of an idea for your next book today. Did he tell you?'

'Colin?' She laughed. 'Cheeky little sod. What does he know?'

'I proba'ly know even more'n you, Messy!' Colin shouted back at her. He always shouted. 'So you can hire me as your helper if you want.'

She smiled. 'Come on then. What's the idea?'

'Did you know, for example, Messy—' Colin yelled, so loud even Jo and Maurice were temporarily distracted. 'Did you know that the ancient Romans used to eat so much so's they couldn't fit nothin' more in their bellies, and then they used to go and sick it up and start all over again! In't that disgustin'?'

'See?' said Grey. 'He says you should do a history of dieting. Since the Romans. Since the Greeks. The Egyptians. Since they invented bloody diets. God knows. Maurice, you probably do. When did they invent dieting, do you think?'

'Ha ha. Grey, you flatter me. I'm afraid I've absolutely not a clue!'

'Probably,' said the General, winking and beaming at the assembled company, 'on the same day they invented ladies!'

It was breathtaking. Maurice Morrison managed to flash a grimace of schoolboy enjoyment at the General and somehow simultaneously roll his eyes with perfectly pitched, world-weary correctness at the women. And not a single person spotted it. 'Mind you,' he said seamlessly, 'I have a sneaky little feeling the book may already have been written. Not that it matters. *In the least*. And well done, Colin, by the way. Only goes to show how great

123

minds . . .' But his last few words were drowned out by the sudden and deafening bray of the entryphone, newly installed at the bottom of the drive for people trying to get through the remote control gates.

'Good Lord!' exclaimed the General, sitting bolt upright. 'Isn't that the gate buzzer? Did anyone else hear it?'

'Aye, General. Well spotted. That'll be the Royal stripper then. Anyone with jokes about the Queen an' all o' them? Let's get 'em out now.'

'Really, McShane,' chuckled the General. 'You are a shocker.' He shuffled away, laughing merrily, to go and buzz her in.

There was something altogether very festive in the air at Fiddleford that night. Everybody felt it. Grey's dinner had been exceptional. Jo had sold syndication rights to Messy's exclusive, Charlie had put off the water inspector again, and with the presence of Morrison, and the imminent arrival of Princess Anatollatia and Nigel the tennis player, it seemed to Charlie suddenly – and not just to Charlie but to Jo and to Grey and the General – that their refuge was now not only a reality but a success. A success. Even the chickens had started laying again.

As soon as his father came back into the room, Charlie stood up. 'Sorry everyone,' he said. 'Sorry to interrupt. I just thought, you know, before the stripper arrived – it was a good moment to propose a toast.'

Morrison offered one of his less believable chuckles. 'Who *is* this stripper you all keep talking about?'

'She sounded rather lower-class,' said the General, frowning slightly. 'Jo, you've spoken to her. Can you explain that?'

'I wanted to make a toast,' persisted Charlie. 'Very

very quickly. Before she arrives. Just to say thank you all for being here, really. This house has been – a not particularly happy place in the last few years. Of course you all know about the animal slaughters a few months ago. But some of you may not know, my sister – my twin, actually – Georgie, Georgina, died nearly two years ago. Two years ago in December. And in many ways Fiddleford – I think Dad would agree – has not been – has been a very quiet place since then. But we all do love it – I do. Dad does. I think Jo does . . .' He smiled. 'I *know* Grey does. Anyway, we've had a lot of problems, financial and otherwise, and there have been times when I've wondered if we shouldn't just accept the inevitable and sell up. This refuge idea – which we all four sort of created together – is Fiddleford's last ditch . . . If this doesn't work then I think we all know the game is pretty much up . . . But now that you people have been brave enough, *generous* enough, to take the gamble and come to this madhouse—'

'*Shame!*' rumbled the General nonsensically.

'. . . and with the income you're all bringing in: Maurice; Messy; Annatolah—'

'Anatollatia,' corrected Jo.

'Anatollatia . . . And Nigel, tomorrow. And of course the miraculous chickens. Everything suddenly seems— well. Maybe it's a bit premature, but this evening, standing here now . . . I just can't see how we can fail.'

'Too bloody right,' said Grey. 'Well done all of us! And God bless Fiddleford.'

'Also. Just one more thing,' said Charlie. 'Sorry. I'll hurry up. But, er, just one more thing . . .'

He looked at Jo. She grinned at him.

'Without wishing to be coy . . . But it seems like a good time to throw it in . . .'

'Do get on with it, Charles,' said the General.

'But er – the point is – I mentioned Georgie earlier because,' he cleared his throat, 'the point is, I just thought people – Dad, especially – might be interested to know that er . . . the reason Jo is so *grotesquely* fat at the moment—'

'Hey!'

'—is because we're actually expecting twins.' He looked from Jo to his father. 'So – er. Here's to the new twins!'

The General didn't say much. Like everyone else, he mumbled 'to the twins' as he lifted his glass. But his hands shook slightly. Afterwards he stood up and crossed to where Jo was sitting. He hovered over her uncertainly, patting her shoulder. And then in a sudden awkward rush, he swooped and dropped a kiss on the top of her head. 'Wonderful news,' he said. '*Wonderful news.*' It was the first time he had ever kissed her.

'Right then,' said Charlie very briskly. 'Sorry. If that was embarrassing for everyone. Now am I alone in thinking that before the stripper arrives, perhaps Colin and Chloe ought to be persuaded to go to bed?'

'I've seen loads o' strippers before now,' yelled Colin.

Everybody laughed.

'What strippers?' asked Morrison tetchily. 'I do wish you'd let me in on the joke.'

'Oh dear,' said Charlie, 'did Dad not say? She's called Anatollalia—'

'Anatollatia,' said Jo. 'Anatollatia von Schlossenerg. She's some sort of European princess. About fifth cousin of the Queen. And she was a bridesmaid at Princess Di's wedding. Or rather she was going to be, but they had to pull her out at the last minute because she wet her pants, poor little thing. And wouldn't stop crying.'

'You what?? And now she's a *stripper*?' bellowed Colin.

'*Shh!* No! Yes and no,' said Jo. 'It's complicated. Colin, I thought you were going to bed.'

'We got Princess Slozzyberg comin' here takin' her panties off,' shouted Colin, 'an' you think I'm goin' to bed? You're as mad as a hornet's nest, you are. Bugger off!'

'*Shut up!*' But even Jo couldn't help laughing. Everyone laughed. Until, from beneath the laughter, there came a sound of someone clearing her throat; it was a refined enough little sound, with more than a hint of refined impatience.

'Ah-*hem!*'

She was standing at the door that opened onto the hall, smirking slightly, obviously wanting to make an entrance. But she didn't look in the least as anyone had expected.

She was a small woman, barely five feet tall, with a strong stout body and gargantuan breasts which burst forth and sideways, at right angles, from beneath each armpit. She wore a tight, pale beige jersey with a polo neck which stopped around her second chin, making it hard to know where her face began and the chins and jersey ended. Her dark blue knee-length skirt, stretched tight across the hips, left no one in any doubt that she'd remembered her pants that morning.

She cocked her head to one side, a large, pale head with a mousy blonde bob on the top. And smiled. Her bright little eyes creased up tight, and then tighter still, until finally they disappeared completely beneath folds of smiling skin. 'Sorry, people,' she said brightly. Her little eyes pinged open and darted quickly from face to face, looking at everyone, taking everything in. 'Sorry all and sundry,' she said. 'I really *hate* interrupting!'

'Hey!' said Chloe in disgust. 'You don't look like a princess!'

'You don't look much like a stripper, neither,' said Colin.

The eight faces at the dining-room table looked at her in resentful confusion. This was no Anatollatia.

'Who the fuck are you?' asked Grey.

Sue-Marie Gunston was not a princess or a stripper. She was an Environmental Health Officer for Lamsbury District Council, come to do one of her spot checks. And should she encounter any cause for it, she explained apologetically, temporarily blinding herself with her own apologetic smile, she would be within her legal rights to 'close this place down before you people have actually finished your – *what is that?*' She peered over Maurice's shoulder at his pudding plate. 'Your cakey-gateauy-chocolatey thingummy! Ha ha ha!'

'Is that s'posed to be funny?' said Grey.

'Ooo, but not to worry!' she said. 'I always like to tell people, so as we all know where we are. But it's ever so unusual. I'm sure it won't come to that.'

## SOME USEFUL SUGGESTIONS

Disabled people are individuals just like everybody else . . .
If someone looks 'different', avoid staring. Concentrate on
what they are saying, not on the way they look . . .

If you are talking to an adult, treat them like an adult.

*Insert to Department of Education and Environment's leaflet DL170. The Disability Discrimination Act 1995. What Employers Need to Know*

# • OUTSOURCE NON-HIERARCHICAL INTERPERSONAL NEEDS

'. . . Crikey,' said Charlie eventually. 'Well. I suppose you'd better have some coffee.' He headed off to the kitchen to fetch her some and she sat herself down in Anatollatia's seat. Neatly, unselfconsciously, she opened a depressing-looking black plastic briefcase, pulled from it a depressing-looking walnut-veneer-style plastic folder and from that, an equally depressing yellow form. She immediately started writing.

'Goodness,' said Morrison, 'you're working late.'

'I tend to,' she agreed, scribbling away. 'Sometimes it's a job to keep up. Especially now. Every failed farmer in the country seems to think he can open up a bed and breakfast. Hotel. Thingummy-whatsit. You know, tourist facility.' She looked up suddenly and glared at Morrison. 'But they *can't*. It's that simple.'

'Oh, I'm sure,' said Morrison soothingly.

'These characters wake up one morning. They say to themselves, 'Hello, hello, the farm's gone belly up! Not to worry – let's pop in a couple of beds, serve up a bit of toast and marmalade for breakfast, bingo! Bankruptcy: bye-bye. But they have *no idea*! Not a clue! I shouldn't say this, but it's this sort of any-which-way, give-it-a-try attitude which really annoys me.'

'Is that right?' said Grey. 'Why's that then?'

'*Why?*' Sue-Marie looked at Grey as if he was stupid, and then back at Morrison, and then at Messy, and then back at Grey. She frowned. 'You all look very familiar . . . Have we met before?'

'It's coz they're all ever so famous,' said Colin. 'In different ways. An' we got another one turning up in a minute an' another one tomorrow called Nigel who's gonna show me tennis! An' they're *all famous*!' He pointed at Morrison. 'That one's—'

'Colin,' said Jo. 'Time for bed.'

'But I haven't—'

'*Now,*' Jo said.

'Go on.' Grey gave him a friendly wink. 'Fuck off, will you?'

'And you too, Chloe, darling. Time for bed. And please. Don't listen to Grey's silly swearing. It isn't funny.'

'*So,*' said Sue-Marie playfully, as soon as they'd gone. 'Are you going to tell me what you're all famous for? Or are you going to make me guess?'

The question sent a frisson of panic through Morrison which slowed down his naturally charming responses. So unfortunately it was Grey who broke the silence first.

'If you don't mind my sayin', it's none o' your fuckin' business,' he said.

'Oh!'

'*Grey!*' said Jo.

He ignored her. 'Now you've marched in here interruptin'

132

our dinner and threatenin' to close our place down. I don't think it's too much to ask that you do whatever it is you feel you need to do and then leave us to enjoy our anonymity and what's left of our evenin' in peace.'

'Dearie me,' Sue-Marie said with valiant facetiousness, the playful grin apparently cemented to her face. And, without another word, returned to her paperwork. Silence fell over the table. She scribbled hard, unaware of the frantic scowling and grimacing taking place all around her. She didn't notice Messy signalling emphatically to Jo, and then both of them tiptoeing out of the room towards the kitchen. She didn't look up until Charlie came in with the coffee tray.

'Super,' she said to him. 'Are you Food-and-Beverages?'

'No, this is coffee,' said Charlie and then, realising that wasn't what she was asking, added, only a little more helpfully, 'I mean I'm Charlie Maxwell McDonald. I'm the owner, if that's what you were asking. Sorry. What did you say?'

'That's super,' she said patiently. 'I take it you're Food-and-Beverages as well?'

Charlie looked no less confussed. 'As part of your job description?' she added, more patiently still. Sue-Marie was very patient.

'My what?'

'Your—'

'I do the cookin',' interrupted Grey. 'What do you want to know?'

'Excellent.' She offered him one of her gruesome, heartless smiles. The flaps of soft white skin which closed over her eyes prevented her from registering his horrified response. He shuddered, like he'd eaten a lemon. 'And

133

are there other food handlers,' she continued, 'within the organisation? Or do you take sole responsibility?'

'Aye.'

'Aye – what?'

'Aye. It's just me.'

'Except I can see Mr— McDonald here, conveying coffee,' she said, sharp as a hawk. 'Is that usual practice?'

'Aye, sometimes. We all do the coffee from time to time.'

'*Tripping hazards*,' she muttered softly to herself, turning the page of her yellow form and jotting something down. 'And I'm sorry. Whether you like it or not I am going to need a name.'

'Aye, I know.' He paused. 'It's McShane. M-c-S-H-A-N-E. Grey McShane.'

She wrote it down. She looked at it. '. . . *McShane?*' Her mouth fell open. '*Grey McShane? . . . I KNOW WHO YOU ARE!*' She stared at him for several moments in blatant, self-righteous disapproval and then, suddenly remembering something, broke off from what she was about to say and pointed at the space where Colin had been sitting. 'You *winked* at him!'

'So I did. Aye,' drawled Grey, his mouth already curling at the humour of what he planned to say next. 'Later on I usually pop upstairs for a wee bi' o' what I like to call *toast-an'-marmalade*, darlin'. An' we bugger each other senseless until mornin'.'

'McShane!' thundered the General. 'Don't be so bloody disgusting!'

'For Christ's sake, Grey! That *wasn't funny*!'

'That really was *loathsome*.'

Everyone yelled at him. Everyone except Sue-Marie. Grey

134

McShane took a gulp of his wine and waited for the storm to pass. Sue-Marie watched him. She made another quick note on her yellow paper and then, with an even gaze, continued with the usual line of questioning. 'Before I take a look around the kitchen,' she began, 'I assume you've attained your Basic Hygiene?'

'My what, darlin'?'

'It is a prerequisite for all food handlers, as I'm sure you're aware,' she said. 'I'll need to take a look at your certificate. If you could provide that for me.' But Grey didn't move. '. . . As soon as that is convenient. Please.'

He laughed. 'I don't know what certificate you're talking about,' he said, draining his glass and slowly pushing back his chair. 'But I certainly haven't got it. Come on, I'll show you the kitchen.' He laughed again. 'I don't know what you're hoping to find there, mind. It's just a bloody kitchen.'

Grey didn't really notice untidiness, or understand why people minded about it so much. Charlie, on the other hand, though he'd never before encountered a professional such as Miss Gunston, and had no idea what, exactly, she would be hoping to find, strongly suspected she would take offence to whatever she found in Grey's kitchen. 'Actually, Sue-Marie,' he said hurriedly. 'Miss Gunston – *Sue-Marie*. Can I call you Sue-Marie? This really isn't a very convenient time. We're expecting another guest at any moment. As you can see we're in the middle of dinner. Would it be very inconvenient for you to come back later?' But she was shaking her head before he'd even finished.

'. . . Or perhaps,' he added hopefully, 'you could come back in the morning? For example. Everything'll be tidy by then.' Charlie was already sidling towards the door. As he drew closer to it he could hear the clattering of plates. Messy and Jo were on the case. But it had been chaos in there only a moment ago. They needed more time. 'Or why don't you just sit down for a bit? Relax! Finish your coffee!'

'I'm sorry,' she said, offering another of her blinding smiles. 'I wish I could oblige. Truly. However, it is a legal requirement that you submit to an EHO inspection, when and if an inspector calls. Where is the kitchen? If you just pointed me in the direction I could probably let you all get on.' By the time her smiling folds were lifted Charlie had already slipped out of the room. She frowned. 'Where's he gone?'

'To the kitchen to fetch some sugar, I sincerely hope! I simply can't drink coffee without sugar. Can you?' Maurice Morrison had been paying rapt attention to the toings and froings of the last few minutes, hence the uncharacteristically low profile. Since when several important jigsaw pieces had fallen into place, and he now, very reluctantly but nonetheless clearly, understood:

A) that he was spending his purdah not in dignified rural isolation, but in the company of a stripping princess and nationally reviled pervert.
B) that this was something which the British Public (& Mr TB) should never be allowed to find out.

Which meant

C) that the repulsive Sue-Marie Gunston should *under no*

136

*circumstances* discover his identity, lest she mention it to someone who might mention it to the press.

And therefore

D) that although *per se* he admired the stalwart work of all EHOs he would be feeling a lot more comfortable if this one could be persuaded to get the fuck out of the house.

So it was time to act. 'Miss – Gunston,' he said charmingly. 'You seem like a sensible woman.'

'Well, thank you.'

'Would you perhaps allow me to make a small suggestion?'

'Certainly.' Sue-Marie blushed. *You're gorgeous*, she thought. She was finding it difficult, in fact impossible, not to focus her eyes on the V of sun-kissed chest which glowed between the top two buttons of his shirt.

'Because of course you're quite right,' said Morrison. 'It is a legal requirement, and a very sensible one, that our friends here agree to giving you a tour of their delightful – food preparation area. But I think you'll find – if you refer to your notes – a proprietor/proprietress *is entitled* to ask you to come back at a more convenient time. And as you can see, we are all in the middle of dinner. I would have thought . . .' He smiled at her. 'Of course I realise that you must be dreadfully busy, and it is entirely at your discretion, but if you could find it in your heart . . .'

'We-ell,' she said conquettishly, 'I'm not saying I *can't*, but you have to understand it puts me in a difficult position. As soon as I set a flexible precedent at a given location, so to speak, I find people tend to start walking all over me.'

'Oh, I do assure you, we have no intention—' but he noticed she had raised her eyes from his golden chest and was suddenly staring at his face. All his senses warned him that full recognition was now only seconds away. He broke off abruptly and stood up.

'I must say,' she said, squinting at him more than ever, 'you look *super* familiar.'

'And so do you, Miss Gunston. So do you . . . Perhaps we both simply have one of those faces.' He gave her one last smile, one of his very best. 'Or perhaps we had the good fortune to have met up in a former life. Now if you'll excuse me, I really must . . .' He left the room without even bothering to finish his sentence.

The General stood up next. 'I think,' he said, 'on this confusing but happy note, I might take myself off to Bedfordshire. And I shall look forward to meeting the young stripper in the morning. So good evening, Miss – Ahh. Miss . . . Yes. And no doubt I shall see you tomorrow, McShane.'

'Aye.'

The General winked at him as he walked by.

'Well,' said Grey, once the General had left them. 'For a woman who really hates interruptin' things this must all be pretty devastating. There was eight of us in here half a minute ago. What do you suppose went wrong?'

'I don't know, Mr McShane,' she said pertly. 'You tell me.'

They were born enemies. It had nothing to do with her job or his name. Grey and Sue-Marie glared at each other, silently acknowledging their mutual revulsion, until slowly he drained his glass once again, refilled it, stood up. ''Scuse me,' he said simply, and left the room.

In the kitchen, the emergency clear-up had ground to a dramatic halt. Crowded together and all yelling in front of the open fridge, Grey discovered Charlie, Jo and Messy fighting over a packet of uncooked chicken breasts.

'You've got to put the raw meat,' Messy was shouting, snatching for the packet (which Jo was holding), and missing, and trying again, 'you've got to put the raw – put the bloody raw meat on the bottom shelf! I did it in *GCSE*.'

Grey burst out laughing and the three of them turned on him, each one in such a high state of panic they were delighted to find someone new to vent it on.

'*Fuck off!*' they all yelled at once.

And then suddenly Jo, sounding unusually hopeless, let out a peculiar whimpering sound. Her head lolled, her knees buckled and the packet of chicken fell to the floor. Messy, Charlie and Grey leapt forward and caught her, just as the refined accents of Miss Gunston pierced through the adjoining dining-room door—

'Hello? Hello?'

'Jesus Christ!' cried Charlie. 'Jo? Jo, are you all right?'

'Hell-oh-ho! Is anyone there?'

'Someone. Please,' he snapped, 'get rid of that ghastly woman.'

Jo gave a wan smile. 'My darling,' she said, as the three of them slowly lowered her onto a kitchen chair. 'You're beginning to sound like your father.'

'I'm calling an ambulance,' he said.

'Don't be ridiculous, Charlie. I'm fine. I'm *fine*.' She stood up, sooner than she ought to have done, no doubt, but Jo hated being an invalid. She wobbled slightly. 'I just need some air . . .' She would have liked to stay around to deal with Miss Gunston first, but Charlie didn't provide her the opportunity. With his arm wrapped tightly around her, he more or less forced her out of one door just as Sue-Marie, who in the meantime, and for reasons best known to herself, had changed into a doctor's coat and bath cap, burst triumphantly through the other.

'Ah,' she said with beady satisfaction. 'Here we are!' Slowly, unselfconsciously, she stood at the door and scanned the room. Her eyes flitted over the old stone floors (still covered in vegetable peel), the Aga (still covered in dirty saucepans), the General's leather armchair (still floating on its sea of newspaper), the large Victorian pine kitchen table in the middle of the room, and the vast eighteenth-century pine dresser, which had been leaning against the same wall, beneath piles of changing clutter, for as long as anyone called Maxwell McDonald had owned the house.

The kitchen was a large scruffy room, pretty in an old-fashioned way, worn and very homely. It had been scrubbed every weekday morning, probably since the day it was built, certainly since Mrs Webber had first come to live on the estate. But Sue-Marie Gunston looked around her and all she could see were *old things*, and all she could think of were *dirt traps*. She shivered in revulsion. 'So this is the kitchen, is it?'

Jo and Charlie felt relief wash over them the moment they stepped out into the moonlight. They were both so busy

140

now and there were always so many people in the house, it had been a long time since they'd last been outside together, alone. In the moonlight. Slowly, happily, arm in arm, they walked the hundred-odd yards to the cedar tree and then they sat down beneath it in the frozen grass, and looked at each other and kissed, just as they had in the olden days.

'We should come out here more often,' she said.

'I know we should,' he said, stroking her hair. 'What's the point of living in a beautiful place like this if we never have time to—' He glanced up at the house. 'I mean, *look* . . .'

There was a layer of frost around the lake and on the sloping lawns which framed either side of the house. Rustling ivy glistened around the windows and the soft red stone seemed almost luminous in the moonlight. In the kitchen Miss Gunston, making notes about safety rails, disabled toilets, non-slip easi-clean surfaces and non-porous cooking utensils, could do her very worst. But outside Fiddleford was unbowed, after all these years: old and solid and dignified and utterly, magnificently peaceful.

'I love it here,' she said suddenly, as if only fully realising it for the first time.

'Even with all the maniacs we have to share our lives with these days? . . . And Miss Gunston . . . And two more maniacs arriving . . .'

'Especially,' she said seriously. 'I love the maniacs. Most of them. They give the whole place a point.'

He kissed her again. 'Including Grey?'

'Of course including Grey.' She sounded slightly shocked. 'It wouldn't be Fiddleford without Grey. You know that.'

'And Colin Fairwell?'

'Yes, yes,' she laughed. '*And* Colin Fairwell.'

'And the shrinking but otherwise physically repulsive Messy Monroe and her funny little daughter?'

'That's not funny,' she said.

He kissed her. 'I know it's not. Sorry. Let's forget about her. What about the psychopathic Government Minister, who I would guess *you* have rather a soft spot for . . .' He kissed her again. 'And of course my almost – completely – impossible father?'

'I love them all,' she said, laughing and pushing him away. 'More or less. *Especially* the psychopathic Minister, who incidentally isn't in the least psychopathic. He's very interesting.'

'And I love you,' he said seriously.

'And I love you, too. Even more than Maurice Morrison . . .'

'Jo, that thing in the kitchen—'

'It was nothing. I'm fine. I'm completely fine.'

'Because if anything happened to you. Or the twins . . . Don't you think you should spend a couple of days in bed?'

She laughed.

'No, seriously.'

'Honestly, Charlie. I'm fine . . . In fact I've never felt better in my life . . .' She leant across and they kissed yet again, falling gradually as they did so back onto the frozen grass: Jo on her side, to accommodate the bump; Charlie stretching to put his arms around her shoulders. But it wasn't comfortable.

A moment or two later, after a valiant effort by both of them to pretend that full-blown sex was a realistic and desired option, Charlie grinned at her and said, 'It's getting pretty cold out here, isn't it?'

She laughed. 'It's bloody freezing. And I must admit I'm beginning to wonder if we've gone completely mad, leaving Grey alone with the woman from Health and Safety.'

Slowly Charlie pulled himself up onto his elbows. 'You were going to faint,' he said uneasily. In fact he'd been thinking just the same thing.

'I think we should go in.'

'I know,' he said, springing nervously to his feet. 'He'll have the place closed down before we can fucking blink.'

She shuffled a bit, tried to stand up and fell back again, the way heavily pregnant women tend to. Jo had always assumed she would glow through her pregnancies, just as she glowed through everything else. It was usually only a question of willpower, and one or two useful techniques. And Jo worked hard at her glowing, of course. Jo always worked hard. But the task was proving more difficult than she had imagined. With every day that passed, the harder she felt she had to work at it, and yet the more cumbersome, dependent and generally dismal she felt. 'I think,' she said, lunging forward and falling back once again, pretending to laugh but suddenly feeling oddly tearful about her intolerable state, 'I think I'm going to need a bit of help.'

Slowly, carefully, Charlie levered her back up to her feet, and as they were walking across the lawn towards the house she tried to make a joke of it: 'God knows what it's going to be like in a month's time. I'm already the size of a small car.'

And Charlie chuckled warmly, because whatever size she was it didn't occur to him; he could not imagine how it would ever matter. 'I know,' he said, giving her shoulders a squeeze. 'You are going to be *vast*. You're going to look like a bloody bus!'

Back in the kitchen things were slightly worse than they had imagined, when they were lolling beneath the cedar tree, imagining the worst. Nobody was shouting at anybody. In fact Messy and Grey were hunkered together whispering in one corner of the room, while Gunston worked away in the other, scribbling furiously, her mouth so pinched the lips had turned white. She stood, bent rigid and awkward over her labour, left hand resting on her paperwork, writing hand clasping its pen at the furthest end, to maximise the distance between her flesh and the detested, potentially germ-infested wooden dresser she was leaning on.

'Hello, hello,' said Charlie. He and Jo hurried in, bringing with them a burst of cool fresh air. 'How's it all going? Everything OK?'

Gunston didn't look up. Grey and Messy, both white in the face, looked from him to Jo and back to each other.

'What's happened?' said Jo.

Messy and Grey stared back at them, dumbstruck apparently. Lost for words.

'*What's happened?*' said Charlie. 'For Christ's sake—'

'She's closin' us down,' said Grey, his voice low and lifeless. 'The fuckin' bitch is closin' us down.'

'I'm issuing,' she said primly, but still without looking up, 'what we call a prohibition notice, effective immediately. Should you wish to contest it, and—' she glanced at Jo and Charlie and offered a little laugh, 'I don't honestly recommend it, you'll find details on how to appeal on the reverse of the form. In the meantime I would advise you that failure to comply with this notice carries a fine of up to £20,000 and/or two years' imprisonment.'

'But why?' said Charlie incredulously. 'I mean . . . *why?* What have we done that's so wrong? Of course I realise the vegetable peel probably isn't—'

'Vegetable peel? Mr Maxwell McDonald,' she said, laying down her pen and slowly, assiduously, fitting the completed form into an envelope. 'If I didn't know better I would assume you were joking. Frankly, where do I start?' She laughed a little recklessly and, with the envelope neatly glued, indicated the space around her in exaggerated despair. 'The inadequate lighting? The total lack of temperature control documentation? The primary food handler smoking – *smoking* – and apparently inebriated whilst stationary and without an HACCP.' She pointed, as if it would clarify anything, at an electrical socket a metre or so from Charlie's left elbow. 'The absence of an appointed safety representative or any hazard analysis records; the absence of an approved first aid kit; the absence of any first aid kit at all; no visible kitchen staff overalls; no staff cleaning facilities; inappropriate sanitary conveniences for guests or staff; *wholly* inadequate food storage facilities; no visible pest control systems; a total omission of maximum load notices on the shelves; inadequate plate stacking and storing facilities; ditto cutlery. No safety viewing panel on significant traffic route outlets in the food preparation area, no fire safety equipment, incorrect positioning of potentially hazardous disinfectants and sanitisers . . . *and you talk to me about vegetable peel?'*

'Yes!' said Charlie, who had listened in fascination to Sue-Marie's impassioned spiel and, like everyone else in the room, had drawn from it only one nugget of reliable

145

information: that they were in a lot of trouble. 'But for Heaven's sake, don't worry about the vegetable peel! It's nothing! We can clear it up!'

'Have you,' said Sue-Marie severely, 'ever actually slipped on vegetable peel?'

'Never!' said Charlie adamantly. But the question suddenly seemed so ludicrous he started laughing. 'That is to say I have never— ' he repeated solemnly, hearing Grey and Messy both stifling their own laughter, and desperately trying to focus on what was actually at stake. 'I am glad to say I have never in my life suffered that misfortune.'

'Thank goodness,' Jo said earnestly, scowling at Messy and Grey. 'Because we all know how slippery vegetables can be.'

'They can be *lethal*,' corrected Sue-Marie. 'And I'm sure I don't need to tell you, poor balance in later stages of pregnancy can increase the risks from slippery surfaces. Spillages should be cleaned immediately and sensible footwear should be worn. Don't, Mr Maxwell, try to make light of these hazards. Or my work. Did you know that four hundred people every year are killed in accidents caused by work or work-related activities?'

'Goodness,' said Jo. 'How terrible.'

'1.7 fatalities per 100,000 workers in Great Britain. As opposed to 3.2 in the US. And 3.9 across Europe.'

'Goodness,' said Jo. 'I didn't know.'

'Thanks to the likes of people like me,' she said, crossing the room and holding out the envelope to Charlie, 'Britain has one of the best Health and Safety records in the world. And I, for one, intend to keep it that way.'

'Amazing,' said Jo. 'Fantastic. *Well done*. But, Sue-Marie, if you don't mind my saying, this isn't a chemical plant or a nuclear power station. Nobody's dying at Fiddleford. We just haven't cleared up dinner.'

To Jo's dismay, her three allies responded to this quite reasonable observation with nothing more useful than muffled guffaws.

Gunston glared at them. 'Oh,' she said. 'Very humorous, I'm sure.'

It was the 'I'm sure' that finally did it. Like a group of schoolchildren, all four of them, Grey, Messy, Charlie and finally even Jo, disintegrated into nervous, helpless and entirely unhelpful giggles.

Upstairs Maurice Morrison heard the door bang as Charlie and Jo returned from their night-time walk and assumed it was the sound of the Environmental Health Officer leaving. He wasn't tired (Morrison was rarely tired) and he longed to rejoin the social throng. But the spectre of encountering Gunston again made him hesitate. What if she came back again? He forced himself to wait a little longer.

Maurice Morrison hated his own company at the best of times. He was a people-person, so he explained to them. Without people around him, swooning at his energy and charm, Morrison's mind tended to race very unpleasantly, and his whole being began to feel weightless, as if he were sort of evaporating into the air. But he had checked for messages and there were none – not at home, at his offices, nor on either of his mobiles (he always travelled with two), and though he racked his brain he could think of nobody to telephone. Or nobody, at this hour of the night, who would have been willing to take his call.

Alone in his beautiful, grand old bedroom (magnificent

plasterwork, he noticed. Original. Perfect condition. This house was a remarkable find), his mind was racing even faster than usual, hopping manically from one subject to the next. From the monstrous EHO woman downstairs; to Messy Monroe's miraculous weight loss; to his own precarious position here at Fiddleford and the ghastly humiliation of being caught by TB, cowering here, with a bloody stripper. He thought of the comatose Albanian boy (name temporarily forgotten), lying in his NHS hospital bed. Maurice couldn't help hoping that the boy's – situation – might be resolved, one way or another, without too much more unnecessary hanging about. Apart from anything else there was his parents' anguish, of course, which-must-be-unbearable ... and while the boy insisted on clinging on, Morrison's entire ministry – actually Maurice's entire life – was being forced into pointless suspension, which really wasn't good for anyone or anything, least of all, of course, all the genuine recipients of unkindness in the country who were here quite bloody legally ... Mostly, though, what he thought about were all the Boys out there (some of them not so Boyish any more) who might be reading of his downfall, and remembering ... Had he maltreated any of them? No! Certainly not. He'd always been very considerate. Very generous. Unless you counted – well, but that was years ago .... Or the other little chappie. Little Afghan. Little shit. What was his name? Who'd started asking for money ... But Maurice had threatened to have his entire family deported. Which had shut him up.

Sitting on the edge of his red velvet four-poster bed and running, once again, through the names on his mobile memories just in case someone to talk to had slipped through the net, Maurice realised that what he really needed in life were friends. And a house like this to entertain them in. And a wife to organise the flowers. A charming new wife! (That would shut everyone up.) And a new family, why not? He wasn't very old. And he looked years younger. He could start all over again.

He threw his two mobiles onto the bed and stood up in restless disgust. Never mind bloody wives. Right now what he needed was humans. Anyone. Distraction. Morrison paced the room, picking up ornaments, putting them down again, evaluating the little oil paintings on the walls (mid-nineteenth century mostly, he noted. Farm animals and so forth; charming but virtually worthless). He could buy the whole place, lock, stock and so on – if he wanted. A few authentic touches would be nice . . . and he could always throw out what he didn't like. Had that bloody woman left yet? He thought so, but he couldn't tell. Well, of course she bloody had. Anyway, he couldn't wait any longer. The silence was driving him insane . . .

So he pushed open the kitchen door (without safety viewing panel: hence the mistake) with the kind of intensity expected from a man at the end of his solitary confinement. By which time it was too late. He couldn't turn back. Charlie, Jo, Messy and Grey were just recovering from their unhelpful bout of giggles as the door slammed into Miss Gunston's solid torso, sending her thundering gracelessly to the floor.

'Oh, my dear!' exclaimed Morrison. 'I am so sorry!'

He had no choice but to bend over and help her up. And something, perhaps the impact with the floor, or the angle of his head as it loomed over her, provided the jolt she'd been looking for. He held out both hands to her and started heaving her up, and suddenly she exclaimed:

'*I* know who you are! Of course!'

'I do apologise, Miss Gunston,' he said hurriedly. 'Are you all right? That was quite a tumble.'

'You're Maurice Morrison, aren't you?'

He concealed his anger perfectly. Nobody would have guessed, from his concerned smile, how violently he was cursing her inside. 'There's a little . . . ah—' He pointed delicately at a piece of vegetable peel which had attached itself to the hip of her white doctor's coat. 'I think it's carrot . . .'

She flicked it off impatiently, and turned back to gaze. 'This – is – such – a – complete . . .' She shivered, apparently lost for words. 'This – is – such a . . . completely . . . amazing . . . *honour!*' she gasped at last.

'Oh!'

'Do you know, Mr Morrison—'

'Maurice! *Please!*'

'Maurice,' she corrected, flushing slightly. 'Do you know, Maurice, we actually used your company's safety procedures as a *model* at college! A model! At work in the real world . . . That's why I was so sorry to hear what happened. To you of all people. You didn't deserve it.'

'You're too kind,' mumbled Maurice, looking appropriately hangdog. 'Really, too kind.'

'*He* didn't deserve it,' muttered Grey. 'What about the fuckin' busboy?'

'Well, quite,' added Morrison smoothly. 'The poor lad is still in a coma, I gather. I spoke to the hospital this evening. It's terrible. Too terrible. My heart breaks for the family . . .'

'Well,' she said, her soft moon face flabby with concern as it peeped up at him. 'If there's anything I can do. Anything at all . . .'

150

He smiled at her. What, he wondered, did she think she could possibly do to help him, under the circumstances? Except die. Perhaps. Get off the estate and crash into a tree and die. 'You're very sweet. Very, very kind. And I do apologise for that unfortunate— *bump*. Are you all right? Did you hurt yourself?'

'Oh, not to worry,' she said cheerfully. 'I'll probably pop in for a check-up tomorrow. But I don't think there's any serious damage.'

'I'm so pleased.'

She stood there grinning and everybody waited. 'But what are you *doing* here, Maurice?' she said eventually. 'I don't mean to be rude but I mean to say – no offence – only I wouldn't imagine this was exactly your sort of a place.'

'On the contrary, Miss Gunston, this house is a very remarkable . . .' He broke off, briefly defeated by her plainness, and the absence of any observable advantage in going on. But she waited expectantly, and so he tried again. '. . . Certainly one of the most delightful country houses I've had the pleasure . . . but er— I'm really only down here helping out an old—*friend*. Isn't that right, Charles? Joanna? Giving them a little advice on, er, safety matters. And of course . . . Anyway. In these tragic circumstances perhaps, I would be awfully grateful if you didn't mention our, ah. So if you could—'

'She's closing us down,' said Charlie bluntly.

'Closing the place down?' he said. Slowly Maurice looked around the room, at Charlie, Grey, Jo, Messy . . . They all looked back at him in silence, waiting for his reaction. He glanced down at Gunston, barely a foot in front and at least a foot below, her pallid moon face still gazing up like a lovesick teenager, entirely in his thrall. With a single word, he realised, he could put a stop to it. If he wanted to. And they all knew it.

'*Really?*' he said at last. '. . . But *why?*'

She blushed. '*Why?* Why? Well . . . Where do I start?'

Where indeed? Faced with Maurice Morrison, utterly unable to break from his inquiring eye, she suddenly couldn't remember. She hunched her shoulders together for lack of anything else to do. And laughed.

'Inadequate lighting,' said Grey sardonically. 'It's where you started before.'

'Well, exactly . . .'

'And vegetable peel,' said Charlie. 'But we were about to sweep that up.'

'And the plate stacking . . . precarious . . . plate-stacking procedures,' she stuttered. But she still couldn't bring herself to break his gaze, and while she drowned in his cool blue eyes, the kitchen she had taken such exception to faded into oblivion.

Another long pause while they all looked at Sue-Marie, and she looked at Morrison, and he inhaled through his teeth – thinking – and slowly exhaled again. Until finally he smiled, and said—

'Well, goodness, Sue-Marie. It's wonderful to see you – being so industrious at this late hour. And so conscientious. I couldn't fault it. Marvellous! It's what keeps Britain's safety records so ahead of the game! But I'm a great believer in giving people a second chance, aren't you?'

'Oh absolutely,' she said limply. 'Where there isn't any danger to the general public . . .'

'I mean I can *see*,' he said, incorporating all his surroundings in a vague but thoroughly obliging hand gesture, 'that there is some room for improvement. But isn't it perhaps a little *draconian* to close the place down. Just like that? At eleven o'clock at night?'

She left just before midnight, having withdrawn her prohibition order, provided Grey with an application form for the course in Basic Food Hygiene – to be held at the council offices on Monday of the following week – and enthusiastically, by way of reward, accepted Maurice's offer of a little drink with him, alone in the drawing room.

So while Charlie, Jo, Grey and Messy tidied the kitchen, Maurice sat with Sue-Marie, listening patiently as she sipped at a glass of Baileys and bored him senseless about the need for protective eyewear in commercial kitchens.

'I'm thinking particularly,' she said, 'of steam and smoke situations. For example when relocating oven-fresh products from one food receptacle to another.'

He gave her a business card and implored her to contact him directly with all her safety-related observations, whenever they occurred to her.

'Or anything else, for that matter,' he said, 'because of course what we need, what *every* government needs, is the grassroots voices: intelligent, informed communication *directly from the coal face*. Yes? Otherwise, Sue-Marie, let's be frank, how can we ever really know where we're going wrong?'

As he guided her out to the front door she assured him, for reasons only fuzzily understood but satisfactory nonetheless, that she wouldn't breathe a word of their magical encounter to anyone. Ever. After all, even Government Ministers needed a bit of privacy once in a while! It would be their little secret.

\*     \*     \*

Charlie and Jo went to bed immediately after Gunston left, and Maurice Morrison followed soon afterwards. Which, just as the clock in the hall began to strike midnight, left Messy and Grey loitering awkwardly at opposite ends of the kitchen, trying to guess what move the other might want to make next. They weren't ready to say good night to each other yet, but as the clock chimed on it became clear that they couldn't think of much else to say to each other either.

'Hm!' said Grey, who never, never used platitudes. 'That was a lively evening!'

'Yes, wasn't it?'

'And a close one. With the inspector there.'

'Wasn't it just?' she said, straightening a chair that didn't need straightening. 'Wasn't it *just?*'

'Aye. Shockin'.'

'I didn't think I'd ever hear myself saying it, but thank God for Maurice Morrison.'

Grey certainly wasn't willing to go that far, so he didn't reply. Which left Messy's last comment floating, begging to be rescued. 'In fact I'm beginning to wonder if I didn't seriously misjudge him,' she burbled, and regretted it at once. She didn't want to talk about Maurice. Obviously. But she had to say something. She wanted to stay up saying things all night – and if she left a pause he might seize on it to announce he was going to bed.

'Maybe so,' he muttered, watching her.

'Which isn't to imply – I mean, Maurice is hardly—'

'So,' he interrupted. 'What are you doing now?'

'What? What am I doing? Oh nothing. Maybe . . .' It had been a long time since she'd last been in this situation. Her confidence had taken a ferocious battering since then, and her technique (what there ever was of it, because, with that bellybutton, she'd hardly needed one before) was more than a little rusty. She lost her nerve. 'Well, I thought I'd probably turn in.' She faked a yawn and hated herself. 'What time is it anyway?' The old grandfather clock was still chiming. 'Ah. Midnight . . . Still midnight, then.'

'Aye.'

'Amazing . . . It's been – dinging – for ages . . . D'you think it's broken?'

'No,' said Grey.

It stopped, and another painful silence descended. She'd said she was going to bed, so she should do it. Now. She should leave the room. But she looked down at the table, traced a knot in the wood with her finger, and still didn't leave, and still came up with nothing to talk about. She traced the knot again. No inspiration. And all the while she could feel him watching her.

He could see the colour rising in blotches around the top of her neck, and he longed to say something that would make it OK. Except it wasn't OK. Grey wasn't OK. He was torn between wishing they had never met, and wishing they might never be separated, and with every second she stayed there she wore his defences a little lower. As he watched her, and revelled in everything he saw, he trawled for the strength to walk away, and never found it.

'Messy,' he said, 'would you consider having a drink with me?'

'Yes! I mean . . . Well, I mean, yes. Definitely. Why not?'

He chuckled and turned to take a couple of glasses out

of the cupboard. 'Come on, then,' he said, as much to himself as to Messy. 'Let's go back in the drawing room. There's a fire in there.'

Things ran a bit more smoothly once they'd settled in the drawing room. They sat on opposite armchairs in front of the fire, Messy knocking back what was left of the red wine, Grey, his usual gin with Angostura, and whiled away an hour or more, dissecting their hosts and fellow guests, contemplating the future – for Fiddleford, for Grey's cooking skills, for Messy's non-existent new book.

'I don't want to write about diet,' she said. 'It's boring. I want to write a book called *What to Do When a Safety Inspector Calls*.'

He laughed. 'Knock her out.'

'Or I could do *Recommended Diets for Fat Safety Inspectors. When They Call* . . . So it's in the same theme as the last book . . .'

'I don't see it sellin', darlin'.'

'Or alternatively I could forget about the bloody book altogether, and see if Charlie and Jo would let me spend the rest of my life taking care of their kitchen garden.'

Looking at her now, she seemed, or so it seemed to Grey, a different woman from the suspicious goliath who had stomped into Fiddleford Manor nearly a fortnight earlier. This new Messy, with her thick hair tumbling around her face, her cheeks shining from the wine, and the air and the arguments about raw chicken, was brazenly, blindingly alive. She was magnificent. 'Messy?' He leant towards her suddenly, sounding unusually earnest.

'Mmm?'

But he didn't speak.

'Come on, Grey,' she murmured, laughing softly, '. . . it's not like I'm going to say no.'

Grey had been in love only once before. It was fifteen years ago, and it had been the catalyst for a lifetime of trouble ever since. She had been young, fifteen years old – unattached and underage – and for most of the time he knew her, until she miscarried, pregnant (by somebody else). They had kissed each other for the first and last time on the day that she died, a month after she had lost the child. They had been eating magic mushrooms. They were on their way home, and Grey, then aged twenty-three, had been at the wheel.

And of course he shouldn't have been. Which was why he lacked the will to deny it when her parents, in their grief-filled desire for revenge, claimed Grey had been the father of the lost baby. He refused to make any comment at all. Fifteen years ago his stubborn silence had infuriated his barrister. Last year, when Grey's handsome face was plastered all over the front pages, it had infuriated his record company and most of the nation too.

'You know, Messy,' he said at last, 'there's stuff you probably read about me . . .'

'And stuff you've read about me—'

'Aye, but we both know mine was different . . . I just want you to know that I was driving when she died, and that's the thing I'm ashamed of. But I didn't do what they said I did. In the papers an' that. I'm not some fuckin' weird pervert.'

'Grey! For God's sake. Of course you aren't. *Either way*.

I know you aren't! I just don't understand why you didn't defend yourself.'

'And bring all Emily's past out? On top of the rest o' the stuff her parents were dealing with? No. I didn't have the heart.'

'I mean with the press. Last year.'

'It was none o' their fuckin' business,' he said. 'It was nobody's fucking business but my own . . . And yours,' he added quickly. 'Now. I mean that. I'm tellin' you now because if we're goin' to . . .'

'I certainly hope so.'

He laughed. 'Only I don't want you to think—'

'I don't. Think anything,' she said. 'I mean *right now, about that . . .*'

Gratefully he crossed over to her and held out a hand. 'Come on then,' he said. She got up and for a moment or two they stood there opposite each other, close enough to hear each other's heartbeat, to feel each other's breath. 'Well?' she murmured. So close they could feel the warmth of each other's lips. He bent to kiss her.

. . . and finally, without another word, they headed out into the hall, and across the hall towards the stairs—

'Remember when you first came through that front door?' he said, pausing at the bottom step. 'I've been wanting to do this since the moment you walked in here.'

'*No!*' she said.

'Aye an' you knew it.' He grinned. 'I bet that's why you couldn't go on wi' all the eatin'. You fancied me that much!'

'And it's why you started asking how the washing machine works. A year after you came to live here!'

'Aye, bugger off,' he said, kissing her again, to shut her up.

Just then the front door burst open, letting in a gust of frosty air and a six-foot female stick figure with a curtain of plastic blonde hair. She carried no luggage, except for a tiny silver clutch bag which sparkled and shimmered in the Fiddleford hall half-light, and she was wearing no overcoat. Instead, on that cold night, she wore a silver silk shirt, floaty and undone to the navel, and beneath it no bra, nor even the faintest hint of there being any necessity for one. Her long spillikin legs, encased in sparkling, shimmering skintight silver evening trousers, looked critically balanced above pencil-thin, pointed silver boots. Her face was orange – from Guy Fawkes in St Barts – and very plain in spite of everything, with a fat, round nose like a potato and a jaw like a horse.

'Hi there,' she boomed, her voice husky from the week's socialising. 'Jesus, it's fucking freezing out there! Have you noticed, guys?' They stared at her. Confused, momentarily, and, for at least thirty seconds, too appalled to speak. She gave her head an impatient little shake. 'Hello! Can you hear me? . . . Or am I invisible or something?' At which point something obviously struck the princess as droll, because she threw back her thin, plastic head and hollered with laughter. Messy and Grey, minds lingering yet on more pleasurable matters, still couldn't manage to speak. They stared.

Anatollatia von Schlossenerg stopped laughing as abruptly and unreasonably as she had begun. 'Oh God, sorry,' she said. 'Am I interrupting something? Sorry. Oh! Bugger, it's cold! God, I hate the fucking country, don't you? Anyway . . . sorry it's so late and all that . . . Got lost . . .

I think Les is bringing up the luggage. At least I certainly hope he is! I left him grappling with some dudes down at the gate! *Journalists* of course! *Loathe* them, don't you?'

Finally Grey said, 'Actually, we're just going to bed.'

'Oh bloody hell,' she said, 'just my bloody luck! I've had to sit next to Dog-Doo-For-Brains all the way from London. Poor guy and all that, I know he probably can't help it. But I've been longing for a chat with anyone fucking *half* human for *hours*! Know what I mean?' She looked at them hopefully.

'Sorry,' said Messy. 'It's very late.'

She sighed. 'Well ... That's a fine bloody welcome, I must say. I don't suppose you know where I'm sleeping?'

'I don't,' said Grey distractedly. 'Of course I don't. And I'm not wakin' up Jo and Charlie, not after what they've been through tonight. You'll have to sleep on the sofa in there—' He indicated the drawing room. 'There's a fire.'

'Oh ha bloody ha-ha. Very funny,' she said, not sure, at this stage, whether to register hilarity or rage. 'Tell me you're joking!'

'Of course I'm not bloody jokin'!' Grey snapped. He was a man, after all, who'd spent several years sleeping under bridges. 'Wait there. I'll see if I can find you a blanket.'

Slips account for about 86 per cent of the total slips and trips injuries. In 90 per cent of cases the floor is wet.

Table 1 indicates ways you can keep floors dry. If that is not possible the floor has to be sufficiently rough, the environment, footwear, task have to be suitable and people have to walk in an appropriate way.

*Slips and trips: Summary guidance for the catering industry. Health and Safety Executive*
*Catering Information Sheet No 6*

# • TARGET IDENTIFIABLE HAZARDS

Upstairs in her bedroom Jo didn't hear Anatollatia come in, but she wasn't asleep either. Jo didn't sleep at all that night. Her mind raced. The twins kicked. However she lay she was uncomfortable. Meanwhile the hours ticked silently by and all she could do was listen to Charlie's easy breathing and try not to feel resentful, not just of Charlie but of everyone. It was something, as the night crawled on, which she found increasingly difficult.

She tried breathing exercises. She tried rhythmic belly rubbing and quiet chanting: *Contented Mum makes Contented Baby* . . . just as they advised in the books; *Contented Mum makes Contented Baby* . . . *Contented Mum makes Contented Baby* . . . Nothing seemed to work. Jo hated feeling so angry. She knew perfectly well that the ideal pregnant state was one of healthful serenity. That babies who suffer second-party emotional trauma in the womb are twenty to thirty per cent more likely to exhibit dysthymic behaviours in early childhood. But she couldn't help it. In fact the waves of violent emotion she had so carefully camouflaged ever since her pregnancy began were growing more intense every week. The more slowly her body was forced to move, the more energetically her brain seemed to whip itself into frenzy.

There was Sue-Marie Gunston, threatening to return to the house and ruin everything. There was Charlie comparing her to a bus . . . And then of course there was Messy. Increasingly slim-line, safety-literate Messy Monroe and her fucking GCSE in food storage. Maurice Morrison must have commented three times on Messy's improved appearance during dinner. And Charlie was obviously incapable of not bringing her into every bloody conversation they ever had.

How in Hell was she meant to compete? When she was thirty-five weeks pregnant with twins? And how in Hell had it ever come to the point where she felt that she *should* compete? Whatever happened to fucking feminism? Whatever happened to women sticking together? She resented Charlie for sleeping through all her angst; for being so carelessly unpregnant. She resented Grey for— she wasn't quite sure what. But by five a.m., the worst of her rage was focused on Messy. Who floated about the house, flirting with everyone, patronising Jo about packets of chicken, and purposely antagonising her by losing weight just as she was piling it on. Not until the dawn began to seep through her bedroom curtains did Jo's anger finally begin to burn out.

At six o'clock in the morning, she fell asleep. Just, coincidentally, as Maurice Morrison was rising. He too had lain awake most of the night, worrying about this and that: about Sue-Marie Gunston, all the boys lying latent in the woodwork, his newly discovered loneliness . . . He had come to the reluctant conclusion that Gunston's secrecy could not be relied upon, and that therefore, in spite of its many attractions, he would have to leave Fiddleford at once.

So he took his first shower of the day, very quietly, before it was properly light. He rang his chauffeur and ordered him back to Leigh Delamere service station and then, using Charlie's name, ordered a local minicab to come and pick him up at the end of the drive. Fifteen minutes later, carrying his own matching Mulberry suitcases, dressed in a long black cashmere coat and, for anonymity, an old shooting hat he found in the boot room, Maurice Morrison slipped out by the back door. He left an effusive note of thanks on the kitchen table, together with a cheque for £1,000. Though he didn't have the time to bid them farewell that morning, there were various reasons why Morrison wanted to leave the inhabitants of Fiddleford with a good impression. A thousand pounds, he reckoned, for a single night's sleep, ought to do the job.

He walked quickly through the rose garden along the side of the house, constructing his usual plots and counter-plots along the way, and yet was still able to register the incredible sculpture-work in the garden's central fountain (broken, he had no doubt). It would all be so different when the place was his, he thought happily. He gave an involuntary skip of pleasure. Maurice Morrison loved possessions, but he had so many already. The trick, these days, was in discovering something he truly wanted, and didn't yet have . . . And Fiddleford Manor, he had realised in one of numerous flashes of clarity last night, fitted the bill exactly. It was perfect; a perfect new project. He would put a gym in the old stable yard, he thought. And convert the cellar, if there was one (and he assumed there was) into a vast indoor swimming facility. And of course there would have to be some sort of conference room at the back for tax purposes . . .

It was turning into another beautiful, crisp autumn day. As he passed beneath Messy Monroe's empty bedroom he paused to blow a theatrical farewell kiss.

'A bientôt!' he whispered.

. . . Because in the lonely spirals and blinding flashes which had shaped so much of Maurice's thinking last night, Messy Monroe had also featured very heavily. Messy Monroe and the role she might play in his new, friend-filled Fiddleford existence . . . He had grand plans for her. She would certainly be hearing from him again.

She was intelligent, he thought (but not too intelligent); potentially ravishing, and with none of that awful strident confidence other women had. Of course he would try to discourage a second book, but the occasional little pep talks to the Socially Excluded (re bodies etc) would allow her to maintain a show of independence without requiring her to stray too far either from their new country house, or from his £9.6 million Hampstead home. Which she could certainly redecorate if she liked.

At thirty-one, she was perhaps a year or two older than he would have initially chosen. But even Maurice Morrison couldn't have everything. And as the British Government's most newly appointed Minister, what he required was not, unfortunately, a teenybopper with perfectly rounded breasts – or even (God forbid) a full-lipped, finely chis-elled, downy-cheeked—. No, what he required was a softly cerebral sort of a *wife*, who could look intelligent for the cameras. That Messy was also a single mother, and of an exceptionally pretty (and vaguely ethnic-looking) young girl, could only work in his favour. Besides which, of course, Messy was a delightful woman, and clearly at something of a loose end. He had no doubt she would make their little wedding look enchanting.

But not just yet. Not this morning. Maybe this evening he would call her from London and then send some sort of trinket down: books probably. Would go down better than jewellery. And then in a few days he would drop in with the helicopter (always impressive, even with book readers). He might make some sort of declaration there and then, if possible – which it tended to be, when Maurice set his mind to something. At any rate he needed to get the thing wrapped up and public within a week – or two, max – if it was to serve its purpose . . .

But right now dawn was breaking and he wanted to be well clear of the house before the new working day began, so that should Gunston's tongue feel tempted to wag Morrison would be in a position to refute everything at once, either from the doorstep of his Hampstead home, or – better still – from the bedside of the dying Albanian. After which, with Gunston being such an ugly and charmless woman, the media would be disinclined to give her silly claims much more of an airing. And the entire silly subject would very quickly be dismissed.

He hurried on towards the gates and the end of the drive, choosing instinctively the less direct, more camouflaged route, across parkland. Just in case. Maurice's years in the spotlight had taught him that even here at a media refuge (or perhaps especially here; the previous twelve hours had hardly left him with much faith in the operation) there was always a danger of photographers.

He passed the cedar tree without bothering to appreciate it this time; actually he was picturing that first introduction between the Morrison Bride and the stupendous, mesmerising Mrs TB, who was no doubt fascinated by the social implications surrounding self-esteem, body image and so on and forth. Or she certainly ought to be, with an arse like that; oops. Where had that come from? He giggled mischievously. And with a carefree swing of the Mulberry suitcases he strode out from the last knot of rhododendrons, into the final bend of the drive. He froze. Twenty yards in front of him was the gate. Thirty yards in front of him was the minicab, its engine running, waiting to transport him back to civilisation, and between the two – what looked like a major glitch. One . . . two . . . three reporters clustered around the remote control intercom, buzzing it aggressively, waiting, buzzing it again. And behind the reporters, two photographers; all five, apparently, too stupid to notice he was standing right in front of them.

'FUCK!' he whispered.

How the Hell had Gunston managed to work so fast?

'FUCK!' he said again, and backed silently away.

About five hours later, at eleven o'clock, Charlie woke Jo with a cup of coffee (decaffeinated). He pulled open the curtains at the two long windows opposite their bed, and paused briefly to revel, once again, in the beauty of his park, which looked more beautiful to him every day and which, this morning, was bathed in the softest of autumn sunlight.

When she first came to Fiddleford, before the money ran out, Jo had wanted to transform their bedroom into an oasis of urban good taste, something to retreat to when her new life became too unbearably rural. She'd covered the 1970s floral wallpaper with white paint, and had a sisal carpet laid beneath the rugs. Above the marble mantelpiece she'd hung a very fine and very large, simple, modern oil of something green and yellow. Whatever it was it looked magnificent.

But by the time her pièce de résistance – an ankle-height rubber and worsted-steel bed – finally arrived from its showroom in Westbourne Grove, the old-world charm of Fiddleford had seduced her. She sent it back. And replaced it with a brass bed she'd discovered in one of the junk-filled corners of the old stables. The result, a mild-mannered mixture of old and new, was a lovely, welcoming room: a room which lightened her spirit every time she walked into it.

'I left you sleeping,' Charlie said, collecting pillows from around the bed and propping them up behind her so she and her belly could sit up. 'I know you've got lots to do. But after what happened last night—'

'It wasn't anything,' she said. 'Honestly. My knees just went a bit funny.'

'Messy says she fainted when she was pregnant with Chloe a couple of times. She says you probably ought to stay in bed, at least for a bit. They made her stay in bed for a fortnight.'

'Well,' said Jo, her hackles rising immediately, 'she's hardly a doctor, is she?'

'Mm? No, she's only—'

'So I presume she doesn't know what she's talking about.'

169

'Of course not. She was just being friendly, I think.'

'Yes. Right.'

'Well – *yes*,' he said, looking at her cautiously.

'Anyway, Charlie, I'd prefer it if you didn't discuss my medical situation with our guests. It is private.'

'Private?' he laughed. 'Jo, you've discussed your "medical situation" with anyone who'll listen every day for the last eight months. And you passed out in front of her! What was she supposed to do? Pretend not to notice?'

'And in case you were wondering,' she said, ignoring his question and, feeling unjustly wrong-footed, beginning to shout, 'in case you were wondering, the last thing I want to do is spend the next sodding fortnight in bed!'

There was a moment's silence as her words reverberated. She caught his eye and chuckled sheepishly.

'Slept well then?' said Charlie.

She shook her head, took a gulp of coffee and he watched her, a faint, distracted smile on his face. 'OK,' he said carefully, 'I'm going to mention a person's name to you. That's all. But please, promise me, before I give you the name, promise me you'll stay calm . . .'

She stared at him. '. . . *Anatollatia*! Jesus Christ!' She tried to climb out of bed, immediately lost her balance and fell back onto the pillows again, spilling coffee over her chest as she did so.

'No, it's OK. Everything's *fine*. She's downstairs at the moment, and she's *very happy*. She's spent the last two hours scouring the papers like a bloody drug addict, looking for stories about herself. And as you know there are an awful lot of them. So she's having a wonderful time. She got here last night. And though she says it wasn't her, it obviously was. At any rate *somebody's* tipped off the press. We've got reporters crawling all over the village, apparently. In fact they've been so annoying I've had to disconnect the intercom.'

Jo groaned.

'But she's actually quite sweet. Thick as pig shit, poor little thing. And *hideous*—'

'Looks-not-relevant, Charlie,' she said automatically. 'Please. Don't be sexist.'

He ignored her. Possibly didn't even hear her. Jo's endlessly appropriate interjections had long ago lost their power to impinge on his consciousness. 'But sweet,' he continued blithely. 'Quite boring. But definitely sweet.'

Jo sighed. 'Sweet or not, she knows perfectly well not to talk to the press. Who let her in anyway?'

'Grey and Messy from what I can work out. Though I must say they're both being bloody obtuse about it. And then Grey told her it was too late to ask us where she was sleeping.' His face cracked into a grin. 'So she slept on one of the sofas in the drawing room.'

'No!' Jo hauled herself out of bed faster than she had managed in weeks, spilling coffee everywhere again and hardly even noticing it. 'Please,' she said, reaching for the first piece of clothing she could find – last night's black woollen maternity trousers, with a blob of chocolate on the belly – 'tell me you're joking! Tell me it's not true!'

'But the thing is, Jo . . . *Listen*. I've shown her the bed-room now. She's had a bath and all that. She's actually – to be fair to her, she's actually taken it incredibly well. She's made a lot of feeble jokes about sofas and sofabeds, but honestly, I think she thinks it's all a tremendous adventure. I keep telling you, she's having the time of her life.'

\*　　\*　　\*

Back in his bedroom, having been careful to retrieve the effusive letter plus cheque on his way through the kitchen, Maurice Morrison put a call through to his PA. Twenty minutes later she called back to reassure him that, so far as she knew, nobody in the media had any idea where he was hiding, and that the reporters at Fiddleford Manor were in pursuit of a girl called Princess Anatollatia von Schlossenerg. If her tone suggested she would have liked to know more, Maurice didn't choose to pick up on it.

Instead, mightily relieved but still angry, he snapped shut his mobile phone, swallowed a handful of vitamin pills, and changed into his jogging pants. Apart from yelling at his staff, which he couldn't do here in case the others heard him, Morrison's favourite way to work off any frustration was by sprinting very fast around Regent's Park. On this occasion the park at Fiddleford would obviously have to do.

It had the desired effect. By the time he finally came down to the kitchen, where the rest of the household was still lingering over breakfast, he had run, stretched, showered for a second time, and made at least a dozen more calls. He was one hundred per cent his ebullient and charming self once again.

The Albanian, he'd been informed, had not died overnight. But TB's people had suggested he wait a couple more days before putting in an appearance at the bedside. In the meantime Maurice could manage most of his affairs from here. And then of course there was Messy to be thought about. And various schemes. Various things to organise. He had already spoken with Gunston. After an interminable eleven-minute conversation, during which she had proposed several changes to the current degradable refuse legislation, he judged his secret, after all, was safe with her, at least for a while yet.

He found Messy and Grey sitting silently side by side at the kitchen table, staring at their newspapers. He noticed they didn't look up when he came in. He also noticed that Grey was examining share prices, which was intriguing. He found the General putting down his magazine and rising from his leather armchair beside the Aga to welcome the Minister in. And the Sleazy Stripper, in tight white jeans and cream-coloured cashmere turtleneck, discussing shoes with his hostess, Joanna. Who looked a mess, he noticed: red eyes, dirty hair and last night's trousers.

'See the problem with tan, I think,' Anatollatia was saying, 'especially with the teeny-tiny heels, is you're always running the risk of looking a bit *Susie*. Do you know? Do you know what I mean?'

Jo nodded enthusiastically. 'Absolutely,' she lied. 'Anatollatia, I am so sorry about last night.'

'Oh forget about that,' said Anatollatia impatiently.

'Also, perhaps after you've finished breakfast I think we need to have a quick natter about the ground rules here. OK? Because it is essential, for everyone's security, that while you're at Fiddleford you really *don't* talk to the press. At all. Except through me. Are you clear on that?'

'*Totally!* But, Jo, I really swear—' Like a child she gazed across at Jo, an expression of entirely unconvincing innocence in her wide blue eyes. 'I mean, I know you think I rang that particular journalist – or whatever. Whichever one it was. But I *absolutely swear* I didn't. Honestly. I *swear!* Cross my heart!'

'I'm sure you didn't,' said Jo soothingly. 'Just for future reference, yes? No more chats with anyone in the media.

While you're here, Anatollatia, the aim is not for *you* to get *yourself* any more *bad* publicity. It's for me to try and turn the bad publicity around.'

Anatollatia gave her a double thumbs up and grinned. 'You got it, dude!' she said. 'But seriously though, Jo. I really think if you're going for teeny-tiny, *plus*, you know, with the tan, you've just got to be subtle. That's all. That's actually all I'm saying. Or you're going to end up looking like a slut. Frankly. Don't you think?'

'Couldn't agree with you more,' said Maurice, holding out a hand to the new guest. 'How d'you do. You must be Anatollatia von Schlossenerg. Maurice Morrison. So sorry to have missed you last night.' He turned to Jo. 'May I impertinently inquire what all the apologies are in aid of?'

'Oh God, Maurice! *Our hero!* The man who saved us from Sue-Marie Gunston!' Jo stood up to hug him, found her belly in the way, and patted him awkwardly on the shoulder instead. 'How can we ever repay you?'

'Don't even think about it,' said Maurice. 'It was nothing! Nothing! As a matter of fact I rather got the impression the poor lady was new to the job, didn't you? Probably told her at college, *go in with a firm hand*. All that nonsense. I think she was actually desperate for a little guidance.'

'Well, Messy and Grey have very kindly volunteered to go to Lamsbury this morning and fetch a lot of easi-clean paint and things. So at least when she comes back it'll look like we're making an effort.'

'Excellent!' said Maurice automatically. Sue-Marie Gunston would not be fooled. But that was hardly his problem. Quite the contrary in fact.

'Good morning to you, Maurice,' said Grey pleasantly.

'And thank you kindly for savin' our bacon last night. Can I get you a cup o' coffee?'

'Goodness! And good morning to you, too, Mr McShane. And good morning to *you*, Messy.' He beamed at her. '. . . Oh, by the way, I've got some— I hope you don't mind. I was so touched by your enthusiasm last night, Messy, I rather took it into my head—' He paused, delved into the inside pocket of his lightweight Donna Karan leather driving coat, and pulled out a scrap of paper. 'Here we are— I put in a couple of calls, because of course there's a large school just down the road in Lamsbury. I spoke to the head and he's *longing* for you to drop in for one of those little chats—'

She looked blank.

'Which we were talking about,' he prompted. 'To the sixth formers.'

'Oh. Of course!'

'Any day next week, he says. You can have the whole sixth-form for an hour. So I should take a few signed copies of the book, don't you think? Anyway it's all written down here.' With one of his most charming and self-effacing grins, he slid the scrap of paper across the table.

'That's— Maurice, that's amazing,' she said. 'Thank you.'

'Don't mention it, please. It's just a little something. Just to get you going. Until you're ready to start the next book.'

'Thank you so much.'

'Think of it, if you bother to think of it at all, as a wholly inadequate attempt at recompense for my dreadful behaviour on *Question Time*.'

'But it wasn't your behaviour that was dreadful!'

He held up a hand. 'For which,' he continued, 'I really

am truly sorry. Especially, if I may say so, now that I've had the pleasure of getting to know you better.'

'Bloody hell,' muttered Grey, without looking up from his newspaper. 'Any more of this an' I'm gonna vomit.'

'Shh. Shut up, Grey,' she said mildly. 'And, Maurice, thank you. Really . . . So thoughtful.' The idea of discussing body image with the adolescents of Lamsbury – petrol bombers all of them, no doubt – was not entirely uplifting. But it was clear he had gone to some trouble. And she couldn't help it, she was flattered.

'Well! I should probably apologise to you, Messy,' said Jo irritably, 'for not having thought of something like this myself.'

Messy laughed. 'I should think you've got enough on your plate. How are you this morning by the way? Shouldn't you be in bed? I remember when I was having Chloe—'

'Yes, Charlie told me. I'm fine, Messy, thank you,' Jo said sharply, and tried to sweeten it with the flash of a professional smile. 'I think this could be an excellent rehabilitation vehicle for you. I suggest we hand-pick a couple of journalists to come down and cover it. What do you say?'

'Oh.' Messy sounded apologetic. 'I'd much prefer not . . . I mean unless you're thinking about the . . . money—'

'No!' said Jo. 'No, of course not.' She laughed. 'You've more than paid your way. I'm just thinking about your image.'

'Well, in that case I'd definitely prefer to keep it private.'

'There you go again,' exclaimed Maurice. 'Hiding your light under a bushel! But you need to get *out there*, Messy. Brave the world again! Show 'em what a star you really are!'

'No. Not at all. I was just saying—'

'Me and my kids used to adore you on *Top of the Pops*,' lied Maurice, who, between his other adventures that morning, had ordered Messy's biog to be e-mailed to him, and had spent several minutes examining it. 'We used to watch you religiously. Every Friday night. It was the highlight of our week. My son absolutely worshipped you . . . and so, I might add . . .' he said, setting his head to one wry side and pausing, so she could interrupt—

'*Oh hogwash*!' she cried, flushing with pleasure. 'Honestly, Maurice, for such an incredibly successful man you do talk rubbish!'

'Right.' Grey closed his paper and stood up. 'I'm off to Lamsbury. I'll see you all later.'

'Oh! No! Grey! Wait for me!' As she jumped up she knocked the scrap of paper Maurice had given her to the floor. He strode forward to help her retrieve it, and in doing so managed with perfect daintiness to obstruct her path to the door. She thanked him profusely as he handed it back to her; she tried as politely as she could to dodge around him. But she moved too slowly. Or the men moved too fast. By the time she was free Grey was already gone, and, for once in his life, he'd closed the door behind him.

An awkward pause followed while Messy, looking crestfallen, quietly sat down again.

'Bloody Hell!' yelled Anatollatia. 'Hope he buys an extra bedroom while he's out! 'Cos I wouldn't mind actually sleeping in a *bed* tonight! D'you know what I mean?' She threw back her long thin head and howled.

'Oh do shut up,' said the General.

'Sorry. By the way has anyone got a copy of the *Daily Star*?'

'We don't tend to get the *Star*,' said Jo. 'But I can certainly order it for you, if you'd like.'

'Oh no, don't bother. I just thought there might be something in it, you know, about *me*. Incidentally, when's that dishy tennis player turning up? Is he dishy in fact? Does anyone actually know?' She sighed. 'I bloody hope so. Here I am, stuck in the dreaded country with *two* bloody gorgeous blokes in the house, and they're both taken! Just my luck, hey? Oh. And you, Maurice. Sorry.'

'And the General!' said Jo quickly, smiling at him. But he was embarrassed. He pretended not to hear.

'Well!' sighed Maurice, stung, but managing to rise above it with his usual grace. 'Messy! I must say I find myself at something of a loose end this morning. I don't suppose you could use any help in your marvellous garden?'

Just then Grey poked his head round the kitchen door. He winked at Messy. 'Are you comin' then?' he said.

'What? Yes, of course I am!' She stood up to follow him, and then remembered Maurice's question. 'Oh goodness, sorry, Maurice! And thank you! What a generous offer. You'll find a fork in the greenhouse, if you feel like doing any digging. So thank you . . . And thanks for the er – you know. The speechy thing.' And once again, Grey closed the door behind them.

Nigel wasn't dishy, as it turned out. At least not in any obvious way. He arrived alone, silent and humourless and utterly innocuous, the only obvious proof of his presence at Fiddleford the vast amount of food he put away. He was beefy, pale and, like a lot of professional sportsmen, catatonically incurious. Nigel's world ranking had been slipping every year for the last six, and since then, what with the injuries, the work-outs, the interminable conversations with advisors (all of them, thanks to the cheating scandal, now leaping at the opportunity to dump him), he had lost the habit of wondering about anything except his failing career. He'd been staying at Fiddleford for three long days before Colin Fairwell happened to tell him what all his fellow guests were in for.

Colin had campaigned for a lesson in 'being a Tennis Champ' from the instant Nigel arrived. But when he finally succeeded in dragging the world's 87th-ranker to the moss-covered court, he discovered that the game was a lot more boring and difficult than it looked. So while Nigel obligingly threw him balls, every one of which he missed, Colin chattered, and along the way delivered a garbled rendition of the standing of everyone in the house.

'You've got to move your feet,' Nigel interrupted him every now and then. 'It's no good just standing there swiping.'

'So I reckon Sleaziburg's got a bit of a thing for you,' Colin said, flapping his racquet in the air while another ball drifted peacefully past his elbow. ''Cos o' the way she looks at you. And they wanted her naked in the magazine, so she's proba'ly got lovely boobies when she acsherly gets 'er shirt off. Even if you can't exactly see . . .'

'You're not looking at the ball,' said Nigel methodically.

Nigel was not generally open to any new suggestions, but Colin's comments about Anatollatia left quite an impression. Partly because Nigel, although too shy to answer when she spoke to him directly, had spent the last three days quietly admiring her. He liked her yellow hair and the glamorous way she changed her clothes each evening. He liked the way she was always laughing. Also, and for obvious reasons, he hadn't noticed how dense she was.

'You've got to step into the ball, Colin,' he said. 'Watch the ball, and then step into the ball.'

'Plus I reckon she needs a fellow to take care o' her,' Colin puffed, swiping and stepping this way and that. 'She's not as bright as all that, you see. Whereas you're good at sport. You see? An' you know what? Bein' a Royal lady and all that, I bet she's loaded.'

At supper that night, Colin insisted on organising the seating. First he put himself next to Chloe, then he put Messy next to Grey (for a moment it looked as though Maurice had shimmied his way between them, but then Grey, without saying a word, slowly walked all the way round the long dining-room table and sat himself down on her other side). Then he put Anatollatia and Nigel together.

'Don't worry if he's a bit shy at the beginnin',' he yelled at Anatollatia as they settled side by side. 'Why don't you ask him stuff abou' playin' tennis? 'Cos that's somethin' he definitely feels super about. And don' ask him about the cheatin' thing, OK? Not unless you want your head bitten off!'

Later, when he could squeeze a word in, Charlie interrupted Anatollatia and Nigel to ask him how Colin's tennis lesson had gone, and Nigel said evenly, 'Colin's very enthusiastic, but we had a bit of trouble getting him to focus on the ball.'

'Did he manage to hit it?' asked Charlie. He glanced down the table to the end where Colin and Chloe were flicking peas at each other. 'Colin? How did it go this afternoon? Nigel says he can't get you to concentrate, which seems hard to believe. Did you manage to hit the ball even once?'

'Bloody nearly,' yelled Colin.

Everyone laughed, except Nigel, who explained that it wasn't really Colin's fault. It was the tennis court.

'The moss is very bad, isn't it?' said Charlie. 'But everyone's so bloody busy. There's never time to do anything about it.'

'Well, I'll do it,' said Nigel. 'If you've got the weedkiller. I can't stand seeing a court in that kind of a state.'

At some point during supper the General had commented to his neighbour on how tired Jo was looking and soon afterwards, much to her annoyance, a table-wide squabble had broken out about who among them should relieve her of which mundane chores. Jo resented even the mildest suggestion that at eight-and-a-bit-months-pregnant-with-twins she was any less capable than she usually was of anything. Her father-in-law's observation had turned it into a matter for discussion by the entire household, and now Messy – *Messy* – was insisting on doing the shopping for her. The conversation must have coincided with an upsurge of some dreaded emotion-enhancing pregnancy hormone, because poor Jo, normally so self-controlled, dissolved into quiet tears.

Messy was the first to notice it. She leant across the table, across Maurice (surreptitiously reading a text message on his mobile), and reached out for Jo's puffy, pregnant hand. 'Jo!' she whispered warmly. 'Please don't worry! You *mustn't* worry. It's just a – fucking *nightmare* being pregnant. But it does – I mean – I know it's hard to believe but you *do feel normal again* . . . eventually.'

At which point Jo lost it completely. Her shoulders heaved, everybody stared, Charlie leapt from his seat at the opposite end of the table and rushed to comfort her. Suddenly they were all demanding that she and Charlie take some time off together. With swollen, blurry eyes she looked across at Charlie. He looked back at her and smiled. And through all the clamouring voices they lost themselves for a moment, just imagining the pleasure of being somewhere on their own . . .

But the next morning as they were packing their suitcase and it seemed that nothing could puncture their happy mood, the subject of Messy's departure date came up. It was a subject they'd been skirting around for several days. On this occasion their carefree mood made them less cautious than usual, and within seconds the conversation had turned into a row.

Except during the small hours, when Jo lay awake and fretted about the threat she posed, she was never entirely clear what it was about Messy which offended her so much. She was good company. She was helpful and very kind. She spent hours hard at work in the kitchen garden, and just as many with Colin and Chloe, either teaching them both to read, or 'optimising productivity' as Colin had learned to call it, searching for stale eggs around the chicken run.

'But it's something we're going to have to get tough about at some juncture,' Jo said to Charlie. 'She's not exactly front page news anymore, so there's really no need for her to be here now. And unless we lay down some sort of precedent none of our guests will ever leave again.'

Charlie laughed.

'It's not funny.'

'I know it's not funny. But it's not very likely either. The whole point is that people should stay until they feel up to facing the world again. That's the whole idea. And, Jo, thanks to you she's paid us a bloody fortune.'

'Yes, but it's our bloody *home*, Charlie,' she snapped. 'And I should have thought we'd both be allowed to decide who lives in it and who doesn't. Don't you think?'

'But it's also our business, Jo. And you can't just turf people out because they're— Because you're— Because they're making you feel—' He stopped.

'Making me feel *what*?'

'Nothing.'

'What? Making me feel what?'

'. . . Oh come on, Jo. It's obvious. She's looking . . . I mean she's lost a lot of weight, and Maurice and Grey are buzzing around her like a couple of moths . . . And you're pregnant, for Christ's sake. You're probably feeling—'

'Fuck you!' She stormed out of the room.

Charlie looked regretfully at the half-packed suitcase on the bed and considered going after her, as he assumed she was assuming he would. Distantly he heard her office door slam, and thought better of it. She was right, of course. It was her home. It was outrageous to expect her to share it with anyone she didn't want to – however stupid the reason. But he didn't feel like admitting as much just yet. He didn't feel like going anywhere near her.

He strode angrily out into the autumn sunshine, and headed, as he always did, for the farmyard, where he found Les having a tea break outside the sheep pen. He was struggling over one of the tabloids.

'Hello, Les,' said Charlie. 'I didn't know you read that old rag!'

'I'm not,' he said, stuffing it under his jersey.

'Oh. OK.' Les denied everything, regardless of what it was, or of the evidence. It was one of the reasons, Charlie suspected, he was quite a boring conversationalist. 'Have you seen the children?'

'Children? No!'

'Thought they might like to see the new piglets.' He signalled the pen behind him. 'Must have farrowed last night. By herself. Five of them. Have you seen?'

'I don't know where the children are.'

'Right then . . . Never mind.' Charlie put his hands in his trouser pockets and was about to move off. 'Incidentally, Les,' he said mildly, 'I hate to be meddlesome but why are you here? I thought you were in the bottom field today.'

'That's right. I'm just on my way.'

'Fine . . . Good.' But Les still sat there. 'Well, go on then,' said Charlie.

'. . . Only I was jus' wondrin', Charlie,' said Les, obstinately refusing to budge, 'I was jus' wondrin' if you happen to know much about these plazmie television screens?'

'These what?'

'One of them reporter chappies was tellin' me it's like havin' a cinema in yer own home.'

'Really? How lovely,' Charlie said vaguely. 'No. I know nothing about them at all, I'm afraid. Never heard of them. If you see the children will you tell them the sow and her litter are down in the pen? And Les,' he added as an afterthought. It was so obvious it seemed almost rude to remind him, but then – as Jo so often remarked – nothing was too obvious for Les. 'These reporters hanging around . . . You know, don't you, never to let them in?'

'Yes I do, sir,' he said quickly. 'Yes I do most certainly.'

184

'I mean, I hate to say it, Les, but you shouldn't even be talking to them, really . . . Because once they know you're working here they're not going to leave you alone. They'll offer you money to get information out of you.'

'Will they?' said Les, registering the surprise with such enthusiasm his voice leapt at least an octave.

'Yes,' said Charlie seriously. 'And you've *got* to refuse. Are there reporters in the village today?'

'No, sir. I don't know, sir. I haven't seen.'

'OK. But if you do see any you won't let anyone in, will you?' Les didn't reply at once. 'Les, you are clear on that, aren't you? It is vital that you *never* let anyone in through the gates. Not without passing it by Jo or me first.'

'Yes, sir. Have you tried the tennis court? Young Colin's been going on abou' the tennis.'

'Oh! Good. Fine.' Charlie frowned. 'Why do you keep calling me sir?'

Instead of the children, he found Anatollatia, sitting on the spectators' bank and cheering monotonously as Nigel, a basket of balls beside him, slammed one perfect serve after another over the net.

'Amazing, isn't it?' said Charlie wistfully.

'God, it's absolutely . . .' she tried to think of another way of putting it, '*amazing*. Isn't it? What are you doing here, anyway? I thought you and Jo were having a little holiday.'

'Bit of an argument,' he mumbled. 'So we cancelled.'

'Oh! Shame!'

'By the way, Nigel,' he shouted, to discourage her from pursuing the subject, 'if ever you're looking for someone to knock up with . . . I used to play quite a lot.

And I would be . . . Well, I'd be *honoured*, as a matter of fact.'

'Yeah?' said Nigel, pausing to wipe the sweat from his forehead with the bottom of his shirt, and revealing, to Anatollatia's delight, a meaty but decidedly masculine stomach. 'Yeah, well, maybe. Nothing much else to do round here, is there?'

'Ooh, I wouldn't say that!' said Anatollatia flirtatiously.

He smiled at her blankly, awaiting specifics, and it occurred to Charlie that he should probably move on.

He was making a reluctant path back towards the house, preparing himself to forge some sort of peace with Jo, when he thought he heard voices coming from the hay barn behind the old stables. Les had complained about the children always being in there so he took a detour to get them out. But as he drew closer he realised that the muffled voices did not belong to children.

'Who's in there?' he shouted. 'What's going on?'

He pushed past the tractor, between the hay bales and almost fell on top of them, just where he was about to put his boot, both of them naked, except for a few strands of hay.

Charlie burst out laughing.

'Yeah, yeah, yeah,' Grey said irritably. 'Fuck off, will you, Charlie? I thought you and Jo were away today, anyway.'

He stepped back, tactfully looking away while Messy fumbled to cover herself. 'Sorry to butt in,' he said unconvincingly, and chortled. 'I mean barge in. I thought you were journalists.'

'Well!' Messy said gamely. 'Reassuring to know you're so vigilant!'

'Reassuring to see our guests are getting on so well.'

186

'Very funny,' said Grey.

'All right. I'll, er – leave you to it then.'

'No, no, not to worry,' said Messy. 'Funnily enough we were just leaving.'

'No we bloody weren't,' said Grey, pulling her with him back into the hay.

And so Charlie moved on again.

It occurred to him as he walked away that he and Jo had created a matchmaker's paradise here at Fiddleford, a love nest which seemed to work wonders for everyone except themselves. They were so embroiled in the running of the place they never seemed to have any time alone. And when they did he was probably talking about the council, or the water board, and she was boring on about her sodding pelvic floor. Or they were squabbling about Messy . . . Messy . . . looking good, he couldn't help noticing. Better than good . . . Oh shit. It wasn't his fault. It wasn't Jo's fault. But the fact was, thanks to the twins, he and Jo hadn't managed a decent fuck for well over a month . . .

He sauntered on, still more unwillingly, back towards the house and his angry wife. He was feeling uncharacteristically self-pitying. Did all marriages unravel as quickly as theirs was, he wondered, or was it his fault? Or was it hers? Or was it nobody's? Or everybody's? Or Messy's? Or Maurice-bloody-marvellous-Morrison's?

But then, as he approached the old stables, he was distracted by voices once again.

'. . . This was undoubtedly the concern, Derek. So I believe . . .' came the unforgettable, nasal, monotonal whine which was Sue-Marie Gunston's. '. . . Very hazardous, yes indeed. This isn't strictly speaking my area, as you'll be aware. But I would certainly envisage formal proceedings being the next logical step . . .'

They were standing side by side, she and the man called Derek, in the archway beneath the stable yard's rickety clock tower, both wrapped tight against the autumn warmth in brightly coloured anoraks with hoods which sat up and rubbed against their ears.

The old stables had been built in the 1890s, soon after the original stables were destroyed by fire, and they were handsome but they weren't exceptional. Built in the same red stone as the house and set around a paved courtyard, they were, however, exceptionally decrepit. One end was still used for his sister's retired hunter, but the rest had for years now been used mostly for storing junk. So the stables were a magical place, filled with forgotten spoils: old paintings, dining-room chairs, sewing machines, broken sofas, old jewellery boxes, writing boxes, broken gramophone players . . . Somewhere amid all the mess, in one of the loose boxes to the left of the tower, there still stood a barouche which had belonged to the General's great-grandmother. As children, Charlie and his twin had spent many forbidden hours rummaging around in there, searching for hidden treasure in the debris of their family's past . . .

'What the Hell,' said Charlie, 'are you two doing here?'

When she saw Charlie a flicker of panic passed across Sue-Marie's face. But it was swiftly replaced by the sprightly, blinding smile.

'Hello there – Charles! Goodness! Certainly didn't expect to see you. Out and about. Not on a chilly day like this!'

'Who let you in?'

Sue-Marie didn't answer. 'May I introduce you,' she said instead, 'to my colleague Derek Stainsewell? Derek also works with the Environmental Health Unit. He's in Structure, Preservation and Planning.'

'Mr Stainsewell,' said Charlie, choosing not to notice the hand that was proffered, and keeping his own in his trouser pocket. 'How did you get in here?'

Derek Stainsewell didn't answer either. Instead he said, 'As a matter of fact I was just on my way to find you. Apologies, Charles. I should have done so right away. However since you're here, perhaps we could have an informal chat about these tremendous old stables . . .' He looked politely at Charlie and waited for a response. When Charlie didn't offer one, he continued anyway. 'Apart from the preservational point of view, which I shall come to shortly, I'm sure I don't need to tell you, in its current state this building is a real hazard to public safety.'

'It's on private property. As of course are you.'

'But there's a public footpath four hundred yards that-a-way,' chipped in Sue-Marie. 'If a pedestrian should stray from that path . . .' She shrugged, unable to articulate the horrendous possibilities. 'Also of course, there are your "celebrity guests" to think about . . .'

'Indeed I was saying to Sue-Marie, as a precautionary measure we really ought to be in our hard hats today.'

Out of the corner of his eye Charlie spotted Les slithering off towards the village. For an early lunch. Or possibly another elevenses. 'Les!' Charlie shouted. Les jumped, but otherwise pretended not to hear. He continued walking. 'LES!' Charlie shouted again. 'I'm over here!' Les threw a guilty look over his shoulder, which was a mistake,

189

because he caught Charlie's eye. 'Could you lend me a hand, please?' Les shuffled reluctantly over.

Charlie waited patiently until Les had joined them. 'I don't know – I can't imagine – how these people got in, Les,' he said coldly.

'*I* didn't let 'em in! I never seen 'em before in my whole life.'

'—But could you show them out again, please? And lock the gate behind them. And when you've finished could you come and see me? I'll be waiting for you at the house. I think you and I need to make a couple of things clear.' He turned back to Derek and Sue-Marie. 'And by the way you're trespassing,' he said. 'Next time, either make an appointment. Or keep to the footpath, please.'

## OPENABLE WINDOWS AND THE ABILITY TO CLEAN THEM SAFELY

Openable windows, skylights and ventilators should be capable of being opened, closed or adjusted safely and, when open, should not be dangerous.

*Workplace health, safety and welfare, a short guide for managers. Published by HSE Health and Safety Executive*

- # TACKLE AND DEMOLISH NEGATIVE-
  OUTCOME VENTURES AND SITUATIONS

Maurice was disconcerted. After all, at thirteen stone (or whatever she was), a single mother, a washed-up TV presenter, and until recently a figure of national mockery, Messy could hardly be described as the most eligible bacheloress in the stock room. She ought to have been flattered by his intentions. *Att*entions. But in the five days since he'd decided to marry her, Maurice had been forced to acknowledge an unexpected and somewhat degrading obstacle. In the form of Grey McShane. It was something which he assumed he would overcome but it was irritating all the same.

They thought they were being discreet and yet it was perfectly obvious – to him at least – that Messy and Grey were at it. Like fucking rabbits. It was conceivable, actually more than conceivable, highly probable that they imagined they were in love. So he needed to prise them apart. And to do that he almost certainly needed to get Messy away from Fiddleford, which wasn't going to be easy.

He had just found them in the kitchen together. They

were repainting the cupboards with an infuriating air of joyful incompetence while Charlie, Colin Fairwell and Chloe attempted to re-tile the floor (with non-approved tiles, Maurice noted, so they would have to do them all over again. But who was he to interfere?) He loathed DIY. He thought it was brutal and disgusting and – in this instance – an insult to the craftsmanship of the original house. So after a few well-chosen remarks regarding his own ineptitude in the decorating department, he had quickly escaped the kitchen and left them all to it.

It was nearly a week since he had arrived at Fiddleford, and – absurdly – the Albanian debacle remained unresolved. He was itching to get back to his ministership, but the prissy little sods had now told him it would be 'inappropriate' to be seen in Westminster without visiting the hospital first. Which was all well and good. Except the auntie in charge of the boy (name now entirely forgotten; he would have to check his notes) was still refusing to allow him anywhere near the sickbed. Which was ridiculous. It wasn't as if the boy would notice one way or another. That morning he had ordered his lawyers to make her a few delicate suggestions regarding money. A risky strategy but since the boy clearly wasn't dying, it seemed the only one left open to him. He hated being made to wait for things.

Now he was waiting again, pacing through the rooms at Fiddleford, making mental notes – a patch of damp here; a superb piece of cornicing there – waiting nervously to be informed of Auntie's response. But his telephone wasn't ringing. So when he discovered *La Monumentale* Jo with her office door ajar he was delighted.

He had noticed some tension developing between Jo

and his adorable intended, and he was curious. In fact, with the exception of Nigel and Anatollatia who tended to loll harmlessly and wordlessly about the tennis court all day, too wet to broach the single subject so obviously on both their minds, he had noticed tension developing between *La Monumentale* and everyone in the house. Even her charming husband. It was most intriguing.

Intriguing, and possibly quite useful. Though of course he couldn't be certain about that. What he needed, in order to progress from this stultifying position, was information. About Fiddleford (financial state of/Jo's attitude to). About Jo and Charlie (marital state of). And of course about Messy. Did Jo know Messy and Grey were *shtupping* each other? Did Charlie know? If not, why not? And so on. By the miserable look on Jo's face he judged she would welcome some friendly company. He seized the moment.

'Hello, Jo,' he said warmly, sitting himself down on the chair beside her desk and then asking politely if he could join her.

'Please do!' She sounded absurdly delighted. They both noticed it. With a light sigh to redress the balance she closed her newspaper (already discarded by the General) and dropped it onto the floor with the others. 'Been trying to find a new guest,' she said. 'But I can only think of Prince Edward's wife. And she won't take my call.'

'Isn't the house full already?'

'Yes, of course it is,' she said quickly. 'Anyway . . . Would you like some coffee?'

Maurice spraddled his knees, rested his forearms one on each and leant towards her, his body, his face a picture of masculine concern. 'Jo, darling,' he said softly, 'will you forgive me for speaking out of turn?' He didn't wait for her reply. 'Only frankly, I'm worried about you. You've been looking so unhappy these last couple of days.'

'Actually I'm fine.' She gave him a very stiff smile. 'But thanks for asking.'

'Well, you don't look fine. If you don't mind my saying so, Jo, you look dreadful.'

'Thanks a lot!' She tried to laugh but it sounded pitifully unconvincing. He waited, a look of the most tender attention on his face, and suddenly she was overcome by the need to talk to someone – and not just to someone but to Maurice, who wouldn't report back to her friends, who wouldn't judge her for complaining about her perfect new marriage so soon after it had begun . . .

In their enthusiasm for peace a week ago she and Charlie had settled on a compromise, regarding Messy's departure, which had satisfied neither of them. They had agreed that Messy should be asked to leave, but only when they could provide a decent excuse for it, i.e. a new guest in exceptional need of her bedroom. Since then Jo had searched high and low for a candidate, re-churning all the ground her father-in-law had already worked over, but without success. And in the meantime Messy remained, quite oblivious to all the trouble she was causing, in fact blissfully happy and getting slimmer and more beautiful by the day.

But the subject of Messy had now become such a fraught one between them, they found it easier not to refer to her at all. Charlie hadn't even mentioned the entertaining encounter in the hay barn, for fear of upsetting her. It was a great mistake. Because Jo, spinning off in her own lonely bubble of hormone-induced insanity, had become so absorbed by the threat Messy posed to her own marriage, she was the only person in the house who still hadn't noticed what was going on. All the currents of electricity flying between Messy and Grey, Grey and Maurice, Maurice and Messy had completely passed her by.

'You know,' said Maurice quietly, patting her on her knee and, in doing so, making her tired eyes immediately fill with tears, 'of course I'm hardly one to offer advice. Twice divorced and so on. But sometimes, Jo, it helps just to chat about these things . . . I mean none of us is perfect. Nothing's perfect—'

Jo knew all that. But she couldn't speak in case he noticed she was crying. So she nodded instead, causing, to her dismay, one fat tear to overspill. They watched it plop onto the back of his hand.

'Oh angel!' he said, quickly wrapping her in both arms. '*Angel!*' His sympathy was the final straw. Jo had reached a point of such exhaustion she couldn't control herself any longer. She cried like a child – sniffing, hiccupping, dribbling, her whole body shaking – and all the while Maurice rocked her, and patted the back of her head.

'Come on,' he said softly, when she was calm enough to hear him. 'Talk to me, Jo. Tell me what's going on.'

'You're such an amazing man, Maurice,' she said, wiping the tears away. 'So kind. I'm so sorry.' She smiled. 'God knows what you must think of this madhouse . . . We're supposed to be helping *you*, not the other way round.'

'Oh nonsense.'

'Seriously, Maurice,' she said. 'I don't know how you do it. You've got all these things going on in your own life.

197

I mean the last thing you need is some mad pregnant cow—'

'Hey!' he said, giving her another of his electrifying knee taps. 'Enough of that. You're a beautiful woman, and you've got two perfect little poppets growing inside you. That's a wonderful, incredible thing and you of all people should appreciate it. So come on, give yourself a break! Now *talk to me*. We're friends, aren't we? Tell me what's going on.'

'I'm not even sure I know where to start,' she mumbled. 'I mean it's nothing. I know it's nothing. I know I'm incredibly lucky and everything. It's just . . .'

. . . *Well, well . . . so* the finances were pretty desperate, were they? But that was no surprise. He'd already guessed as much. And she felt fat and ugly and redundant blah blah blah. And she didn't realise that Messy and Grey were at it like the proverbials. At it like *rutting pigs*, more like. Which was interesting. She thought Messy was after Charlie, of all the absurd ideas! So she was jealous of Messy. Very interesting indeed. No reference to any frisson between Messy and himself, then. Which was disconcerting after all the effort he'd put in. But which might possibly be made to work in his favour. . . . Poor old thing. Funny to think how impressed he'd been when he first met her. She'd seemed so grounded. In fact it was a sad, strange thing about most women. They almost always did turn out to be a disappointment. He picked his next words very carefully.

'The problem with your beloved husband,' he said, 'is he's a flirt. He's a terrible flirt, isn't he?'

'I suppose so,' she said unwillingly. Because she didn't

think he was a flirt. Or not so that it mattered. People warmed to him, that was all. And he warmed to them. Nobody involved could really help it.

'And by the way, Jo, you're not imagining it. Of course they bloody fancy each other! *I've* noticed it. We all have. OK? So you can set your mind at rest about that. Just because you're pregnant it doesn't mean you've gone crazy, OK?'

'. . . Well.' It wasn't quite what she'd been hoping for. 'I know that.'

'So . . . *yes*,' he said, 'Charlie does flirt with Messy. Of course he does. And *yes*, Messy flirts with him. They're both very flirtatious people. And perhaps, you know – who knows? Under other circumstances *who knows* what might have happened? But that's not the point. The point is, Jo, sweetheart, it's *you* who married him. He's *your husband*. He's the father of *your* twins.'

'Right.' She gave him a sickly smile. 'So he's stuck with me.'

'Don't be silly! I'm just saying – Jo, darling – *let them flirt!* Who cares, eh? After all you'll be back, fighting fit, and knocking 'em all dead in no time! A few months. Well, maybe a year. But until then, Jo, darling, realistically – *what can you do?*'

'I don't know,' she said miserably. 'Nothing.'

'Exactly! You can't compete! So don't waste your precious energy trying. Lesson number one, darling girl, in the secret of Maurice Morrison's success. Actually the secret of anybody's success. Don't waste time competing until you know you're going to win!'

'But he said he loved me!'

Morrison paused. She looked ready to cry again. 'Well, *of course* he loves you! I can see that! We can all see that!

But come on, Jo, you're a sophisticated woman. Love him or hate him for it, but, angel, nothing ain't gonna change it. The guy's got testicles, OK?'

That zapped her a bit. As intended. 'What? For Christ's sake, Maurice, I don't give a fuck what he's got. I don't care if he's a fucking hermaphrodite. It's not the point. He married me. He got me pregnant. He should bloody well appreciate we're in this together.'

Much better. 'Take my advice,' he said. 'Don't say a word about it to anyone.'

'I wasn't going to.'

'Just keep an eye on him. And if the worst comes to the worst – well, Jo, it's your house, too. Whatever Charlie may say, the best thing may be for you to ask Messy to leave. Yes? Yes?' He was tapping her knee again, trying to chivvy out a smile. 'And in the meantime,' he stood up, straightened his cashmere jersey and grinned at her, *'get some rest, girl! Yeah?'* With a meaningful squeeze of both her shoulders, a meaningful eye-to-eye moment, he left her to stew in the juices he'd so meticulously coaxed to the boil. *'Watcha!'* he said with a final wink, and walked out into the hall again.

Right then. Still no word regarding Auntie Money-Grub. Next job: the one he always dreaded. Time to put in another call to Sue-Marie.

'Sue-Marie? Hello! So sorry. Meant to call back yesterday. But you know what it is. Busy-busy-busy. How's it going with you?' Maurice was always careful when talking to his new friends at the Lamsbury Council never to do it within earshot of the house. So he had taken his mobile to a place behind the sheep pen, where there was always a good reception. 'Now then. Where were we? Any word from Derek? What? Oh yes, yes, of course. Ha-ha. Sue-Marie! *Trust me!* I've already set my researchers onto it! Degradable refuse! Absolutely. They're beavering away on your marvellous suggestions even as we speak, that's right. And they'll be calling you— Yes . . . Well, goodness, thank *you*, Sue-Marie! Yes. Splendid! Any word from Derek?'

Derek, Maurice decided, would probably benefit from one of his one-to-ones. He would put in a call later. But in the meantime he needed to update Sue-Marie with various. They had a lot of ground to cover.

Point One. The Stairs.

'At an educated guess I would say the lower two flights almost certainly exceed the legal width for public use, Sue-Marie, and that bothers me. It's a hazard. I would insist on a central railing. Minimum height, 1200 mm if I'm not mistaken! Am I right?' He laughed, briefly. 'And while we're on the subject of the stairs, it might be worth having a quick chat with the local fire authority. Chivvy them along a bit. They really should stipulate fireproof partitioning floor-to-ceiling all the way along that stairwell. Up the landing and down into the hall. It's going to be costly, I know. But you and I appreciate *where members of the public are involved SAFETY MUST COME FIRST* . . .'

Point Two. The Kitchen.

'I hate to tell you this, but, Sue-Marie,' he laughed, 'honestly I feel such a fool. I should never have allowed you to hold fire on that order. But, Sue-Marie, like it or not, *we have a mouse infestation*. And frankly you need to *re*-present that prohibition order pretty much *PDQ*. Don't you think? We've really got to get that kitchen closed down before something horrendous happens . . .'

'Maurice,' Sue-Marie broke in tentatively. 'No offence. I don't mean to be rude – and don't get me wrong – don't think I don't appreciate it. But why are you doing all this? I mean, sorry, but I actually thought they were friends of yours. You said you were staying there to help them out.'

'And so I am, Sue-Marie. So I am,' he said smoothly. 'The point is, after your timely visit the other week – and then your magnanimous stay of execution – I foolishly assumed that my friends might have got the message. Sue-Marie, I've tried to say it gently. I've tried to say it *less* gently. They're not listening! And the fact is, I hate to make these sorts of generalisations, but I'm afraid we're dealing with the *upper classes* here. These people are so used to *making* the laws it sometimes doesn't occur to them that they may also be expected to abide by them occasionally! Do you see? They tend to think that rules are for other people. Which is all well and good and so on. But after the ghastly – *terrible* – experiences of last week . . . You know the poor lad's still in a coma. It seems increasingly unlikely he's going to pull through.' He left a heavy pause.

Which Sue-Marie dutifully filled. 'I'm so sorry, Maurice.'

'Well, but that's my point. If there's anything to be learned from this tragedy then, believe-you-me, I intend to learn it! And whatever my own personal feelings for the Maxwell McDonalds may be, and I adore them, I simply cannot sit back and watch while they put more people's lives at risk. To be frank, if something happened to one of those kiddies, I'm not sure I could take it.'

'I am sorry, Maurice.' She sounded chastened. 'I truly didn't mean to upset you. I was being silly. It's just . . .' But still she couldn't quite let it go. 'Well, I suppose I was thinking about you and the stables. I just wondered, you know,' she laughed nervously, 'perhaps you had some plan up your sleeve you weren't telling me about?'

'The stables? No, no – goodness! Same reasoning, my dear. Same reasoning.' If she'd been listening more attentively she might have noticed the voice tightening a fraction. But she noticed nothing. All she wanted was reassurance. 'Besides which,' he went on, 'I hate to see beautiful things being left to fall apart. And frankly, Sue-Marie, if Derek doesn't take action about those stables pretty quickly, I shall have to bring the matter up with English Heritage myself. Perhaps you could tell him that . . .' Maurice wondered if he'd sounded snappish, so he smiled and dropped the voice by a note or two. 'Now then, Miss Gunston, might I inquire, when are you and I going to have this dinner you've been promising me?'

Sue-Marie gurgled joyously into his ear. She had a training seminar from 5.30 to 7.30 on Wednesday; Friday night was Scottish dancing night, and there was the fortnightly work-team catch-up on the Tuesday of the following week. 'Beyond that,' she said, 'I'm free every evening all the way through . . . yes . . . well, there'll be the office do at some point . . . but otherwise all the way through until Christmas. You can take your pick, Maurice! When are you free?'

Maurice Morrison's concentration operated on a strictly is-it-interesting basis. So he wasn't listening. But just as she was rounding off he became aware of someone behind him. He turned to see Les standing less than a foot away, open-mouthed and blatantly staring. Maurice cut off the call.

He knew exactly who Les was, of course. Les was the one who'd taken the blame for letting Derek and Sue-Marie

Gunston into the stables. And he was almost certainly the one Maurice had tipped – and quite generously – for carrying the suitcases upstairs on the evening he arrived. Since then Maurice had seen him roaming about here and there, looking slovenly. But until now they hadn't spoken.

'What the *fuck* are you doing?' Maurice yelled, alarming the piglets on the other side of the wall, and setting them all to bleating. 'Are you *spying* on me?'

'I was not,' Les said slowly. 'Only I heard you talkin' away, and Charlie said to watch out for strangers. So I came to see. But it's only you. An' you're stayin' at the house, aren't you? 'Scuse me fer interruptin'.' But instead of walking away he shuffled a little bit closer. He looked slyly (or so, unfortunately, Morrison interpreted it) at the tiny mobile telephone Morrison was holding, and said, 'I love them walkabout doodahs, funny enough. I think they're beautiful things. I wish I 'ad one sometimes. Jus' for holdin' reelly. May I have a look an' see?'

'You little *shit!*' hissed Morrison, outraged. '*You're trying to blackmail me!*'

Les stared at him. 'What's that, Sir?'

'Go on!' Morrison hid his telephone behind his back. 'Fuck off out of here, you silly cunt!' Les stared at him. 'Go on! Fuck off!'

Bewildered, but only a fraction more than usual, Les, who lived in a permanent haze of subdued confusion, wandered away not thinking much, thinking you got some odd sorts at Fiddleford nowadays. And within seconds he'd as good as forgotten the entire incident.

Morrison, on the other hand, who lived in a permanent state of near-psychotic clarity, found it harder to move on.

He did not know how long Les had been standing there. Nor could he know if Les had understood the significance of what he may or may not have overheard. But he knew how much there was riding on it now – too much to leave anything to chance. Which meant Les would have to go.

He redialled Sue-Marie. 'Sue-Marie,' he said. 'So sorry about that. Now. Where were we again?' They made a date for dinner, three or four weeks hence, which he didn't even bother to write down. Then he dropped his voice by another semi-tone and said, 'So tell me, Miss Gunston. What, exactly, are you wearing today?'

Her answer didn't fit the is-it-interesting criteria so while she chortled and chided, and informed him at intolerable length, Morrison made a mental note to give his nails one of those calcium treatments, and bided his time.

Unfortunately, he said, the reason their previous conversation had had to end so abruptly was because he'd discovered an eavesdropper. 'It wouldn't look too good, my angel, if you and I were known to be trading confidences . . .'

'No. I suppose not.'

'Exactly. So I'm going to ask you to do something for me. How do you feel about that?'

'That's OK!'

'You're going to have to trust me.' He smiled. 'Do you think you can do that, Sue-Marie. Can you trust me?'

'Honestly!' she guffawed. 'I should certainly think I can . . . *Minister*!'

'*Good girl!* Now I need you to call the news desk at one of my favourite newspapers and I'll give you a name – Andrew Rampton. Have you got that? I want you to tell him that, while hiding out at Fiddleford Manor, Princess

205

Anatollatia von Schlossenerg – and I'll spell that for you, but he'll know who it is – has fallen blissfully in love with fellow guest, the disgraced British tennis hopeful. Ex-hopeful. *Nigel Harkwell*. Have you got that?'

'Goodness!'

'And if Andrew doesn't bite, I'm going to give you some names for a few other papers, OK? Now then.' He looked at his watch. 'It's eleven o'clock now. In about an hour's time I hope to be able to leave an envelope in the letter box at the bottom of the drive with a film in it . . . If Nigel and Anatollatia do what they usually do at this time of day, I should be able to snatch a picture of them together. OK?

She didn't reply.

'It's all very simple,' he said irritably. 'Have you got it?'

'I don't know, Maurice.' She sounded doubtful. 'It seems a bit cloak-and-dagger to me. I'm not sure I approve.'

Maurice swallowed his first response, and his second. He purred into the telephone something about that dinner date, and she melted. And who could blame her? Until Mr Morrison appeared in Sue-Marie's solitary life, not one man had bothered to look beyond the long, flabby cheeks, the double chin, the short, rectangular body, the self-obstructing beady little eyes . . . No man had listened to her talk as Maurice had; no man had shared so many of her dreams. Not only that, Maurice was no ordinary man. He was *Maurice Morrison*. Rich and handsome and famous. He was more than she had ever dared to imagine – and more besides. He was her prince. Her knight in shining armour. Since their evening in the drawing room together she had thought of no one and nothing else. Day and night she dreamed of their hot, passionate love in Venetian gondolas, of their candlelit dinners when (carnal desires briefly satiated) they would talk with quiet understanding, with mutual respect, about the things that really mattered, and he would listen to her . . . and national policy would be affected . . . and then later, back at the hotel . . . of satin sheets . . . and of sex and more sex and then *room service* . . . Sue-Marie, though unusually plain and bossy, was only human. She would have done anything he asked of her. And he knew it.

When Jo came down to breakfast the following day she found Charlie and Messy alone in the kitchen together, huddled in untimely proximity over one of the morning's newspapers.

'Good morning,' said Jo, very sourly.

Charlie jumped as if he'd been given an electric shock.

'Jo! Darling! Hello, hello! How are you feeling this morning?'

'We only saw each other five minutes ago,' she muttered. 'Calm down.'

'Morning, Jo,' said Messy.

Jo ignored her.

Charlie took the paper from Messy and slid it over to her. 'Bad news, I'm afraid,' he said. 'Anatollatia's been up to her old tricks again. Only this time she must have actually let them in through the gates. They've got a picture.'

Jo scrutinised the photograph. Spread over half a page, and beneath the headline GAME, SEX AND MATCH!, were Nigel and Anatollatia lolling harmlessly on the tennis court as usual. Not touching, probably not speaking, but looking at each other in a way that might have indicated love. 'Bloody hell. That bloody girl. D'you know she was telling me *yesterday* how happy she was

207

here. Because when she got up in the morning she knew there wouldn't be "anything to humiliate" her in the papers. And I believed her!'

'Mind you, there's nothing particularly humiliating about that picture,' Messy said reasonably.

'That's beside the point,' snapped Jo. 'She's a liability.'

'I'm afraid she is.' Sadly, Charlie shook his head. 'She hasn't surfaced yet,' he said. 'But I think when she does, we're going to have to ask her to leave. Don't you think, Jo?'

Jo sighed. 'It's a shame. I know she's ridiculous but I was actually beginning to quite like her.'

'Same here,' said Charlie and Messy. In unison. And then looked at each other and laughed.

Jo counted to three. 'Right,' she said evenly. 'I'm going to wake her up.' She turned towards Messy, sitting innocently at the table, sipping coffee and listening. 'By the way, Messy,' she said, 'I think I heard Chloe crying. She may have locked herself in the bathroom.'

Messy jumped up to rescue her and, as she left, Jo sent a glacial stare to her husband.

Who laughed.

'Oh come on, Jo.'

She walked out of the room.

An hour later Anatollatia was in the hall, packed and sobbing and wrapped in the arms of Nigel. Which was something at least. The sight of his princess's anguish had finally forced him to conquer his reticence. And as they stood together in front of the door, and Les waited nearby to drive her back to London, and Charlie and Jo loitered awkwardly beside them, Nigel had taken her thin orange cheeks in his meaty hands and kissed her full on the lips. It had gone on for ages.

'Come on,' Charlie said eventually. 'Les is waiting.'

Anatollatia pulled back from the long embrace and immediately started crying again. 'But I don't want to go! I love it here! I haven't done anything wrong!'

'I wish we could believe you,' said Jo. 'I really do.' Looking at her bloodshot eyes, her wounded child-like confusion, Jo felt a flash of doubt – and quickly suppressed it. Anatollatia was famously addicted to her own fame. Apart from the Royal pant-wetting incident, and the phantom naked photo-spread, it was pretty much the only famous thing about her. And after all, she had contacted the papers – and denied it – once before.

Nigel held her tight and glared resentfully at Charlie and Jo. 'She's not lying, you know,' he said. 'She didn't do it.'

'Well, who else would have done it?' said Charlie impatiently. 'Look, we can't stand around all day. Anatollatia – please – it's been a pleasure having you here. It really has. But Les is waiting.'

As if from nowhere, Maurice appeared, apparently deep in thought. 'Hello, hello,' he said merrily. 'What's everyone doing here? Anything I should know about?' He glanced across at Nigel and Anatollatia, still clinging to one another, and smiled indulgently. 'How sweet,' he said. 'Isn't that sweet? Don't you think? D'you know I suspected there was a bit of a frisson developing between you two – and of course I was quite right! Isn't that lovely? Well!'

'Yes, yes. We're very happy for them,' said Charlie. 'Maurice, I don't know if you've read the papers today, but unfortunately Anatollatia is just leaving. So if you want to say *goodbye* . . . then NOW . . . is going to be pretty much your last chance.'

'I did read the papers, yes,' he said sombrely. 'Indeed I did. As a matter of fact I was just coming to talk to you about it.'

'But I didn't do it,' Anatollatia wailed. 'It wasn't my fault.'

'I was going to come and find you as soon as . . .' Jo glanced at Anatollatia '. . . I'm so sorry, Maurice. But as you can see we are dealing with it and no damage has been done. I mean, regarding your own position here. Which remains a closely guarded secret. As before . . . Please,' she added lamely, 'will you accept our apologies?'

'Aaah. Jo and Charlie,' he said, raising a hand to his chin and looking very serious. 'Would you mind? Could I have a quick word?'

'But we're dealing with it!' Jo pleaded. 'You can see we're dealing with it! There's absolutely nothing to worry about. The case is closed.'

'My dear Jo – *of course*. But that's exactly my point.'

'Can't it wait?' snapped Charlie. There was something about Maurice, in spite of all the help he had given to Fiddleford and to everybody staying there, which set Charlie's teeth on edge. He couldn't come up with a decent explanation for it and had been forced to the regretful conclusion that it was most likely related to his own jealousy. Which made it even worse. 'I mean,' he added more politely, 'perhaps we should see off Anatollatia first.'

'Only I think you may be doing Anatollatia a tremendous disservice. The fact of the matter is—' He turned, saw Les lolling outside the front door. 'I must say I'd feel a lot more comfortable if I could have this conversation elsewhere . . .'

Not long afterwards Anatollatia was allowed back upstairs to unpack, and Charlie, with a heavy heart, called Les into the library. In spite of Les's angry protestations, half-crazed counter-allegations and finally even his tears, Charlie stuck to his guns, and fired him.

Since that first successful foray into Jo's office Maurice had taken to dropping in all the time, bringing with him a steady trickle of carefully disguised hints and insinuations about the state of her marriage. She had begun to believe that he and the 'poppets' in her belly were the only true friends she had left in the world.

She watched Charlie and Messy constantly, whenever they were together. She watched Charlie passing Messy the mustard; Charlie not passing Messy the mustard – pretending he hadn't heard her asking. Charlie laughing too hard at something she said; Charlie not laughing at something she said. Charlie sitting next to her on the sofa. Charlie sitting on the chair furthest from her in the room. Charlie passing her a coffee cup, and their hands touching . . . or not touching . . . or barely touching . . . She found evidence of a secret connection in the most innocent, non-existent exchanges. And yet she couldn't bring herself to say a word. She was too angry, too proud and – by now in such a hyped-up state – too afraid of what his response would be.

The General noticed something wasn't right about her but felt it wasn't his place to say anything. Grey and Messy noticed it too and finally, at Messy's instigation, Grey asked Charlie what was going on.

'She's beginnin' to look a bit crazy, Charlie my friend. What are you doin' to her?'

Charlie held his head in his hands. 'Nothing,' he said adamantly. '*Nothing*. I wish I knew what was wrong.' He had imagined all sorts of things: that she hated Fiddleford was one possibility – and one that she had denied; that she hated being married was another, or hated being married to him; that she had fallen in love with Maurice Morrison (they spent enough time whispering together in her office.) But the idea that Messy, although clearly an irritant, could possibly have been at the root of Jo's misery simply hadn't crossed his mind. Everyone else seemed to know about her and Grey. He assumed Jo did – and only hadn't mentioned it for fear of putting her nose even further out of joint.

'Grey,' he said miserably, 'I don't know what to do. She barely talks to me anymore! All she does is work. And whisper to that little shit Morrison.'

Grey gave a surprised laugh. 'He's helped us out of a few scrapes, you know.'

'She won't stop working. Whenever I suggest we take a break – or I suggest we do anything together – she says she's got to work. She pretends to be asleep the second she gets into bed. Which isn't to say – I'm sorry. That's more than you probably needed to know. I mean she won't *talk* to me. And then I see her looking at me—' He shrugged. 'I don't know. Like she *hates* me.'

'Messy says maybe she just hates bein' pregnant. Apparently most people do. Plus having twins an' all that ... .'

'She swears it isn't that.' He gave a mirthless chuckle. 'Mind you that doesn't mean much. She can't open her mouth without lying.'

'Aye.'

'Oh God, I didn't mean that . . .'

'I know you didn't. I mean I know you did but it doesn't matter. Only somethin's eatin' at her, Charlie. Whatever it is you should get it out of her.'

'Jesus, Grey. Don't you think I've tried?'

'I'm sure you have. Of course you have.'

'It's got so bad. She's so fucking *angry* all the time. She's making herself ill.'

Later that same day Maurice Morrison tapped politely on the door of the library, where Charlie was diverting his sorrows with the newest batch of incomprehensible government forms. 'Quick word?' he said, slithering into the room.

He was in a good mood that afternoon, having finally been given the OK by the money-grubbing Albanian auntie. She wanted £30,000 wired immediately to a son in the United States. Which was simple enough. If all went according to plan, Maurice would be standing at the boy's bedside within the next couple of days. It gave him the impetus he needed to tie up affairs down at Fiddleford. 'D'you mind? I know you're busy.'

Charlie felt the familiar flutter of ill will when he saw him, but managed to nod politely. 'Come on in.'

'Only it's absolutely none of my business,' Morrison said, rearranging a few papers on Charlie's desk so, like an over-familiar teacher, he could lightly rest his bottom on the edge of it. 'And, as I said to your wife, with two divorces behind me I'm hardly a man to be offering advice. Having said that, I do have some experience of relationships falling apart and frankly . . .'

Charlie smiled wearily. His unhappy marriage appeared

213

to have become everyone's Topic for the Day. 'You're quite right,' he said, laying down his pen, leaning back. 'It's none of your business at all. But go on . . . any suggestions welcome. At this stage . . . I suppose.'

'Quite,' said Maurice. 'I wish *I* had been so wise.' He paused, as if thinking how best to continue. 'Bottom line is, Charlie,' he blurted out. 'It's Messy. She thinks you and she are having an affair.'

Charlie laughed. '. . . She *what?*'

'I know. It's barking. She's barking – if you'll excuse me for saying so. All those hormones probably. My second wife went completely mad when she was pregnant with the second one . . . Marcus. When she was carrying Marcus.' He frowned. 'And frankly I'm not certain she ever recovered. But that's not the point.'

'How can she possibly think anything so stupid?'

Maurice gave the faintest of shrugs.

'And anyway how the bloody hell do you know?'

'Oh—' Maurice ran a brown hand through his blond hair and looked suitably embarrassed. 'God, I don't know, Charlie. You know how it is. Sometimes it's easier to talk to someone else. A stranger . . . Anyway I just thought I'd tell you. Because frankly she's beginning to look very unwell. And miserable. And if I were you, I mean it's unfair, of course I realise that, and I for one shall be sorry to see her go. But if you care for your wife even half as much as I think you do, I should give poor old Messy her marching orders. P D bloody well Q.'

'That's ridiculous! She hasn't done anything wrong. Anyway, for Christ's sake, the whole thing's completely pathetic. She's having it off with Grey.'

'*Is she?*'

'Oh God. Shit! I probably shouldn't have said that.'

'Well, I never,' said Maurice. 'This place is a little hot-house, isn't it? Cupid's GB HQ, nothing less.'

'Not for me,' said Charlie gloomily.

'No. Me neither.'

Charlie laughed.

'I'm sorry, Charlie. To burst in on you like this. Only I didn't know what else to do. After all you've done for me . . . and I like you both so much. I didn't feel I could sit on it any longer. And watch your marriage unravel because of a simple miscommunication. Do you see?'

'Of course. Don't be silly.' Charlie pushed back his chair to indicate that the conversation was over, forced a smile, and thanked him. Once again. 'Once again,' he said, 'thank you. Thank you, Maurice. We seem to spend our lives thanking you.'

'Not at all. My pleasure entirely.' Maurice shook the hand that was held out to him and quickly slithered out of the room again. He stopped at the door. 'By the way,' he whispered, 'if you want Messy, she's in the drawing room at the moment. *On her own.*'

Charlie groaned. He had better get on with it then.

*Tap tap tap.*

Jo was on the telephone in her office. 'Anatollatia isn't doing any press at the moment. None at all. I'm sorry. She's had quite a rough ride recently. She's feeling pretty battered, and she's here just trying to unwind. That's right. It's what Fiddleford is for . . .' He heard her laughing at something.

It was disconcerting, he thought, how professional she sounded when you couldn't actually see what she looked

like. She looked like a hot air balloon. Like a total freak—
*Christ!* What a nightmare thought. What if Messy had
twins? She'd be *disgusting!* Quickly, to distract himself,
he tapped on Jo's door again, a little harder this time.

'. . . Anatollatia doesn't read the papers at all anymore.
No! And, no, she certainly was not responsible for that.
It was a member of staff who has since been fired . . . I
know. Of course I know that and I must admit that was
our initial assumption. But people can change. She—
Well, a little bit, yes, I think she has. She rides – we've
got an old horse here. Plays with the children. Feeds
the chickens. Actually she tidies a lot, funnily enough.
Which is lovely for us! She just potters about, really.
Recovering. She loves it here. All our guests do. In fact
they love it too much. We can't seem to get any of them
to leave!'

*Tap tap tap.* Maurice came in. He hated waiting.

'So anyway, thanks for calling, and I'll certainly let you
know if anything changes. Yes. With Nigel. But he's not
doing press either. No. As I say. Right now neither of
them's giving any interviews at all. So it's a No. No. *No!'*
She laughed. *'Goodbye, Paul!'*

'Sorry to bother you,' said Maurice.

'Don't be ridiculous, Maurice,' she said warmly. 'Come
on in.' Maurice's visits to her office usually started so well.
She still hadn't noticed how depressed they always left
her feeling. He would encourage them to begin with a
lively conversation about Jo's disillusionment with New
Labour, with party politics in general (and so on), during
which Maurice would wait patiently and patiently nod,
and patiently wait and nod patiently . . . Until it was time
to make a delicate reference to the Messy dilemma, drop

a delicate hint that things were getting worse, and mop up with some delicate support.

'Jo, darling, you're going to be livid. I've done something a bit naughty. Actually more than naughty. Something terrible.'

She laughed. 'What on earth have you done?'

'Only I've been feeling so bloody awful for you. I just couldn't stand to watch it any longer.'

'Watch what?'

He took a deep breath. 'I had a word with Charlie. Sort of man to man. Yes, yes, I know.' He smiled ruefully. 'And *all* that nonsense! But I couldn't stand it any longer. I told him— Jo darling, I told him you were *very* suspicious of what he was up to. I'm sorry, angel. I know it's absolutely none of my business and you're probably *furious*. You have every right to be furious. Are you furious?'

'Of course not,' she said automatically.

'But the important thing is he feels *terrible*. Bloody awful. Of course. Who wouldn't? I actually think they *are* a teeny bit in love with each other – in a silly adolescent sort of way obviously. I mean *silly*. A *silly* way. Nothing to worry about. Of course. The point is he *knows* how important you are to him. How important you are to the house . . . So anyway . . .' Maurice shrugged. 'He's in the drawing room now. Telling her to go, I imagine . . .' He smiled at Jo, a little smile of victory, which she was supposed to share with him. 'I think we'll find she'll be out of Fiddleford by lunch time.'

'*Right*,' Jo said finally. She'd had enough. She hauled herself up from her chair and left the room.

'Jo? Jo, where are you going?'

He followed her out into the corridor. 'Maurice,' she

said, 'thank you for everything you've done and said, and I'm sure it was all done with the very best intentions. But I think you'll appreciate in the end this is something between me and my husband. So . . . If you'll excuse me.'

'Yes, of course. Of course. I'm sorry.' He stepped quietly back into the shadows.

When she opened the door to the drawing room she saw Charlie sitting on the sofa beside Messy, one hand pushing back his thick dark hair, the other hovering above Messy's knee. He was looking at her, trying to work out the kindest, most tactful way to begin. He glanced up, saw Jo and instinctively snatched his hand away.

'Charlie?'

He leapt to his feet. They stared at each other while she waited hopefully for some other explanation, an explanation which might persuade her to stay. She clung onto the door handle, saying nothing, while the world around her crumbled. It occurred to her that until then – until that moment – she had never really believed it was true. But the look of guilt on his face, his lack of words, his refusal to say anything to bloody well explain himself . . .

'. . . Charlie?' she said again.

'. . . Jo?' said Messy innocently. 'Are you OK?'

'Jo, darling,' Charlie stuttered, 'I was just— We were just—'

But the humiliation of standing there, trying not to faint, listening while he fumbled for an explanation, was much more than she was willing to wait for. She walked away.

She locked her bedroom door behind her and started to pack. When he followed her, stood on the upstairs landing and pleaded and shouted and even tried to kick the door in, she ignored him. She put on a Walkman to drown his voice out.

And when she came out and tried to edge round him with her great big belly, Charlie had no choice but to carry her great big suitcase downstairs.

And put it into the boot of the car.

'Where are you going?' he asked, as she squeezed herself in front of the steering wheel. 'Please, Jo. Where are you going?'

She tried to close the car door but he held onto it.

'Jo? Tell me, please.'

She started the engine and started driving anyway, but he clung onto the door handle.

*'Where can I find you?'*

Maurice, lingering impotently by the library curtain, could only stand and spy. *'Bugger!'* he muttered to himself as her car accelerated out of view. 'Bugger, bugger, bugger!' Somehow or other he'd gone and got rid of the wrong girl.

He was about to wander away when he saw the Land Rover hurtling up the drive after her. So he was following, was he? Well, well. *While the cat's away the mice will play.* And so on.

Or perhaps . . . He smiled. Perhaps he should have put that the other way around?

Put on protective clothes before entering a food area . . .
Protective clothing is designed to protect food from contamination and you from harm. It should be:

- suitable to the task
- clean and in good condition
- light coloured so that dirt will show easily, prompting you to change into clean replacement clothing
- easy to clean . . .

Typical examples include: overalls, jackets, trousers, aprons, neck scarves, hats, hair nets, beard nets, moustache nets.

Always put on [nets] *before* you put on other protective clothing to avoid displacing hair.

*Food Safety First Principles Workbook, Chartered Institute of Environmental Health*

# • INITIATE ZERO-TOLERANCE STRATEGY TO CONFRONT ADVERSE BEHAVIOURS

It was a subdued crowd which gathered in the drawing room that evening. Nobody had heard a word from Charlie or Jo since they'd sped off in their separate cars, and neither was answering their mobile. So while Messy, Grey and the General gnawed half-heartedly at the bones of a pointless conversation the others – even Colin – sat very quiet and bewildered. Everyone was waiting to start supper, only Maurice – eccentrically, since it had been dark for hours – had disappeared on another of his runs.

They all jumped at the sound of the intercom.

'About bloody time too,' said Grey. 'Stupid buggers must o' gone off without their gate controls.'

'They jus' went off to 'ave the babies,' Colin yelled happily, leaping up. 'So there'll be four of 'em now. And the little 'uns'll be squarlin', for bottles of milk or nappies an' so on.'

But when the General returned from buzzing them in he hardly looked the ecstatic new grandfather. 'It's that abominable council woman again,' he said. 'The plain one. She's banging on about the kitchen. I think we need Mr Morrison. Does anyone know where he's gone?'

They all headed off in different directions to go in search of him. 'I say, McShane,' the General called apologetically. 'In the absence of Charlie and Jo, I don't suppose you'd mind sticking around, would you? Only the woman was talking so much bloody nonsense into the machine, I'm not sure I'll understand anything she says.'

Sue-Marie arrived with her prohibition notice in an envelope which, as she stood on the steps outside the front door, she proceeded to open herself. 'I've addressed it to you, Mr McShane, as well as to Mr Charles Maxwell McDonald . . . Is he here?' She moved her head to one side and squinted into the space between Grey's chest and the General's shoulders. But the hall behind them looked empty.

'He's not,' said the General.

Grey took the papers from her and shoved them into his pocket.

'Will that be it then?' said the General. 'Thank you very much,' and he started closing the door. But she put her foot in front of it.

'Actually it's not quite as simple as that,' she said. 'May I come in?'

'No,' they both said.

'Your emergency prohibition notice, which is effective immediately, will need to be displayed at the kitchen entrance and, as I recollect, there are several doors offering access. So I've provided you with copies. Do you have some Sellotape?'

'Do we have what?' said Grey.

'You should understand that, with regard to preparation

of all or any bibulations and/or edibles, it is illegal for you to continue using the premises, any part of said premises, or any equipments described by me in Paragraph Two.'

'What? What the Hell is she talking about?' said the General. 'Can't you persuade her to speak English?'

'Furthermore,' she continued, 'you should understand that you shall not be permitted to use the specified prohibited premises, part premises or equipments at this location until either a court decides you may do so, OR, as in Paragraph Three, the local authority issues you with appropriate certification to enable such action.'

'But what's the point in speaking,' said the General in exasperation, 'if you refuse to make any sense?'

'Anyone who knowingly contravenes this notice,' she ploughed heedlessly on, 'is guilty of an offence for which offenders are liable to be fined and/or imprisoned for up to two years. Now. I need to ascertain that the notices are duly affixed to all equipments and access points. So shall you open the door or must I refer this to the authorities?'

The General gazed at her. 'Good God,' he said at last, and slowly stood back to allow her in.

'Thank you,' she said pertly.

The kitchen had changed since she'd last been in there. She found Charlie, Colin and Chloe's newly laid, non-porous floor tiles. She found Grey and Messy's cupboards perfectly sheathed in the recommended easi-clean white gloss paint. She found Jo's brand-new probe thermometer, and beside it a book to record the temperature of every dish at time of serving. She found Anatollatia's colour-coded cooking utensils hanging in regimented rows, the General's colour-code chart on the wall, which explained to Grey (as if he honestly cared) that the utensils with green stickers were meant for cooking vegetables. She found a second fridge installed, with a sign on the front which read RAW MEAT ONLY.

'Oh!' she said, obviously put out. 'Goodness!'

Maurice hadn't mentioned any of this.

'Aye. I thought you'd like it,' said Grey.

But it was too late to turn back now. Not without looking a fool. Besides, the floor tiles, when wet, would almost certainly be slippery. And if Maurice Morrison said there was a mouse infestation, then a mouse infestation there clearly was. If Maurice Morrison said the kitchen should be closed, so be it. Emotions aside (impossible of course) Mr Morrison knew what he was talking about. He was a Government Minister whose Health and Safety systems had been used as a prototype at her Health and Safety college. If something happened in this kitchen now, and she had ignored his recommendations, she would find it very hard to defend her position to him, let alone to her team leader. Besides which, anyway, she didn't like the people here. They thought they were so wonderful. They thought they could do what they liked.

So without risking another word on the matter, she set about affixing her notices, and Grey could do nothing but stand and watch.

'What,' he said eventually, leaning against the Aga, which was still (and Grey could only hope she didn't notice it) exuding all the tantalising smells of their dinner, 'are we meant to be doing for food, darlin'? There's ten of us living in this house. Give or take. Should I notify the Social Services that we're in danger of starvin' to death out here? Perhaps they could send us

226

some o' their meals on wheels? Or don't you do those anymore?'

'I'm sorry that's not my problem. But I do reiterate, anyone caught acting in breach of a prohibition order is liable to two years' imprisonment. So I should think, Mr McShane, with your previous experience, you might find it worthwhile to pop that nice dinner you've prepared into the bin, and nip out for some ready-made sandwiches.'

'Och, fuck off.'

During the long drive back to London Jo had racked her brain for an alternative, but after nearly five hours she had been forced to acknowledge that there was really only one person she could face under the circumstances. She swallowed her pride and checked in with her mother.

Mrs Smiley lived alone in a tiny but very tastefully decorated mews house in Hampstead. Recently divorced, she'd taken up painting with great verve and claimed to have started writing a novel. But since she spent most of her time abroad these days, travelling with an old girl-friend to various developing nations, taking interminable photographs of the indigenes looking life-affirming under difficult circumstances, it was unlikely that the novel had progressed far.

Mrs Smiley was not a particularly warm woman, and she had been disappointed by Jo's choice of husband from the start. She didn't approve of marriage anyway – not since her own divorce had come through. And Charlie Maxwell McDonald was a far cry from anything she had envisaged for her advanced, metropolitan daughter. He was pleasant enough, and kind, and certainly good-looking – if you liked the athletic, film star look (which Mrs Smiley claimed she didn't). But Mrs Smiley, who only watched films if they were showing at the ICA, who only ever read unreadable literary novels, who regurgitated the *Guardian* editorial comment on every issue of the day, and still believed she was delivering an independent opinion, who described Umbria as her 'spiritual home' and who loved eating pulses, felt justified in confiding to all and anyone that her heroically attractive and uniquely decent son-in-law was 'ever so slightly dim'.

So although of course she was saddened, she also felt quietly vindicated when she discovered Jo, with whom she had a civilised but distant relationship, standing in floods of tears on her doorstep.

'You're lucky you caught me, Jo,' Mrs Smiley said, as she made her daughter a cup of ginger and camomile tea and settled down beside her at the new wooden breakfast bar. 'Jean and I are off to Uzbekistan the day after tomorrow. But I can rearrange if you like. Really. It's no trouble at all.'

'Don't be silly,' Jo said dutifully.

'Oh. Are you sure, darling? Because of course I can . . .'

There was a knock on the door.

Jo's heart leapt. *'That's him!'* she whispered. And tried again. 'That's him,' this time trying to hide the hope in her voice, not just from her mother but from herself. 'I think he's been following me all the way. If it is, Mum, you *mustn't* let him in!'

Mrs Smiley frowned. Though she loved her daughter as much as she loved anyone, she also happened to have plans for the evening, which she was now obviously going to have to cancel. 'What happened between the two of you?' she said irritably. 'I mean it's terribly bad timing, isn't it, darling? With the twins.'

'*Shhh!*'

They heard another knock and then the telephone started to ring. Fearing it was Charlie, outside and using his mobile, Jo leant across and quickly lifted the telephone off the hook. Mrs Smiley didn't notice.

'Jo!' she heard Charlie shouting. 'Jo! I know you're in there! Jo! Please! Come out! . . . I don't know what fucking mad and stupid ideas you've got in your head, but *please* . . . Jo . . . Please . . . What's happening to us? Come to the door . . . For Christ's sake, JO, I LOVE YOU!'

'This is intolerable,' Mrs Smiley said briskly. 'I refuse to be barracked at inside my own home.' She stood up.

'No!' Clambering to intercept her, sending her chair flying, whacking her tumid belly against the corner of the table, wincing with the pain, Jo grabbed at her mother's cardigan. 'Don't you dare. Don't you *dare* go near that door . . . He can't stay there for ever, can he?' she said. 'Eventually,' (the realisation was accompanied by a fresh wave of misery) 'eventually he'll have to leave.'

But she had underestimated him again.

Sue-Marie forced Grey to throw his fine-smelling supper into the dustbin. She stood beside him and watched while he put the whole thing, including pot and lid, into a bin liner, miraculously produced from her own jacket pocket.

'You can take the fuckin' pot, too,' he said. ''Cos I'm not fuckin' washin' it.'

'I was about to suggest the very same. Those particular receptacles aren't Approved anyway. We don't like earthenware.'

But she left the bag behind. And when she'd gone, he

hoicked it all out again and called everyone into the dining room. Everyone, of course, except Maurice, who was still nowhere to be seen.

Maurice arrived halfway through dinner, full of apologies for his absence and outrage at developments. He vowed to get on the telephone in the morning and do his utmost to get the decision reversed. 'I'll talk to a couple of people,' he promised. 'I'll do everything I can but I fear it may be too late. Once these sort of things enter the wretched system . . .' He gave a resigned shrug. 'You know how it is. However, let's think positive! I'll make a few inquiries on my way to Lamsbury tomorrow morning.'

'You're going to Lamsbury?' said the General. 'Mr Morrison, I do hope you're not leaving us. I mean to say, of course I realise we probably appear somewhat out of sorts, but it's only a matter of time. Oh dear,' he broke off, sounding suddenly petulant, 'I do wish Charlie and Jo would get back. Don't you, Grey?'

Maurice quickly assured everyone that he wasn't deserting anywhere just yet. He simply needed, he explained, to stock up on dehydrated pawpaw, prunes, banana flakes and other high-fibre energy nibbles. 'It's tragic, I know, but I think I may be addicted to them! I assume there *is* a health food shop somewhere in Lamsbury?' The General offered to fetch the nibbles himself. Grey offered to drive him to Lamsbury, but Maurice was adamant that he venture out alone. He was looking forward to it, he said. It would be the first time he had travelled beyond Fiddleford's park walls since he arrived. He said he would order a cab.

'Does anyone else need anything while I'm there?'

'You could get me some fags,' said Grey.

'Ha!' said Maurice. 'You'll be very lucky! I never heard of a health food shop which stocked cigarettes before. However, I shall certainly ask. How much are cigarettes these days, by the way? Ten pounds? Eleven? D'you know I've no idea!'

Early the following morning, at about the same time that Charlie, frozen, very hungry and still in Hampstead, was first opening his eyes and spotting the parking ticket on his windscreen, Fiddleford Manor found itself prey to yet another unwelcome visitor.

Maurice had only just left for Lamsbury. Messy and Grey, having discussed it at dinner the previous evening, were in the process of moving equipment from the prohibited manor house kitchen to the kitchen in the unused 'General's cottage' at the bottom of the drive, and most of the others were still in bed. So nobody apart from Chloe was around to protect the General when the Fire Authority representative pressed the intercom.

The two of them followed the Fire Inspector as he examined every room, every door, the positioning of every piece of furniture. The Inspector was dismayed by the laziness of some household members, and appalled by the evidence of open fires in some of the bedrooms. In fact he was appalled by everything he saw. Or didn't see. He would, he informed the General, be insisting on the installation of approved fire doors throughout, with approved fire door safety notices on each one; also designated fire exits, appropriate fire breaks, fire night-lights, fire alarms and fire extinguishers and recorded evidence of regular fire drill rehearsals. The hall stairway would need to be partitioned off; fireplaces blocked up; much of the furniture removed from common parts and the four bedrooms at the far end of the house either vacated or provided with an alternative stairway, which would need to be built. The improvements, he said, which he would confirm in writing, would need, if Fiddleford wanted to stay open for business, to have been completed before three months were up.

The General was still reeling from this last incursion when the telephone call about the water came through. Fiddleford's private water supply had failed to meet the required standard for use by non-private citizens, he was informed. Fiddleford Manor would therefore need to be connected to the mains as soon as possible, the cost of which they could not estimate over the telephone, but which would be billed, in due course, to the owners of the house.

The traffic had been growing steadily noisier for some time, Jo noticed dimly, and it was light outside – or as light as November in Hampstead ever could be. She'd been lying there for hours, listening to the familiar clamour of the city, amazed at all the racket, amazed that she had lived with it for so long. As well as the cars, there was the patter of winter drizzle against the window, and it made her long for Fiddleford. She closed her eyes and tried to conjure the sounds that would have woken her if she'd been there; drizzle, perhaps, but at Fiddleford even the sound of rain was somehow friendlier. And then Charlie coming in with coffee, because she always slept later than he did. Charlie bringing her coffee, leaning over to kiss her, walking across to the windows, drawing open the curtains and looking out over the park, waiting peacefully for her to wake ... Until Messy had arrived it had been perfect. Perfect. She would smell the coffee and begin to smile even before she had opened her eyes, because they were happy together, because he loved her and she loved him. Or she had *thought* he loved her, she corrected herself, and she had been stupid enough to have loved him . . .

A business-like tap on the bedroom door. Mrs Smiley came in bearing jasmine tea.

'Jo, darling?' she said. 'It's nine o'clock!' She put the mug down on the table beside the sofabed and watched her pregnant daughter struggle to sit up.

'Do you want a hand?'

'I'm fine, Mum. Thanks.'

Mrs Smiley left her to it. She crossed over to the desk (where her novel would again have to remain neglected) and pulled up the window blind.

': . . Good gracious!' she said suddenly. 'How ridiculous! Hasn't your husband got any work to do?'

Jo grinned. She couldn't help it. 'He's still out there?'

'No need to sound so pleased about it, Jo. It's all very well, acting the wounded hero, sitting in a Land Rover all day and night. But what does it really bloody well *mean*? Men only ever want what they can't have. Believe me.' She turned back from the window and smiled at her daughter as if she were being kind, as if one paltry smile could disguise a whole married life of disillusion. 'Don't fool yourself, darling. Once a cheat always a cheat. Seriously. I've a good mind to call the police.'

'The police?' Jo managed to laugh. 'What for? Parking?'

'Yes, well. It's inhibiting, isn't it? It's *threatening*.'

'Oh, rubbish.'

'After how much he's hurt you I don't see why you're defending him. He's a disgrace. He should be ashamed of himself.'

She sighed. 'Perhaps he is.'

'But it's a bit late for that, isn't it? Anyway I don't want him camping out there. In that . . . *Land Rover*. I'm going to have a word.'

'Mum. Please. I'm asking you. Please. For me. Please, please don't.'

Upstairs at the cottage meanwhile, lying entangled on the bare floorboards of what was meant to have been the General's bedroom, Grey and Messy should have been exceptionally happy. They would have been, but on the final trip from the house, as they both stood in the hall struggling not to drop any saucepans, the General had told them about the morning's new crop of official requirements. He had said that as soon as Morrison returned he wanted to call a meeting. He had sounded entirely despairing.

'Ah! I'm fuckin' stupid, Messy!' Grey said suddenly. 'Why did I not think of it before? We could *buy* this little place! If they let us. And your garden! *We could buy it!* It would answer everything. Their money troubles. Us staying put.'

She laughed. 'But I told you I'm skint.'

'And I told you, I've got money. We could open a restaurant.'

'What? And have Sue-Marie Gunston breathing down our necks for the rest of our lives?'

'Aye. But it would be worth it . . .' Tenderly he ran his thumb over her cheek and lips. He smiled. 'Worth a thousand Sue-Marie Gunstons. If I can stay here wi' you and Chloe the rest o' my life.'

She leant across and kissed him.

'So?' He pulled back to take a better look at her. 'What are you thinkin'?'

'Well . . . For a start, Grey, I'm thinking I love you.'

'Aye.' He sounded unimpressed.

'*Aye?*'

'So are you interested or aren't you? You could forget about the stupid book for a start and turn that kitchen garden into a sort of – what do they call 'em? You can sell all the vegetables and flowers and so on.'

'Oh!' she said. 'Ha! What a lovely idea! But let's face it, Grey, I don't know anything about gardening.'

'It strikes me you don't know much about writing books, darlin',' he said casually. 'You don't even bloody enjoy it . . .'

'I don't know, Grey,' she said, trying to keep the elation out of her voice – just in case he was joking. Or the sound of her own words made her wake up suddenly, alone with little Chloe again, cowering from the hostile world inside their rented cottage. 'I'll have to discuss it with Chloe.'

Grey laughed. 'Och, come on,' he said. 'She loves it here. You know what Chloe'll say!' He rolled onto his side and leant his head in his hand, so his lips hovered an inch from hers. 'I should take that as a yes then, should I?'

Messy agreed that he probably should.

'Clearly, Charlie and Jo are having a few – difficulties – at the moment,' the General began, once everyone was seated. They were all in the dining room. 'Their minds aren't quite on the job. Or so one assumes. Though of course one can't know, because one can't bloody well get hold of them. However.'

'It's a very stressful time for a young couple,' said

Maurice. 'They probably needed a little bit of time alone.'

'The fact of the matter is,' continued the General, 'for those of you who aren't aware, we've had – ha! – rather a rocky twenty-four hours here at Fiddleford. Without wishing to state the obvious. And there's no doubt about it, with or without Charlie and Jo, we are going to find it a bit of a struggle to keep our heads above water. We need—' The General breathed in, and almost laughed. 'Ladies and gentlemen, to bring about the changes these people are asking we need a great deal more money than we actually have. And a great deal more money, I fear very much, than we can reasonably hope to raise in the time allowed . . . Something,' he added despondently, 'about our little outfit appears to have awoken the wrath of the gods. Or the wrath of our ghastly council, at any rate.'

'Oh! Surely not!' cried Maurice, chewing gently on his pawpaw.

'Now I realise that in time you would all – at some point – have been wanting to move on, but I've really . . .' He paused, uncertain how to continue. 'Well, I suppose I called you all together to warn you that it may happen sooner than you think. The way things are going, with the financial demands being made on us, as well, of course, as all the wretched legal implications of staying open without their bloody silly requirements already being in place, there is a very real danger that Fiddleford may be forced to close its doors within the next couple of days.'

A silence fell over the table.

'I'm fairly certain,' said Maurice, 'that so long as you are in the process of implementing the changes . . . General, if what you need are workmen—'

'What we need, Mr Morrison, is money.'

'Ah!' Maurice dithered between sliced banana and prune.

'There's still our eggs, you know,' mumbled Colin. 'I know you don't believe it, but there's a fortune waitin' to be made in those chicken runs.'

'Colin,' said the General, 'I don't doubt it for a moment. But unfortunately we don't have very much time and I fear—' he shrugged, 'even with the eggs, the odds are very much stacked against us. So I'm sorry. I think we should prepare for the worst.'

'I wish I could think of something to help,' said Nigel, clasping tight onto Anatollatia's hand, and blushing furiously. 'I'd put on a display match, only no one decent would play me. Everybody hates me now.'

'*I* don't hate you, darling,' bellowed Anatollatia, before leaning across to nuzzle his solid neck.

'Extremely kind,' mumbled the General. 'Where was I? Yes . . . So, er. There we have it. In the meantime, please, all of you, once again on behalf of Jo and Charlie, feel free to hang on until the very end! As long as you like. Until the authorities give us our final marching orders!' With a brave little chuckle, he sat himself down.

A heavy silence descended. Grey and Messy exchanged significant glances. They both self-consciously cleared their throats.

'Well then,' said the General. 'So. Do we have anything else to add? Anyone? No. Good. Right then. Well. Thank you all for your time. And once again, I'm sorry to be the harbinger of such bloody awful news. No doubt we shall all see each other again at luncheon.' He stood up. 'In the cottage of course. Don't forget, everyone. All food to be served in the cottage from now on. Except breakfast,' he added as an afterthought. 'Don't you think? We can bloody well have breakfast in our own house.'

'Wait a minute,' Messy shouted suddenly. 'Sorry, everyone. But wait a second. If you don't mind . . . Only Grey and I had an idea, didn't we, Grey? We were going to put it to Charlie and Jo first. Obviously. Only with things so desperate it seems stupid not to say something. Don't you think, Grey?'

'Aye. For sure.'

'HA-HA!' Chloe burst out. 'Mummy, are you going to say what I actually *think* you're going to say? Are you? I *definitely* know what you're actually going to say because you've already just told me! Haven't you, Mummy?'

'She bloody is, too!' Colin grinned at Chloe. 'And you told me it was a bloody secret, you big berk!' He cuffed her round the ear, and within seconds they were squabbling.

'If she could get a fuckin' word in—' laughed Grey.

'Grey, darling. I'm not joking. I know you think it's pathetic. But she's only four. You've got to try to stop swearing when Chloe's around. It's the only thing—'

'Aye aye,' said Grey impatiently. 'The point is—'

'Ah.' Maurice gave a tight little smile. 'So we do have a point?'

'The point is, General,' Grey said irritably, 'the point is Messy and me have been doin' a few sums – sort of pooling resources an' all that.'

'Something like that,' mumbled Messy. 'Yours plus my nothing—'

'Aye, never mind the specifics. We'd like to buy the cottage. And the walled garden, if Charlie an' Jo are amenable. God knows what they're worth, but we were thinking maybe £100,000 can get you out o' your troubles.

Isn't that right, Messy? We thought we'd open a restaurant. And one o' them garden centres.'

'A *restaurant*,' said the General vaguely. 'A restaurant, how delightful . . . But, Grey, I'm sure that sort of price would be well over the – er – and so on. We should have it valued, etcetera.'

'Well o' course. We'll work it all out so it's fair. Only I don't know what Charlie and Jo might have to say—'

'Of course you don't. How can you?' said the General, impatiently waving them aside. 'Since the buggers have disappeared off the radar. But, er, seriously. Without wishing to, er— how quickly do you suppose you could get hold of—'

'Och, not long. Next week maybe.'

'Ha!' The General leant back in his chair and clapped his hands. 'Ha!' he said again. 'Grey – you're a . . . You're a . . . Everyone. For Heaven's sake! Why didn't you say so earlier? We should open some champagne, don't you think? To the happy couple and so on! And to *Fiddleford*! Ha! *Still* surviving! In spite of everything! Do we have any champagne? I think poor old Caroline and Jasonette may have had the last of it.'

Maurice Morrison's mind was reeling. He munched silently on his papaya, watching Messy, watching her stupid, fat face glowing with pleasure. Did she not realise what sort of a future he had in store for her? Had she not *noticed*? Had he not already made his intentions excruciatingly clear? Was she blind? Or mad? Or simply very, very rude?

'Messy dear.' His face looked peculiar: twisted and blotchy with shock, and his voice, he noticed, was coming out in a strangulated whine. They all turned to look at him.

He could see their confused expressions gazing back at him, and yet he couldn't stop himself. The desire to puncture her joy was overwhelming. He said the first thing that came into his head. 'Whatever happened to that little talk you were going to do at the Lamsbury Comprehensive?'

'Lamsbury Comprehensive?' said Messy politely. 'God! St George's! Maurice, do you know I completely—'

But before she could continue, Maurice remembered himself, bared his even white teeth and offered a tinkle of his lightest laughter. 'But what on earth am I talking about?' he exclaimed. 'Am I mad? At such a happy moment, to be wittering on about one's social responsibilities and so forth! Bugger the sixth-formers! Ha! Bugger the fat little bastards!'

'You do acsherly *sound* a bit nutty,' said Colin helpfully.

'Do I, Colin, dear? It's because I'm so happy! Happy that my good friends are so happy! Now then, wait there, everyone. If I nip outside a moment . . . I know nothing about Caroline and Jasonette, but your very own Maurice Morrison *never* travels without an emergency bottle of champagne in his suitcase!' he lied; he had bought it that morning, for the moment he proposed to Messy. It was sitting in a shopping bag beside the front door. 'Somebody, go and fetch glasses! I'll be back in a trice . . .'

'. . . To the loving couple,' he said, standing at the end of the table with his intended on one side and her intended on the other, with the whole party – even Nigel who didn't drink – holding champagne glasses aloft. 'I hope you'll be very, very content. In your teeny house! Absolutely enchanting. Many congratulations to you both.'

'Aye. Thank you, Maurice.' Grey leant across while the others drank. 'And I'm sorry. I know there've been times I've been bloody rude. But you're a good man. Yeah, you are.'

'A good loser, you mean?' said Maurice.

'Och no, I didn't mean that.'

Maurice laughed, threw back his head and laughed wildly. When he straightened up and looked at Grey there was a glint in his eye, an angry flush to his cheeks. On any other occasion Grey, normally so astute, would have spotted it at once, but he was too happy that day, and too unaccustomed to happiness. His alarm mechanisms weren't working properly.

'I never imagined it possible, but do you know,' Morrison gleamed, 'I begin to think all this marvellous passion is turning you a bit soft around the edges, Mr McShane!' He patted Grey on the back. 'And so it should, my dear friend. So it bloody well should. Ha ha ha. Now then, Colin and Chloe, about this egg venture of yours. What stage are we at?'

'Well, we've definitely got about a million of eggs, in fact,' said Chloe, 'we've actually definitely got about seventy-one. Plus—' She held up three fingers and a thumb.

'That's true, Chloe,' Colin bellowed. 'We got loads of 'em. We don't even know what to do with 'em we got so many!'

'Splendid! Splendid! *Well done you!* Now I need to make a couple of calls, and after that, what say you we set off on a little jaunt, hey, kids? Just the three of us, hm? Let's see if together we can't broker some sort of deal with that little village shop of yours.'

Maurice Morrison was shaking with rage as he climbed

the stairs to his room. He, who could pull the wool over the eyes of a prime minister, who had, in his climb to the top, outwitted some of the sharpest brains, some of the wiliest operators in the country – in Europe – in the world – had been foiled by a bunch of fucking yokels. All he had wanted, after all, was a crumbling house and a fat companion to look respectable beside him at functions. Was it so much to ask? It was not. Not for Maurice Morrison, who often asked for much more and always got it. He felt slighted. He felt insulted. But the thing he felt most was anger, white hot and well hidden, and what he wanted now was not just the house and the fat, stupid woman. He wanted revenge.

Soon afterwards, then, Colin, Chloe and Maurice were heading off towards the village with Maurice's mobiles, Maurice's small change dispenser, Maurice's Palm Pilot, Maurice's baseball cap and dark glasses, and a basketful of eggs covered in felt-tip. 'In fac' me and Chloe was always hopin' for this,' Colin yelled, as the three of them strode off across the fields together. 'We was definitely thinkin' abou' you helpin' us doin' the acshull deal. We collected twenty fresh eggs this mornin', didn't we, Chloe?' He grinned at her. 'Chloe wanted to colour 'em in, didn't you, Chloe? I told her it's not such a bad idea seein' as how it's almost nearly Christmas time. At leas' it nearly is. The lady at the shop used to be a friend of my nan, Mrs Hooper did. So she'll take 'em when I tell her. 'Specially when she sees I'm not in trouble no longer.'

'Now remember, kids,' said Morrison, who hadn't been listening, 'what are you going to call me when we get into the shop? Colin, what are you going to call me?'

'We're goin' to call you Mr Davison, o' course ... Mr Davison!'

'That's right. And, Chloe? What are you going to call me?'

She beamed at him. 'I'm going to call you Mr Morrison.'

'No. Wrong. You're going to call me Mr *Davison*. So what are you going to call me?'

She looked confused. 'Mr Maurice?'

'Come on,' he snapped. 'Don't be dense! Colin, tell her. What are you going to call me?'

'Mr Davison.'

'Well done. Right. Are we ready? Let's go.'

Mrs Hooper had indeed been a friend of Colin's nan. But she explained regretfully that she couldn't sell the eggs. They didn't comply with the Ungraded Egg Legislation, she said. (Maurice, of course, looked suitably astonished.) Eggs had to be supplied, she explained wearily, from a '*"registered packing station"*, if you please!'

'Ah,' said Maurice, glancing at his watch. 'What a shame.'

'Don't be daft, Mrs Hooper!' bawled Colin. 'They're perfect eggs. Aren't they, Mr Morrison? Aren't they, Chloe? We pick 'em all up this morning!'

'Colin!' said Chloe triumphantly. 'You called him Mr Morrison, you stupid old fool! That's wrong! You actually definitely got it wrong!'

Fortunately for Maurice, Mrs Hooper wasn't listening. 'I'm sorry, Colin, but I can't risk it,' she said. 'They'll be down on me like a ton of bricks. But wait there a moment.' She disappeared into the back of the shop and came back carrying a bale of literature. 'The inspector people gave me these ones last time. I can't make

243

much sense of them myself, but if you're set on the idea . . .'

They were about to leave when Maurice asked Mrs Hooper to keep an eye on the children for a minute and slipped out of the shop to make a few more urgent telephone calls. First he telephoned the local council. Where developments were going according to plan, he learnt, but running a little late. They needed another half an hour. Fine.

The next few calls needed to be more easily traced to the village, so Morrison pulled out his coin dispenser and crossed over to the telephone box. Within a few minutes, and in an impeccable West Country burr, he had informed the reporters of four national newspapers that Schedule One offender Grey McShane was living in a house with an unaccompanied pre-pubescent boy and a fatherless girl of four. The children were in danger, he said. And it was illegal. Something had to be done.

He returned to the shop wreathed in magnanimity and blinding smiles. The three of them would be continuing their afternoon's adventure, he informed Colin and Chloe, in the East Wood, where he had no doubt there was plenty of kindling to be gathered.

'No thanks,' Colin shouted, nodding at the leaflets. 'I'll be gettin' crackin' on all this rubbish, Mr *Davison*. It's goin' to take me about six years to read this stuff! 'Cept Chloe says her mum'll help me.'

'Anyway the wood's boring,' said Chloe.

'Nonsense,' snapped Maurice. 'Come along.'

So Maurice was still out when Derek and a colleague from Preserving Britain arrived to serve the owners of the stable yard with an Emergency Notice of Listing and an Emergency Notice of Repairs.

Derek Stainsewell may not have been in love with Maurice Morrison. But during his telephone calls with the government's Minister for Kindness he had recognised a man to be obeyed. And unquestioning obedience was something which Derek was generally happy to provide. 'Anything,' as he would often drone to himself, or anyone lazy enough to listen, 'anything for an easy life'. Especially, of course, with the added incentive of a cheque from the kind Minister for £7,500. What with one thing and another, Derek had a very easy life, and he wanted to keep it that way.

'Under Section 115 of the Town and Country Planning Act 1971,' he began, standing at the front door before Grey and the General, hands in anorak pockets, shoulders softly sloping . . .

'Oh dear Lord,' sighed the General. 'Here we go again!'

'May we speak to the proprietor of the stable block?' said Derek's companion.

'I wish you could! You'll have to make do with us,' said the General.

'May we come in?' said Derek.

'No.'

'You should be aware that as of this morning your stables are protected by an Emergency Grade Two Star listing. This brings with it numerous implications, and you may find it more desirable to discuss them inside.'

'Absolutely not,' snapped the General. 'I do wish you'd get on with it.'

With a lazy sigh, and an arse which quivered for a chair, Derek began again. 'Under Section 115 of the Town and

Country Planning Act 1971 we are hereby serving the proprietor of the Grade Two Star listed stable block with a notice.' He handed the General an envelope. 'This notice specifies the works which we consider necessary and urgent for the proper preservation of this Grade Two Star listed building. Further,' he went on, and paused for a breath – a nervous breath, 'since this Grade Two Star listed building is unoccupied, there can be no reasonable excuse for delay. If the aforementioned refurbishments have not commenced within the next seven days we – the local authority – can and will commence repairs ourselves, and shall recover the cost from you in due course.'

The General opened the envelope.

'You're jokin', aren't you?' said Grey. 'And how much are your a-fuckin'-formentioneds expected to cost?'

'Good God!' cried the General, goggling at the paper. 'Are you all stark staring barking bloody mad? We'd be better off knocking the entire building down and starting again.'

'I'm afraid this would not be permissible,' said Derek.

'But we can't do it! We can't even begin to do it!'

'In which circumstances we'll be looking at a compulsory purchase, after which the authority will, of course, be at liberty to redevelop the site for whichever use it deems necessary at the appropriate time. With regards to cost of repairs,' Derek added blandly, 'I would estimate all building works coming to something in the region of £750,000.'

Maurice, of course, was long gone by the time the newspapers arrived at Fiddleford. He had already told everybody the previous evening that he'd be heading off early to visit Gjykata Drejtohet, the sick Albanian busboy. If things went according to plan, he said, he would be back in time for dinner. They had all wished him the very best of luck.

'I shall probably bring my helicopter, Colin,' he said. 'Would you like that?'

Colin stared at him, his pale-blue eyes open wide.

'Hm, Colin? What do you say to that?' said Maurice. 'Would you and Chloe like a ride in my helicopter tomorrow evening?'

'Is that a joke, Mr Morrison?' Colin said at last.

'Do I look like a man who would joke about his own helicopters?'

'. . . I don't think so, sir,' he whispered.

'Well exactly. So I shall see you here, shall I? Eight o'clock sharp? And Chloe too, I dare say. Don't forget!' He had ruffled Colin's pale-red hair, and wished him good night.

But by eight o'clock sharp, as Morrison knew only too well, the children would be gone. And Grey would be the focus of hatred once again. And Messy would be distraught, and Maurice and his helicopter would only be dropping in to pick her up and fly away again.

Maurice Morrison always got what he wanted.

At six that morning, as the newspapers were being delivered at Fiddleford and as Morrison was slithering into his limousine at Leigh Delamere service station, Charlie Maxwell McDonald awoke with a start. Mrs Smiley, in slippers and a South American cardigan, had shut her front door with a slam that woke up half the street. She was scowling as she made her way over to him. But when she noticed the look of hope on his tired face

247

she wavered a fraction, and the line she had prepared – something aggressive about calling the police – came out surprisingly half-hearted.

'Never mind the police, Anne,' Charlie had said, yawning a bit. 'I just want to talk to my wife. I won't leave – I can't leave – not until I've talked to Jo. Will you tell her that?'

'You're disturbing the peace. You're disturbing my daughter. Why don't you just piss off?'

He laughed, partly to dispel some of the tension. 'Well, look,' he said. 'You say I'm disturbing *your* peace. But you've just woken me up, so I'd say it was you who's disturbing mine. Anyway I'm not going to piss off. I'm never going to piss off. I want to talk to Jo.'

'Yes, and she doesn't want to talk to you . . . Anyway,' she added suddenly, 'have you listened to the radio this morning?'

'But she's all right, isn't she? You'd let me know if there was something wrong?'

Mrs Smiley ignored the question. 'I said have you listened to your radio today?'

'Of course I haven't. I was asleep.'

'I'm just saying,' she said, turning back towards the house, 'you should probably get yourself down to that house of yours pretty sharpish. Only it sounds like things are turning a bit nasty.'

'Is this a trick?' he said.

She didn't answer.

'Why, what the Hell's happened?' But she was leaving already, and he didn't want to talk about Fiddleford. 'Mrs Smiley – Anne,' he shouted after her. 'Please. At least— will you tell her— please, Mrs Smiley. Will you tell her she's gone mad. Will you tell her she's gone barking fucking – *mad* . . . *Please*. Will you just tell her I love her?'

She laughed. 'Love? *Pah!*' she said. 'You don't even know the meaning of the word!' He looked at her, looking back at him, and of course he couldn't be sure; his eyes were bleary and it was still only half light, but he thought he saw her smiling at him. 'And don't say "fuck" in front of your mother-in-law,' she added, before hurrying back inside again.

At the newsagent's he discovered there were stories in almost every paper. Pictures of the old Grey – debauched and demonic – and, beside them, the pictures of Fiddleford, taken after his sister had died and before they'd put the gate in. The coverage was as vicious as might be expected. The papers were having a field day.

Of course an Anti-Media Refuge could only have been an execration to the people it kept out. Fiddleford Manor, a place which protected the publicly persecuted, which only existed to defy Popular Opinion, and yet which was funded by Popular Opinion's most boisterous, bullying voice, had more than simply infuriated the press. It had revolted them. It had enraged them. Until now they had been restrained. For fear, of all the humiliating reasons, of losing out on exclusive interviews with any future nationally reviled guests. Now they believed they had the ammunition to bring the place down, and they had no intention of holding back . . .

'**BRITAIN'S HOUSE OF SHAME,**' the headlines yelled . . . '**Have we really come to this?**' '**THE SUMPTUOUS MANSION WHERE BRITAIN'S DETRITUS REVELS**

IN THE BEST THAT MONEY CAN BUY . . .' . . . '. . . Where only the vicious, the corrupt and the depraved are given a welcome . . . '. . . '. . . **Cads, lechers, strippers, con artists and crooks lounge in opulent luxury quaffing top-drawer vino from the palatial cellar', '. . . while evil child abusers frolic openly with innocent young kids . . .'**

There was no mention of Maurice Morrison in all this. Not that Charlie noticed. He barely even noticed what they were saying about his house. But Grey McShane – who was more honourable than anyone, more honourable than all of them – had been *happy* this time two days ago, when Charlie left him. And not just any-old-happy; happy for the very first time. And now, for the sheer Hell of it, they were trying to ruin his life yet again. Charlie knew how to help him. But first, he realised guiltily, it was about time he called home.

Meanwhile, inside the mews house, Jo lay on her sofabed oblivious to all this, oblivious to everything in fact, except the loss she felt for Charlie. When she tried to imagine a future without him she found she couldn't. She felt empty. She felt numb. She felt half-dead. And after a day and two nights of listening to his shouted denials, after reading the scrawling letters he kept jamming through the door, she was even beginning to wonder if she hadn't got it all wrong. He'd camped out there in the freezing cold for two long nights . . . Didn't that prove he loved her? Wasn't it almost enough? Except Maurice had said . . . What *had* he said exactly? Christ, she couldn't even remember now.

She and Charlie had to talk. Now. Before she changed her mind. She heaved herself out of bed, glanced in the mirror, glanced quickly away again, put on a dressing gown and tiptoed onto the landing. It was only quarter past six, but she could hear her mother moving around in her bedroom. She tiptoed over the landing and reached the bottom of the stairs without disturbing her. But then she hesitated: straight on to the front door, or left to stand in the kitchen while the kettle boiled? He was cold. He was bound to be cold. It could be a sort of peace offering, semi-peace offering. Just in case he'd never actually done anything wrong. She'd waited this long, she could wait another two minutes . . .

Slowly, carefully, her heart pounding, she carried the two steaming mugs of coffee to the door, threw it open—

'Charlie?'

But it was too late. Twenty yards up the street and accelerating quickly away she could see Charlie and his Land Rover, deserting her and her enormous belly to their lonely Hampstead fate.

Be honest. Do you sometimes juggle priorities, so that safety is not a main consideration? Have there been occasions when day-to-day pressures of running your business led to actions that put people's safety at risk?

*Health and Safety Towards a Safer Workplace. Brought to you with the compliments of 3663 Foodservice in association with the Hospitality Training Foundation, as part of the Quality Business Initiative, which is funded by the Department for Education and Employment*

## • ACTION A FULL AND FRANK ASSESSMENT OF CORE VALUES

A cheerless, prohibited breakfast was spread out over the prohibited table. Nigel and Anatollatia gazed at the papers, drinking prohibited cups of coffee. Messy was already in tears. Grey was already packing. The children ate their prohibited toast and Marmite in silence. It was a truly woeful crowd which gathered in the Fiddleford kitchen that morning.

This time, at the sound of the intercom, they didn't jump, they flinched. It had become impossible not to associate the sound with trouble. Without a word they slid the evidence of breakfast into a nearby cupboard, and awaited their fate.

The Social Services had arrived.

'So soon?' Messy said. 'Didn't you tell them Grey was packing? Didn't you tell them he's never done anything wrong?'

'There's a policeman with a warrant down there, too, Messy,' said the General.

'Trouble is,' said Colin, who knew all about these things,

'you got a couple of YPs in the house with a Schedule One-er. And that's against the law, that is, Messy. Chloe knows. 'Cos I already explained to her. Even if no one's done nothin' wrong, see? You can't have YPs with a Schedule One-er. They won't have it. Any road it's not Grey they're after, is it, Chloe? We know who they've come 'ere for.'

'I haven't let them in yet,' the General said quietly. 'Thought I'd give you children a head start. Are you ready?'

'Ready for what?' snapped Messy. 'Are you mad? We'll talk to them. For Christ's sake, they'll understand.'

The General landed an awkward, hurried pat on Colin's shoulder. 'They're saying they'll force their way in if they have to.'

Slowly Colin reached across the table for Chloe's hand. 'Chloe,' he said. 'You remember all that stuff I tol' you? About when I was in the Home that time? And the kids was bashin' me, and the fella set fire to the bed and the other little fella tried to bleed 'isself to death an' there was all the blood in the bath? You remember I tol' you all that?'

'Yes I do, Colin,' she said solemnly.

'That's where they're takin' us, Chloe.'

'But I don't want to go there.'

'O' course you don't.'

'*I don't want to go there.*'

'Don't be silly. O' course you don't. Neither do I, Chloe.'

With a loud clatter, she dropped the spoon she'd been clinging onto, and jumped down from the table.

'Are you ready then?' he said.

'Chloe.' Messy tried to sound calm. 'Chloe, come back here and sit down.'

'I have a nasty feeling,' the General said, 'that the poor boy knows what he's talking about rather better than we do.'

'That's right, General.'

'Stop it, Colin! Both of you! Everyone! You're frightening her! Chloe, come here. Come and sit on my knee.'

'Chloe,' said Colin, 'are you ready?'

'Yes I am.'

'. . . *RUN!*'

And Chloe did.

She and Colin both ran. Out of the kitchen, out of the back hall, behind the old stables, past the tennis court and the old croquet court, round the walled garden, until they reached the chicken run. By the time Messy caught up with them they had hidden themselves beneath straw and chicken shit, in the corner of the hut where the eggs were laid. Messy could see the straw moving. She could hear them breathing. Without saying a word, she slid down the wall and into a heap beside them, rested her head on her knees and began to cry.

'It's all right, Mummy,' Chloe whispered. 'You've just got to cover yourself, like we have. They won't find us here.'

But they did. The General tried his best to put them off – first by denying any knowledge of any children, later by claiming he did remember them, but that they had both gone to Finland for a break. Eventually the police and the social workers forced their way in. After searching the house, they searched the park: the old stables, the hay barn, the farmyard . . . They prodded the straw where the chickens laid their eggs and hit against Chloe's foot.

'Here!' bayed the policeman, dragging her out. 'Over here!'

Messy clawed at him to release her. Chloe clawed at him to be released. She kicked and fought. They both kicked and fought until someone came up behind Messy and restrained her. It all happened very quickly.

Over Chloe's screaming, over Messy's screaming, as she stood there impotently and he and Chloe were led away, Colin turned back and shouted, 'Don't you worry, Messy. I'll look after her. She'll be all right wi' me. Only tell Mr Morrison it weren't our fault, nor anythin', won't you? So's he'll give us that helicopter ride some other fine day.'

Perhaps even Mr Morrison might have felt a little squeamish if he had witnessed the scene. Or perhaps not. Anyway at the time he was standing in the intensive care unit of the London Central Hospital, gazing through a confusion of wires and tubes at the unconscious, sedated and paralysed body of seventeen-year-old Gjykata Drejtohet. Colin and Chloe couldn't have been further from his mind.

The boy, Morrison fleetingly observed, must have been quite a good-looking little chap in his heyday. Before the accident. He was tall. Dark. Couldn't see his mouth of course, but the eyelashes were marvellous and the jaw was delightfully strong, very well defined ... The money-grubbing aunt would almost certainly have been lying, but she claimed to Maurice's lawyers that he had played for the Albanian Youth football team once. Which no doubt meant a great deal in Albania. And now he was lying here, beautiful but limp, his only sign of life the rhythmic bip bip of the ECG machine beside him.

According to his consultant, Gjykata had shown no signs

of recovery since the day he had been admitted to hospital. The consultant told Maurice that, with the aid of these various machines, Gjykata Drejtohet could persist in his vegetative state indefinitely. Maybe for thirty years. Maybe for fifty . . .

Bip . . . Bip . . . Bip . . . Day after day . . . Bip . . . Bip . . . Week after week . . . Bip . . . Bip . . . Month after month . . . Lying there, unconscious, sedated and paralysed . . . Bip . . . Bip . . . Bip. Year, after year, after year . . . Whatever Maurice did, whatever he said, whatever anyone ever said or thought or wrote about him . . . Bip . . . Bip . . . casting a shadow over Maurice's every move; every public statement, every public appearance, every little interview . . . Bip . . . Bip . . . Bip . . . would be Gjykata Drejtohet, bipping a-fucking-way. Not being dead.

Maurice looked up from Drejtohet's body to the nurse, lingering with flip charts at the end of the bed. He smiled at her and she thought she saw the hint of a tear at the corner of one eye. Blue eye. Blue eyes. Lovely hands. Gorgeous, in that suit.

'Could I . . . if it's all right with you, nurse,' he whispered, 'could I stay a little longer?'

'Of course, Mr Morrison. Minister.'

'Maurice. Please.'

'*Maurice* . . .' She smiled at him. 'Stay as long as you like.'

'Only I was wondering— I'm so sorry. Is there a loo?'

When he came back he asked to pull up a chair and he sat himself beside the ECG monitor, close to Drejtohet's unconscious head. The nurse was flattered to notice that he'd smoothed his hair. She noticed a glistening around his cheeks and jaw and imagined him, with that tear, splashing cold water on his face. What she couldn't have noticed were the two mobile telephones Maurice had switched on and moved to his jacket pocket. Nor would she ever have imagined they were set, the one to call the other, with the touch of a single button, and that his finger was still resting on the button.

He smiled at her. Bip . . . Bip . . . Bip . . . 'Have you worked here long?' he said.

'No!' she said. 'Unfortunately! This is my first week, as a matter of fact.'

'Oh!'

'Everyone thinks ICU's so glamorous. They've seen it on TV. You know, cardiac arrests, CPRs . . . *Stand Back All Clear*. All that rubbish. But most of the time you're just sitting here – listening to that.' She nodded at the ECG, the one which monitored Gjykata's heartbeat. 'Most of the patients aren't exactly up to conversation. So it's just *bip bip bip*. All day long. Can actually be a bit of a snore sometimes.'

'Gosh, I bet!' Inside his pocket the index finger was beginning to feel slippery. 'So, tell me—'

'Elizabeth. Lizzie.'

'Lizzie. Tell me, Lizzie. What happens when the bip machines . . . sort of stop bipping? That must wake you up, doesn't it? What do you do then?'

She rolled her eyes. 'Refer to the bloody handbook in my case! Hasn't happened on my shift. *Yet*. Thank God!'

'Ha ha . . . No, but seriously?'

'Seriously? If this poor lad suddenly went into cardiac arrest?'

'God forbid!'

'Right.'

'What would you do?'

'Well – basically I wouldn't do much. Well, yes I would. I mean. Any kind of ventricular fibrillation and that ECG monitor's going to go crazy. Masses of activity on the screen, and the blips are going to – you know, you'll have heard it on telly. And when I hear that noise,' she grinned, 'I'm going to panic like Hell, because I've never done it before. Not for real anyway. And it'll be just my luck to be doing it for the first time in front of a bloody VIP!'

Maurice smiled.

'I'm going to check his pulse and if there's no pulse then we'll go into CPR. Cardiac Pulmonary Resuscitation. With the two paddles on the chest?'

'Oh yes. I know.'

'We're going to send two hundred joules through that little heart of his, and then we're going to do it again, and then we're going to up the dose and do it again. Basically. Until we can get it working again.'

'And if there was a pulse?'

'What? *Before* the CPR?' She laughed. 'He'd be dead. CPR would have killed him. But that wouldn't happen.'

Bip . . . Bip . . . Bip . . . Maurice looked down at the unconscious body. So good-looking. So hard at work collecting potato skinz when he slipped and fell. He thought of his son Rufus, doing his MBA at Yale, who always looked where he was going. Bip . . . Bip . . . Bip . . .

'Terrible,' he muttered. 'Well! Let's *hope* it never happens!'

'Not on this shift anyway. I'm off in twenty minutes . . .'

'Oh you are? Well – listen. In that case, perhaps – could I take you somewhere for lunch? To be frank I'd be grateful for a little company.'

She blushed. 'I'll have to nip up to the locker room first, though, Maurice. Change into some halfway decent clothes!'

What a shame, Maurice Morrison thought vaguely. He rather adored nurses' uniforms. 'Lovely,' he said. 'Absolutely lovely. Isn't that marvellous?' And pushed the button.

A little vibration in his left pocket, as expected . . . She was trying to remember what clothes she'd left in her locker that morning . . . And then a mass of activity on the monitor. The machine had started screaming. And then Morrison was screaming. *For Christ's sake, Lizzie. He's dying. The boy's dying. Get the CPR! We need the CPR.*

She grappled to feel his pulse but Morrison was shouting so loud she couldn't concentrate.

*What are you waiting for? Lizzie! This isn't a fucking practice! This is YOUR SHIFT. This is FOR REAL. And this boy is dying! He needs CPR! NOW! Somebody, somewhere, this woman has no idea. Find the fucking pulse, you bitch! He's dying! Somebody, get us some fucking CPR!*

. . . and then Somebody was there with the defibrillator. They held the paddles over the boy's chest. They looked across at Lizzie. 'Pulse? . . . Lizzie! Pulse?'

'If there was a fucking pulse she would have found it by now. For Christ's sake, what are you waiting for?'

'No pulse,' said Lizzie. 'No pulse.' But she wasn't sure.

*'Stand back. All clear.'*

Down went the paddles onto his sleeping chest. Two hundred joules of energy coursed through his beating heart, and his heart stopped dead.

Not long after that, Maurice Morrison turned off his mobile telephones, apologised to Lizzie for shouting at her, bent over the bed and allowed her to comfort him while he sobbed, just like a little girl.

Grey was striding alone down the wintry drive when Charlie finally arrived at Fiddleford. He was wearing the same large black overcoat he'd arrived in all those months ago, and carrying a single cellophane bag. But Grey always did travel light.

Charlie stopped the car.

'So you're back,' Grey said, walking right past him. 'About bloody time, Charlie. The place needs you. Where's Jo?'

'Where are you going, Grey? . . . Grey?' Charlie climbed out of the car to catch up with him.

'I don't know. I might go home.'

'This *is* your home.'

'They came an' took the children this mornin'.'

'I know that.'

'I'm not allowed in the house with them.'

'I know. I've heard the radio. I've seen the papers. And I've talked to Dad. Why the fuck do you think I came back here? Without Jo? Grey, wait! Come on!' He grabbed hold of his arm and pulled him back towards the car. 'I've just driven through it,' he said, nodding towards the gate, still out of view. 'There are fifteen fucking journalists out there. Baying for your blood. So wait. *Wait. It doesn't have to be like this.*'

Finally Grey stopped. He looked at Charlie. 'She needs the kid back.'

'Of course she does.'

'I was foolin' myself, Charlie.'

'No, you weren't. Fuck it, Grey. What's the matter with

you? D'you want to spend the rest of your life being a stupid, miserable sod?'

'Aye, and you can talk. Where's Jo?'

Charlie didn't answer. Instead he rummaged in his trouser pocket and brought out a piece of paper. On it was written the name and address, in Scotland, of the people who could clear Grey's name: the people who had lied about him in the first place, whom he hadn't seen or spoken to, except in court, since the day of her funeral: Emily's parents. It had taken one call to Directory Enquiries to track them down. But Charlie had gone further than that.

'What's this?' Grey said, peering at it briefly. 'Where the fuck d'you get this?' He crumpled the paper into a ball and glared at Charlie and for an instant they both assumed Grey was going to thump him.

'They're waiting for you, Grey. They want to talk to you.'

Slowly Grey stepped away and started walking again. 'You'll tell Messy I'm sorry, won't you? And Chloe, when she comes home. Tell 'em I'm so sorry.'

After that, though Charlie continued to argue with him until they reached the gates, Grey didn't say another word.

'You're a fool, Grey.'

'Aye. Nothin' changed there.'

With a final nod Grey opened the gate and pushed his way into the throng. He didn't look up, or speak. He just waited, with his head down. And when they let him, he walked. Charlie watched until they were all out of view, and turned sadly back to the house.

*　*　*

He found Messy alone at the forbidden kitchen table, the telephone receiver resting uselessly in one hand, her head in the other. Charlie put his arms around her.

'They hung up,' she sobbed.

'Who did?'

'Everyone. *They just keep hanging up.*'

'I think,' he said, hugging her a bit, until he thought she would listen, 'you need to get away from here, Messy. As far away as possible.'

'I can't! How will Chloe know where to find me?'

'I've worked it all out. I think . . . You need to go to London and talk to Jo. You need to make a statement. Make a public statement. Make as much noise as you can. Get a campaign going. You'll be nowhere near Grey. There'll be no excuse not to return her.'

'Where *is* Grey?' she said suddenly.

'Grey's gone.'

'Good,' she said. 'He had to go. Of course. He had to go. Oh God.' She started crying again.

'You've got to go to London and get Jo. Trust me. I know it. *I know her.* She can turn the whole thing around. But you've got to go and talk to her.'

'I don't want to. I want to be with Chloe.'

'*I know that.* But Jo can help you get her back.'

'Can't I just telephone her?' added Messy.

He shook his head. 'Messy, you need to be *seen* fighting it out. *Fighting* for her . . . Anyway.' He laughed slightly. 'Jo's taken the telephone off the hook.'

Messy gave a wan smile. 'I'm sorry, Charlie,' she mumbled. 'Only thinking about myself . . .'

'If you do see her,' he sat back, removing his arm from her shoulders, 'or, rather, if she agrees to see you, perhaps you could do me a favour and set her straight on a few things.'

He had to explain why Jo had left in the first place. He had to explain that Messy might need to beg a little for Jo's help. He had to warn her it was possible that Jo would tell her to go to Hell. But Charlie doubted it. Because even if, against any evidence, she persisted in believing that he and Messy were lovers, she would still feel a duty to resolve the situation. It was Jo, after all, who had brought Messy and Chloe to Fiddleford in the first place.

'I seem to remember her calling this place a "refuge",' Messy said wryly.

He laughed. 'It's a total fuck-up, isn't it?'

'Do you think I should sue the management?'

They both laughed, but it was desperate, wretched laughter, and very soon her laughter turned back to tears again.

When Maurice's helicopter touched down an hour or so later he wasn't feeling as cheerful as all that. It had been a disturbing afternoon. A horrible afternoon, really. All the way from London, different parts of the boy's anatomy kept flashing into his mind: the smooth forehead, the lank hair, that pale, defenceless chest. Ever since he'd left the hospital, even while he'd been giving his tearful interviews to the waiting press, he couldn't seem to get the boy's living, dying body out of his head.

It meant he was finding it harder to concentrate than he usually did. As he climbed out of the roaring helicopter and looked up at the handsome house he needed to remind himself of what he was doing here again. He'd come down ... (he smoothed his hair) ... to get the girl. That was right. Tidy that up. And the house. This magnificent house. The very house he'd been searching for all these years.

The children, he knew, had already left. That was straightforward enough. He could say he'd heard it on the radio. Indeed, he had heard it on the radio. So it was the truth, which was potentially confusing. Grey, he presumed, would almost certainly have gone, too. Which left the Three Idiots, as he'd taken to calling them (Nigel, Anatollatia and the General). And Messy. A depleted gathering, then. And the simpler for it.

But the first person he saw when he got to the house was Charlie.

'Charlie! Goodness!'

Charlie was at his desk in the library, writing a letter for Messy to take with her to Jo.

'Hello, Maurice,' he said, looking up but not smiling. 'I suppose that was you, was it, making that bloody awful racket outside? You'll have terrified the animals.'

'Ha!' said Maurice nervously. 'I just – when I heard the news I had to get down here as quickly as possible.'

'Very kind of you,' said Charlie. 'I don't suppose, with your connections and so on, there's anyone you might be able to talk to? Get this bloody thing reversed, somehow. Messy's distraught. *Distraught*. And you probably don't care much about Grey, but he's—'

'As a matter of fact I had rather a bad day myself. Perhaps you heard? We lost Gjykata this morning. I was with him. I was holding his hand . . . Terrible. Heart attack. Out of nowhere. One minute he was with us, the next he was gone.'

'I'm so sorry.'

Maurice raised his hand. 'Don't let's talk about it,

Charlie. It's too ghastly. Too ghastly. I just thought you might have heard. But tell me, how *is* poor Messy? Is she bearing up?'

'Not really, no. She's pretty bad.'

'Ah! Was she there, then, when they came to take the children away? What happened? They were just – what – reacting to the newspaper stories, I suppose?'

Charlie nodded. 'And I can't stop wondering – whoever sold that story must have been here. They must have *known* how happy the children were. They must have *seen* how happy Grey and Messy were . . .'

Maurice blinked. 'The er— Charlie, I hate to state the obvious but haven't you *guessed*— By the way where's Jo?'

'Guessed what? Who?'

'*I* don't know. Well, I mean—' he laughed, 'of course I *do* know. I mean I assume I know. It's so *obvious*.'

'Nothing's obvious, Maurice. I've been away for two days and I've come back to total fucking mayhem. Fucking *devastation*. Who do you think sold the story? Because I have no idea.'

'Come on, Charlie!'

'*Who?*'

'Well, come on! Wake up! Who knows all the ins-and-outs here? Who's already sold one story to the newspapers? And who, Charlie – I can't believe I'm having to say this – *who have you just fired recently?*'

Charlie laughed uncertainly. 'No. You don't realise, Maurice. You don't realise how stupid he is. Poor man. I mean there's one thing spotting a couple of celebrities and taking a snap. But really it's quite another, understanding that because of something Grey did – actually *didn't* – do, nearly fourteen years ago . . .' His voice trailed away.

'. . . There are times, Charlie, when your naïveté astounds me. However,' Maurice shrugged, 'what does it matter? The damage is done. Anyway—' He broke off, bent his head slightly to the side and ran a rough hand through his hair, just like Charlie did. It was a mannerism Maurice had only recently added to his collection. 'The real reason I'm here, deafening you all with my ghastly flying machine – the real reason I'm back here *again* . . .' He looked at Charlie who was frowning, not in the least interested in Maurice's excuses. What wonderful thick eyelashes he had, Maurice thought. What a delightfully strong, well-defined jaw . . . 'Tell me, do you find time to play football anymore?'

'What?'

'I was – I'm looking for Messy.'

'What?'

'I wanted to tell Messy about Drejtohet. Gjykata. I thought she might be interested.'

'She might be. But she's got quite a lot on her plate at the moment.'

'Ah! Yes, of course . . .'

'Are you all right?'

'My dear chap, I've never been finer. By the way where's Grey? Now that Messy needs him so much? Where *is* Grey?'

'Grey's gone.'

'Ah!'

'He had to go.' Charlie turned pointedly back to his letter. 'Messy's upstairs if you want her. Packing. She's leaving for London tonight.'

'Thank you,' said Maurice, backing out of the room. 'Thank you for everything, Charlie. And once again I'm so sorry to have disturbed you.'

\* \* \*

Derek met Sue-Marie in the District Council lift on his way out to the pub that evening. They were alone together, so Derek said—

'Well – we slapped that repairs order on. As specified.'

'Good, good.'

He glanced across at her. 'You put one on the kitchen, did you?'

'Sort of thing.' She smiled at him, a conspiratorial smile, from one hard-working law enforcer to another.

But he misinterpreted it. He thought it was from one crook to another, so he said tentatively, 'So, er. Thanks for that, Sue. Certainly comes in handy.'

She smiled brightly, another of her eye-flapping blinders, because that was what Sue-Marie did when members of the opposite sex addressed her, and she didn't understand what they were saying. 'Super,' she said.

'Yes. My wife's been nagging for years to go on one of those African safari things. In Africa. And Keith and James are ever so keen.'

Sue-Marie inhaled through her teeth, just imagining . . . Savannah grassland, rhinos, little families of warthog, men with spears . . . 'Mmm!' she said. 'Lovely. A dream come true! But I've heard it's *very* dear.'

'Certainly is!' said Derek with a grin. 'The wife's only booked it this morning!'

Sue-Marie didn't say anything. She frowned. Just then the lift bell sounded and the doors opened onto the ground floor. 'Ooh, bother,' she said unconvincingly (not that Derek noticed), 'I think I've forgotten something. I'll have to go back. See you tomorrow then, Derek. Have a good night!'

Upstairs again, Sue-Marie waited patiently for the office

to empty, then she made her way over to his desk. It was a mess, of course, with dirty coffee cups and pieces of paper strewn all over it. Carefully, without disturbing them, she started up his computer and when it asked for a password she typed in the name of his wife. Then the names of his two children. And then DEREK. Which worked. But when she scrolled through his files she didn't really know what to look for. So she found nothing.

The cleaner came in. But the cleaner didn't know where she usually sat. The cleaner didn't even know her name.

'Hello!' Sue-Marie said brightly. 'Working late tonight, I'm afraid!'

'Ye-es,' said the cleaner.

Sue-Marie opened the top drawer of his desk. There were half-eaten chocolate bars in there, and wedges of unopened envelopes. The second drawer was so crammed she couldn't open it more than a couple of inches, and the third was no better. She tutted disapprovingly. It was people like Derek, she thought, who gave public servants a bad name.

And then suddenly she lost heart. She didn't even know where to begin. And she was being absurd anyway. She felt ashamed for suspecting either of them. Derek was lazy but that didn't mean he was a villain. And Maurice Morrison was a *dreamboat*. She shut the computer down, forced closed the three drawers again and was about to leave when she finally noticed the sheet of paper. It was covered in food splodges and doodles and lying directly in front of her, face up, half tucked beneath the keyboard.

He'd drawn a lot of hearts on it, a single giraffe, several pound signs, an outline of Africa and some diamond shapes, partially shaded. And between them, in loopy, adolescent handwriting:

*moneyson moneyson mauricon morrison moneyson mauricon I ♥ U*

She wanted to be wrong. She hoped she was wrong. But it aroused suspicions she'd been repressing for days. She picked up the piece of paper, gave a cheery goodbye to the cleaner, who didn't seem to hear, and headed for the councillors' car park. Sue-Marie needed time to think.

Meanwhile Moneyson himself was sitting on the edge of Messy's bed, watching her pack. He wanted her to stop for a moment, to look at him, to concentrate, but she was bustling about from one cupboard to another, sobbing all the time, and looking, frankly, *appalling*.

'Messy, sweetheart,' he said. '*Listen to me*. Calm down. *Calm down.*'

But she didn't want to listen. He stood up, stood in front of her, took one of her fleshy upper arms in each hand. '*Stop!*' he said.

Irritably she shook him off.

'Messy! . . . Messy!' He sounded hurt.

'I'm sorry, Maurice. But you can see I'm in a fucking state. I can't— there's no point in all this talking. I've got to get to London. I've got to get this—'

'Ah-ha! Then I can help you. Let me give you a lift in my 'copter. Let me do that at least.'

But it only reminded her of Colin. Colin and Chloe, who should have been riding in his helicopter at that very moment. She started crying again.

He said, 'Messy, please. Come outside with me. Just for a few minutes. The cold air will do you good. Give you a chance to think clearly. I can give you a lift back to London. Tonight. And *I can help you get your daughter back.* Of course I can! I'm a Government Minister, for Christ's sake! Ha! Do you think I can't pull a few strings with the local council?'

'You can?' she said, stopping suddenly, looking at him angrily and clearly for the first time. 'But you can't even get anyone to open the fucking kitchen again! Or stop all that crap about the stables that's obviously going to bankrupt them. How can you get me my daughter when you can't even stop some stupid bitch from closing a kitchen?'

'Oh, Messy. Ha-ha. *Messy!* I'm not God!

'But you're a fucking Minister. It's the next best thing, isn't it?'

'No! Well, yes and no. Look, Messy. You're not listening . . . Come outside with me. Please. I need to talk to you. I can get your daughter back. I promise. We'll get your daughter back. But, first, come outside with me. Talk to me. I have a proposition to make. Proposal. Approach. Suggestion. Whatever [nothing sounded quite right]. Come outside with me, Messy. And we'll *talk.'*

In his jacket pocket (where the mobiles had been) there rested a small square box from Tiffany. It was something, he calculated feverishly, as they made their way down the stairs, which he might produce at any minute. Or might not. Might. Might not. Might. Might not. Of course it depended on how the conversation developed.

Outside at last, by the light of the moon, Messy and Maurice walked across the park, over the cobbles past the old stables, towards Messy's walled garden. Maurice, pacing beside her through the cold air, fingering the Tiffany box in his pocket, found himself besieged suddenly by images of the dead boy . . . his fingers, his chest, his feeble adolescent shoulders . . . It was Messy who finally broke their silence.

'I shall miss it here,' she said. 'It's the most beautiful place I've ever been.'

'Yes . . . It casts a sort of spell on one, doesn't it?' he said. 'But never fear! We shall be back!'

She shook her head. 'Not me.' She thought of Grey and the cottage, and Chloe, and of how happy they all might have been. She started crying again. 'Maurice, tell me, please. I can't stand her having to spend a night in that place. Can you get her back tonight? *Please* . . .'

'Messy . . . *Messy*,' he sing-songed, stroking her hair in the moonlight. 'Messy, angel. I can't get her back tonight. You know that. But if we work together—'

'Then what can you do?'

'I can talk to people—'

'So why aren't you talking to them. *Now*?'

Maurice recoiled slightly, but chose to continue stroking. Her voice could be unattractively shrill sometimes, he noticed. It was something else they would need to work on. Something they could work on together . . . That and the continued weight loss, of course. He smiled. At his little rough diamond. They would have such fun, working together . . .

'For fuck's sake, Maurice, why are you smiling?' She pushed his hand away. 'You keep talking about helping us. You zoom around in your fucking helicopter, promising the world. But so far as I can see nothing ever happens. *Nothing*.'

'Ha! *Nothing Ever Happens* . . . Do you know it?' Suddenly he started humming. 'Del Amitri, if I'm not mistaken. Wonderful song.' Again, with a tender smile, he replaced his hand on her hair.

Again, she flicked it off. 'What the hell is the matter with you?'

'Messy, darling – I'll tell you what's the matter with me. Can I tell you what's the matter with me? Can you not guess?'

Her heart sank. '*What?*' she said, with all the discouragement she could muster. 'Maurice, seriously. This isn't the time. Can you help Chloe or can't you?'

But he wasn't listening. '*Messy, I'm in love with you.*'

She sighed, a thundering, heaving, intensely impatient sigh. 'What's that got to do with anything? We were talking about Chloe.'

This was going badly wrong, Maurice noted. He worried if he was rushing things a bit. He laughed, a tittery, jittery laugh, and then, out of the corner of his eye, he noticed the Albanian's hand was moving. *Was that possible?* He spun round. 'What was that?'

'What was what?'

'Did you see it?'

'What?'

'Did it move?'

'What the fuck are you talking about?'

*Concentrate.* He had to *concentrate.* 'Messy, darling.' Without warning, he plopped down onto his knees. He fumbled inside his pocket. 'You make me feel whole. I am besotted. You make me feel alive again. Like I want to live again. Like life is lovable again. Messy, I want to marry you.'

'Christ!' She wanted to shake him. 'Maurice, get up! Stand up! *Belt up*, for God's sake.'

'From the moment I first set eyes on you—'

'I'm not interested. I do *not* want to hear this.' She tried to cover her ears but Maurice grasped her hands and held them.

'You *must* hear this. Messy – I love you.'

'Maurice, I don't— I *do not* love you.'

'No!' he cried triumphantly. 'But you love *this house*. Don't you! Tell me you don't love this house!'

'So what?'

'Well! And wouldn't you love to live here for the rest of your life? Not in a poxy little cottage at the bottom of the drive, but *here. Here!* In the Great House. Tell me you wouldn't love that! Tell me—' He stopped suddenly. A rustle in the rhododendrons. *'What was that? Did you hear that?'*

His face looked so terrified, Messy felt a flash of pity. 'Maurice,' she said quietly, 'let me go. You're not yourself. I think maybe you need to – have a little rest or something. I don't know. Anyway I've got to go . . .'

'Nonsense, I'm – there it was again! What was that noise? . . . Did you hear it?'

'No, I didn't. Of course I bloody didn't. Let me go!'

'Hello?' he shouted, peering out at the bushes. She snatched her arms away and ran. 'No! Messy, wait!' He scrambled to his feet, frantic not to be left alone out there with the rhododendrons and the ghost of Gjykata Drejtohet. '. . . *Messy!*'

Another rustling sound, very close, very loud, and out from the shadows stepped—

'Only me.' She grinned at him.

He screamed.

'You are a dark horse, aren't you, Maurice? First this . . .' She waved her stolen piece of paper. 'Now Messy Monroe . . . And that really upsets me, Maurice. Because I believed in you. I really believed in you. You were my hero. You were! My champion, my idol, my shining light . . .'

'How the fuck did you get in?'

'I was actually on my way to see Mr Maxwell McDonald.'

'But he despises you!'

'I hinted,' she said heavily, 'that I was in possession of some very relevant information. I was just parking my car when I heard you. *Chatting away*. So I thought – wait there, Sue-Marie. Less haste, more speed!'

'What do you want?' he snapped feverishly. 'Can't you see I'm busy?'

'Mmm. Let me think about that,' she said slowly. 'I suppose you *know* Derek Stainsewell's taking his wife and kids off on holiday to Kenya?'

Maurice Morrison's shoulders hunched. Slowly, meticulously, his fingers, hands and arms began to knot together. He looked down, allowing his neck to flop forward. He cleared his throat, shook himself all over, breathed in, breathed out, pulled his head up. 'My dear, *dear* Sue-Marie . . .' She could see his teeth glistening in the moonlight. 'The very lady I was looking for! What a wonderful, *wonderful* surprise!'

She was torn. She could still hear Messy's footsteps sprinting over gravel back towards the house. And yet here was Morrison. Her fallen hero. Her vanquished champion. Her broken idol. But her idol nonetheless. The breathtakingly handsome, adorable, gorgeously irresistible Money

Morrison. Maurice Moneyson. Whatever. At her mercy.

'Then kiss me!' she said.

And he did.

Messy could have run to the cottage, where she knew Nigel, Anatollatia and the General were munching joylessly on the General's ineptly made sandwiches. But the house was closer. And she was frightened. When she ran into the library, half crying, half laughing, there was no sign of Charlie. Only his letter to Jo, which lay half written on the desk.

She barricaded herself in, for fear of encountering Morrison ever again, and ordered a cab to take her on the long drive to the train station. But by the time it arrived, and she had buzzed it through the gate, there was still no Charlie, and the others hadn't yet returned from the cottage. She left Fiddleford without saying goodbye to anyone.

She didn't notice Charlie, running cross-country through the park as she swept up the drive that last time, and nor did he notice her. He noticed very little, in fact. Maurice's words had blocked everything else out. *Sometimes, Charlie, your naïveté astounds me* . . . He'd forgotten everything: the letter, Messy, Sue-Marie. *Sometimes, Charlie, your naïveté astounds me.* Was he really such a fool? *Sometimes, Charlie, your naïveté astounds me* . . . Was that why everything was crumbling? He needed to know, and cross-country, and running, was the quickest route to finding out. He was heading to the Fiddleford Arms, where Les, as Charlie well knew, could always be found at this time in the evening.

He needed to face Les and ask him – *did you do that? HOW COULD YOU HAVE DONE THAT? What did any of them ever do to you?* And the faster he ran the more urgently he needed to know, the angrier he became, and the faster it made him run. By the time he arrived at the Fiddleford Arms, his lungs were bursting.

A contented babble flowed from the little tables. The pub was full but not crowded, softly lit, peacefully cheerful, and Les was sitting by the fire, nursing his Bass. On either side of him sat the reporters, all three of whom Charlie recognised from the gates that morning. As he crossed the room towards them a few people threw out greetings. Everybody liked Charlie. But Charlie didn't answer. He didn't hear.

He only stopped when he reached Les – Charlie stood in front of him, panting. 'Outside,' he said. There was sweat pouring down his face. *'Outside!'*

A curious silence fell, followed by an irritating, baiting 'Woo-oooo!' from the journalists.

'What's the matter, Charlie?' said Les, without moving.

'I said—' Charlie lunged at him. He ducked. His three neighbours shrunk away. 'Come outside. Now.'

Slowly Les stood up. 'You know what?' he said. 'After all these years, it would acsherly be quite some pleasure.'

By the time Maurice Morrison's helicopter flew overhead, half the pub had emptied out into the car park. Though Maurice couldn't have heard it, their baying and catcalling echoed through the village, and in the midst of it, Charlie and Les were going for each other as if their lives depended on it.

In spite of all his trouble, in spite of Drejtohet twitching and spasming on the one side, and Sue-Marie Gunston pawing away at the other, Maurice Morrison managed a little titter. He pulled out his murder weapon and alerted the police of an affray.

Messy stood at the door in the freezing late-night rain, her miserable tear-swollen face looking tentative, trying to read Jo's expression. There was a long silence while they gazed at each other, sized each other up.

'But don't you realise,' Messy said, laughing suddenly, slightly hysterically. 'I'm in love with *Grey*!'

Jo hesitated. 'It's not really very funny.'

'We were going to move into the cottage if you'd let us. We were going to open a restaurant and I was going to do the garden – open a garden centre. And Chloe was going to go to the little school in Fiddleford. We had it all worked out. It was going to be lovely. And then Colin and your little twins would have been running around. And the chickens . . .' It was the chickens, for some reason, which set her crying again. 'And now it's all ruined. Everything's ruined.'

'No, it isn't,' Jo said instinctively. 'Of *course* it isn't!,' and before she'd had time to think she'd turned sideways to avoid the bump, stretched out and taken Messy in her arms.

'They came and took Chloe and Colin.'

'I heard.'

'And Grey's gone.'

'I know. It was on the radio.'

'And then on top of that,' Messy snorted, 'Maurice Morrison asked me to marry him!'

'. . . *Did* he?' said Jo, pulling back to examine Messy's

face. 'He asked you to *marry* him? . . . Are you sure?'

'Certain, Jo.' Messy smiled.

'He asked you to *marry* him?'

'It's quite insulting, isn't it? I thought so. I mean when he's so obviously gay. Don't you think?'

'It doesn't make any sense,' said Jo, only half listening. 'He told me you and Charlie . . . *He* was the one who told me you and Charlie . . .'

'I'm afraid I think he's a bit deranged.'

'He wanted me to throw you out of the house.' Slowly things were beginning to fall into place. 'He thought if he could separate you and Grey . . .'

'Well, he's managed it now.'

'*And then he proposed to you!*' They looked at each other in disbelief. 'Bastard! What a creep! . . . Oh God, I'm so sorry, Messy,' she mumbled. 'I'm so sorry. But I think I need to talk to Charlie.'

'Jo – please. Wait! Will you help me?' Her face twisted, and she started sobbing again. 'Charlie said you'd help me. He said if we got a thing going, a great big thing – with all the newspapers and TV and media—'

'What? Well, *of course*! Obviously! Come on, you're freezing.' Jo backed up to let her in. 'We're going to get the press together tomorrow afternoon. As many as possible. That's what we're going to do. It's going to be fine. It's going to be *fine*. Only first I've got to call Charlie.'

'The General's gone to bed,' Anatollatia boomed down the telephone. 'Nigel and I are just sort of on our way. And everyone else seems to have disappeared. Sorry. We haven't seen Charlie for hours, have we, babe?' There was a pause. '. . . He says no. Anyway, are you all right, Jo? How's the bump? Ya? Hey, Jo, hang on. Hang on a mo—' Another pause. A brief confab with babe . ' . . . I know this probably isn't the time. With everything else going on. But we want you to know, Nigel and I are getting married!'

'Oh! Well, that's wonderful news!'

'We were in the stables, having a quick romp in the junk! Hope you don't mind!'

'Er—'

'Amazing that place. We can't keep away from it! And then suddenly, Jo, out of nowhere – I mean we were merrily shagging away – and he comes up with the Big WYMM! The bloody *Big Question!*'

'Well – congratulations, Anatollatia. Congratulations to you both.'

'So – sort of when you're freed up a bit could you do it for us? Sort of make an announcement and all that?'

'Of course I'd love to!'

'And I know we probably seem a bit dim to you, Jo. You're such a brainbox and everything. But we've worked it all out. *I've* got buckets of cash and *he's* got buckets of talent. Plus I just tend to sort of wilt without the sun.'

'Right . . .'

'Bingo! We're going to open a tennis centre in Ibiza! A tennis centre! Where really fab players can just come and *hit. All year round!* And I'm going to sit around by the pool drinking Cinzano. Or whatever they drink out there. Absolute *bliss!* Don't you think?'

'Anatollatia, it sounds wonderful. Congratulations! And send lots of love to Nigel – but I've got to dash . . .'

'Babe, darling, she's sending *loads* of love . . .'

\*     \*     \*

By seven-thirty the following morning Jo still hadn't heard from Charlie. She'd been calling Fiddleford for hours, ever since five o'clock, but all she ever got was the answer machine. She assumed Anatollatia had forgotten to pass the message on and that the whole hopeless household was still asleep.

She, on the other hand, at thirty-seven weeks pregnant with twins, had spent most of the night making plans. Spread out on the duvet in front of her were various lists: train times to Edinburgh, lists of news editors and journalists; lists of cab companies in Bonnyrigg, and, beneath them all, circled several times, Emily Deagle's parents' telephone number. She could do nothing, she had decided, until she spoke to them. She took a deep breath and dialled.

'Hello, Mrs Deagle? Is this Mrs Deagle?'

'Yes it is.'

'I'm – er. Good morning. Hello. Sorry to call so early.'

'That's OK.'

'You don't actually know me. And really, believe me, I'm sorry to trouble you. On such a . . . delicate . . . Mrs Deagle, I'm so sorry to be doing this . . .'

'Aye.' She sounded unconcerned. Not even curious.

'My name is Joanna Smiley. Joanna Maxwell McDonald. I'm calling you – I'm so sorry.'

'Aye. You said. We was waiting for one o' you to call. He'll be comin' up with you, will he?'

'Who?'

'Who? Whatever the poor bugger's callin' hisself these days.'

'Charlie?'

'Alistair – Grey McShane.'

'You've talked to Grey?'

'No!' she said impatiently. 'I talked to your husband. What's the matter with you?'

'You talked to Charlie? How? Where is he?'

'*I* don't know where he is! Bloody hell . . . Here, Eddie.' She passed the telephone over to her husband. 'You talk to her.'

Two years ago, when Grey had been riding high as the millionaire poet and he had first been outed as the man who had sexually offended their late daughter, Mr and Mrs Deagle had had to deal with a lot of journalists sitting outside their door. They'd felt ashamed (revenge had long since stopped offering any solace), and guilty, because it was their grief-ridden lies which had incriminated him in the first place. But they had said nothing. They knew that by lying in court all those years ago they had committed a crime, and they were frightened.

They would have sat quietly and said nothing this time around, too. Except this time Charlie had called. And after he had spoken to them he had given them a telephone number for his lawyer.

'Aye, I hear what you're sayin',' Eddie Deagle had said to the lawyer. 'And we do, as we said to Charlie, we feel very badly about it. The poor bugger's been to prison an' that. But the wife and I broke the law, didn't we? They might charge us.'

'They might,' the lawyer had said. 'Of course it's very unlikely. *Extremely* unlikely. But it's a gamble. It's something you'll have to refer to your own consciences, I imagine. But really, Mr Deagle, if he didn't do it he didn't do it. I think that's something which needs to be cleared up.'

Mr and Mrs Deagle had slept on it. In fact they had slept better than they had slept in nearly fifteen years. Because once upon a time they had been very fond of Grey (or Alistair, as he'd been called back then). In his own careless way he had loved their daughter almost as much as they did – and there weren't many people they could say that about. So when Jo called early that morning they had already decided: it was time they set the record straight.

Jo said she would arrange what she grandly called a 'press conference' at their house in Bonnyrigg for five o'clock that afternoon. She declared with her usual professional certainty that they would all be there: twenty journalists 'at least'; Jo; Grey's new girlfriend Messy, Charlie, and of course most essentially, Grey McShane.

Wherever the Hell he was.

She called Fiddleford again and this time she caught the General, who was just on his way out. When they heard each other's voices they had both been taken aback by how happy and relieved they felt. So much so that they were embarrassed and tried to disguise it by laughing uproariously at everything the other one said.

'So I'm off to Bonnyrigg!' exclaimed Jo.

'Oh! Ha ha. To see this poor girl's parents, I suppose? Ha ha. Yes! Ha ha. Charlie mentioned he'd spoken to them!'

'Yes! Ha ha! Charlie had already spoken to them!'

General Maxwell McDonald said he hadn't heard from Grey and nor, so far as he knew, had Charlie, who wasn't 'ha ha ha, strictly speaking in the house'.

That pulled her up a bit. 'Not in the house? Where is he then? I've been calling since five o'clock.'

He said Charlie was on the farm, which was a lie. 'With Les away, you know . . . He has to start very early.'

'Well . . . can you *please please* let him know he needs to get on a train to Edinburgh as soon as possible, because we need him in Bonnyrigg by five. And we need Grey, too. Desperately. I'm hoping, actually I'm counting on him calling either Messy or Charlie some time today, so if Charlie remembers his mobile . . . And – sorry – *sorry* to involve you in this, General. But I'm going to give you Messy's mobile number because, if it's possible, I'm not sure I really want to talk to him about all this until we've seen each other face to face, and sorted out a few things of our own . . . I think,' she added heavily, 'I owe him an apology.'

'Ahh!' exclaimed the General. 'I must say I'm delighted you're . . . I shall look forward to seeing you, Jo. I must say . . . In fact we've been finding it quite a struggle without you.'

'And we,' said Jo (referring to herself and her unborn babies, which briefly reminded the General of her more annoying side), 'have been finding it quite a struggle without you, General. We've been missing you all terribly.'

'Right you are. Ha ha. Good good.'

The General hung up, and continued outwards to Lamsbury police station where, when the telephone rang, he had been on his way to pick up Charlie and Les.

He found them both covered in swellings and bruises, Les looking very smug, Charlie looking understandably gloomy. They had spent a long night locked up in the same cell together, and Charlie had quite early realised his mistake. Les may have been with journalists every night. He may have been more than willing to share all his knowledge with them. But Charlie's initial judgement had been quite right. Les had no knowledge to share. He had barely taken in the names of Fiddleford's celebrity guests, let alone their crimes, or their relationship to one another. However many drinks the reporters bought him (as, in fact, the reporters themselves were slowly beginning to discover), Les would always and for ever be useless to them. Charlie had apologised exhaustively and by dawn a peace of some sort had been forged. They were both worn out.

'Maurice Morrison, my spies inform me,' said the General, as they climbed into the Land Rover, 'proposed marriage to Messy Monroe last night.'

'Really?' Charlie said dully. 'He was behaving so oddly, I had a feeling he might do something like that.'

'He told her they were going to live together at Fiddleford.'

'Ah.' Charlie thought about it for a second. 'The little shit.'

'Yes.'

'By the way I've offered Les his job back.'

'Oh good. I am pleased,' said the General.

''Cos you said you was sorry, didn't you, Charlie?' Les explained gleefully.

'I did,' said Charlie. 'Very sorry. Yes I did. Entirely my mistake. And I am. Very sorry.'

'Excellent,' said the General. A silence fell. '. . . You're a bloody fool, Charlie.'

'Yes. Thanks, Dad.'

'Incidentally,' he added tentatively, 'I— er. I talked to Jo—'

'*You talked to Jo?*'

'That's not sayin' I'm takin' it, mind,' Les interrupted

from the back seat. "Cos I ain't. Bein' frank with you, General, the job's all such a damn bother to me. I'm not sure I can be fussed.'

'Oh . . . Ah well.'

'That's what Charlie says to me.' Les laughed. 'He's gettin' more like his daddy every day! I says I'll take one o' them big fat pay cheques fer the thumpin' we gives each other, which I enjoyed heartily, and then we can call it a day.'

'. . . So you *talked* to Jo?'

'From what I understand, Morrison was telling her all sorts of nonsense.' He looked embarrassed. 'That you and Messy Monroe . . .'

'An' *she's* a big 'un!' Les cackled irrelevantly, giving Charlie a hefty prod on one of his many bruises.

Charlie winced. 'And did she sound – what did she sound like?'

'She said you needed to be at the girl's address in Bonnyrigg by five o'clock and I told her I wasn't sure if you'd make it . . . but if we can get to the station by ten . . .' He glanced at his watch, scowled, made a few dramatic gear changes and the Land Rover accelerated. 'You don't mind if we go via Tiverton, do you, Les?'

Les didn't bother to reply and before long he had fallen asleep, and Charlie and the General were silent again. They were only a few miles from the station before Charlie spoke again.

'Someone sent me an anonymous offer on the house, Dad,' he said bluntly.

'Morrison, of course. The little snake.'

'I suppose so, yes. Yesterday afternoon . . . It was well timed. Because we can't run a refuge if they're going to take over the stables. And without the refuge, I can't ask

288

Jo to stay here. I can't, and anyway she wouldn't. While the house falls down around us. Why should she? . . . Dad, I'm sorry – I'm sorry to you, to Mum, to Georgie . . . I'm sorry to let you all down. But I love Jo. I won't lose her. I'm thinking about selling the house.'

By the time they drew up in front of the station the General still hadn't responded.

'Well?' said Charlie, climbing slowly out of the car. 'Are you going to say anything?'

'I don't know what to say,' he said at last. 'The old house is a bloody white elephant. We both know it. And nobody could say you two haven't tried. You do whatever you have to do. Whatever you have to do to get her back again.' The General glanced briefly at his son. 'We've survived worse things together, haven't we, Charlie? Than seeing off an old house.'

Charlie nodded. They both nodded.

'By the way if you don't hear from Grey before, it might be worth trying the poor girl's *grave*. Don't you think? Very keen on graves, McShane is. For some reason. Can't stay away from them. Have you noticed?' (Charlie hadn't.) 'Anyway, best of luck!' And in a clamour of throttle and scraping gear, the General accelerated away.

# MINIMUM CONTENTS OF A FIRST AID BOX

## [HSE Guidance]

Guidance leaflet

20 individually wrapped, sterile, adhesive dressings of various sizes.

2 sterile eye pads

4 individually wrapped triangular bandages

6 safety pins

6 medium-sized and 2 large individually wrapped, sterile, unmedicated wound dressings

1 pair of disposable gloves

*Health and Safety First Principles Workbook, Chartered Institute of Environmental Health*

# • CO-OPT REALISABLE RESOURCES TO OPTIMISE TASK EFFECTIVENESS

Four o'clock. As she stood at Mr and Mrs Deagle's front door Jo felt a sharp twinge in her cervix, which made her lean on their bell rather longer than she had intended. But the babies weren't due for three weeks yet, so she said nothing. She and Messy already had enough to panic about.

The journalists – and as they travelled northwards, there had been numerous confirmations – were due at the house within the hour. As was Charlie, of course. And Grey – or so Jo, in her determination, had blithely promised everyone. At that stage, and with a single goal in sight, she would have said anything to get the press into the same room as Mr and Mrs Deagle and their statement. So Grey would be there, she proclaimed, standing shoulder to shoulder with the parents of his so-called victim, breaking his silence, protesting his innocence after fifteen long years. He was the only reason any media was coming. Which was a serious problem, because with just one hour to go, he still hadn't made contact with anyone. Nobody knew where he was.

Eddie Deagle, tall, thin, pale, bearded and dressed up for the occasion in a V-necked sweater and uncomfortable-looking tie, pulled open the door of his small grey terraced cottage while the bell was still ringing. 'All right. I heard you,' he said. There was a nervous glow about him as he glanced first at Jo's distended belly, and then over her shoulder, over Messy's shoulder, to the taxi, just pulling away. 'Where is he then?'

'Grey? He's on his way. He's definitely on his way.' She felt another stab of pain, leant briefly against the doorframe. 'Do you mind? Sorry. Can we sit down?'

The four of them settled together in the Deagles' tidy front room, which smelled of Mr Sheen and was uncomfortably cold, and endured a quarter of an hour of very difficult conversation. Corrine Deagle – buxom, with bright-yellow hair and a gaudily made-up face which belied the grey, weary sadness in her eyes – made them cups of watery tea, handed round a plate of biscuits, and told Messy and Jo how anxious she and her husband were feeling. As the years had passed, and the anger had faded and the fact of their daughter's death could begin to be separated, just a little, from the way that it came about, they had both slowly begun to acknowledge how much Grey (or 'Alistair') must have loved their daughter. And when, last year, he had still said nothing, still never said a word to defend himself, they had wanted to call him, to comfort him, tell him they had forgiven him. In spite of everything. 'He loved her, you see,' she said again. 'He loved her. So there . . .' She cleared her throat, gave a quick, embarrassed laugh. 'An' we're that keen to set this right now, me and Eddie haven't eaten a thing since your husband's telephone call.'

They wanted to know where Grey was coming from, where he was now, whether he was arriving with Charlie, or on his own, whether he was travelling by train, or bus, or taxi . . . and it wasn't until Messy and Jo were actually sitting there, in the house of the grieving couple and confronted by their hungry interrogation, that they finally understood the cruelty of their situation. Jo, until this point, had been operating on a tidal wave of optimism. Now she could hear the clock ticking on Eddie and Corrine's mantelpiece. She could see the nervous anticipation in their dry eyes, and she felt mortified. An uneasy glance across at Messy, sitting awkwardly beside her, assured her that she was feeling no better. 'Mr and Mrs Deagle,' Jo began, 'I think I should explain—' when she felt a contraction so strong she had to cough to stop herself from crying out.

'You shouldn't be rushin' around,' said Corrine Deagle disapprovingly. 'Not in your condition. You should be putting your feet up.'

'Jo?' said Messy. 'Are you all right?'

Jo could feel herself breaking into a panicky sweat. 'I'm fine,' she said. 'I'll just er—'

She had slipped off to the lavatory and was bending over the edge of the basin fervently muttering antenatal mantras to try to calm herself down when Messy's mobile rang. Messy jumped on it, but it wasn't Grey of course. It was Charlie, ringing for an update.

'Ah! Charlie,' Messy said. 'Have you arrived?'

'I'm in a minicab a couple of miles outside Bonnyrigg, only I thought I'd check—'

'And, er— have you brought any friends with you? Because this is, er. This is very bad. Very bad, Charlie . . . I don't know if you realise . . .'

'No news yet, then? OK . . .' He was thinking. 'How's Jo, by the way?'

'She's fine. What . . . um—' She smiled at the Deagles, neither of whom smiled back. '*Suggestions*. I think. Is what we're after. I have Mr and Mrs Deagle here, very much anticipating your arrival. And Grey's. Of course. And I'm thinking it's about time—'

Suddenly Mr Deagle leant forward and snatched the telephone out of her hand. 'I've had enough of this,' he said. 'You don't know where the bugger's got to, do you? . . . Is that you, Charlie?'

'It is,' said Charlie. 'Hello, Mr Deagle.'

'Do you know where the bugger's got to or don't you? 'Cos we're not sittin' here all afternoon, waiting for the man to turn up if he's never goin' to.'

There was a long pause. 'He said he was going home, Mr Deagle. I think we all assumed he would have contacted you by now. Or us. I'm very sorry—'

Mr Deagle's face sagged. The light went out. '. . . So is he comin' here or isn't he?' he said doggedly.

'Not. He's not.'

''Cos if the silly bugger can't be arsed to save 'is own skin, I'm certainly not doin' it for him.'

'I know. Of course. And I'm so sorry,' said Charlie. 'I'm so sorry to put you through this. We had no right—'

'Aye. It's a bit late for that.' Mr Deagle looked across at his wife, who was listening intently, and slowly shook his head. 'You shouldn't have bothered us wi' this, you know. You shouldn't a' done it.'

Charlie hesitated. He and Jo had already caused them enough trouble. He knew it. He was ashamed. But they'd all come this far. They were so close. He had to ask.

'There's just one possibility,' he said. 'Would you mind very much telling me where Emily is buried?'

And that, half an hour later, at the cemetery on the other side of town, was exactly where Charlie found him. Not looking his best. Because he'd been there ever since he'd left Fiddleford.

It was raining and windy and already very dark when Charlie's driver drew up at the cemetery gates.

'Rather you than me, my friend,' the driver said, keeping his engine running.

They looked out into the Scottish November blackness. In front of them, looming out through the rain, all they could see were gravestones, and beyond them the shadows and outlines of more. 'If you hear any strange noises,' Charlie said dismally, 'you'll come after me, won't you?'

'I shall not.'

He chuckled unhappily. 'But promise me you'll wait.'

'Depends how strange the bloody noises are. How long are you goin' to be?'

Charlie scaled the gates without much difficulty and strode through the absolute darkness for several long, long minutes. When he walked into the second tombstone he started humming to himself to try to keep himself calm, and then, with increasing desperation, he started calling out Grey's name. But Grey didn't call back.

The place seemed to be deserted. All he could hear was the wind in the trees and the rain beating on unseen graves, and it was truly – not very enjoyable. He was about to turn back when twenty or so yards in front of him he thought he glimpsed a lighted cigarette.

'Grey? . . . *Grey?*' He broke into a run. 'Grey, if that's

you . . .' In his haste to reach him Charlie stumbled on something, a loose brick, or a rock, or an empty flower vase – he never saw what it was exactly – and it sent him flying to the ground, and as he landed he thought he heard someone laughing. 'Grey? . . . GREY!' He scrambled to his feet. 'Answer me! Grey, you bugger, if that's you, and you're not saying anything, I swear I'm going to—'

He saw Grey's outline, sitting hunched on the ground against a small cross, taking a drag from the cigarette and then treading on it. He was still laughing.

'Is it my imagination or am I sensing a wee bi' o' *fear* out here in the darkness, Charlie, my friend?' he said.

'Jesus! You wanker. You fucking wanker . . . *Jesus*.' Charlie collapsed onto the wet grass beside him. 'I've never been so fucking terrified in my life . . . How long have you been out here?'

'You get used to it after a while. Until someone comes yelling at you out o' the blackness.' He gave another deep chuckle. 'Callin' you a fuckin' wanker.' He offered up his bottle of gin and Charlie snatched at it greedily. 'How d'you know I was here?'

'I didn't.' He passed the bottle back to Grey and stood up. 'Dad guessed. Says you're grave-obsessed, which I must say I'd never noticed. Until now, obviously. Come on. I've got a car waiting. We've got to go. Messy, Jo, Mr and Mrs Deagle and a load of reporters are waiting to see you. We've got ten minutes. Mr Deagle says if you're not there by five past five he's throwing everyone out. So we'd better hurry.'

Grey didn't move.

'*Come on, Grey*. What are you waiting for?'

'Thank you, Charlie, for takin' the trouble. Thank you kindly. I truly mean that. But I'm not comin'.'

'Why not? Grey, it's all set up. It's ready to go. It's a chance— Please, don't be stupid. It's your one chance to set things straight.'

'It wouldn't be fair.'

'But Mr and Mrs Deagle *want* to see you. They *want* to set the record straight.'

'It wouldn't be fair on Emily.'

'*Why?* Grey, I don't want to— But they're very . . . frank. From what I understand you're about the only person in Bonnyrigg Emily *didn't* sleep with. So what's the fuss? Corrine Deagle told me *Emily* didn't even know who the baby's father was. God rest her soul. Not that anyone's blaming her and all that.'

'Shut up.'

'All right. I'm sorry. But if her parents can say it . . . You've spent fifteen years grieving for her. What does it really matter, anyway?'

'Of course it doesn't.'

'Well then,' Charlie nudged him. 'Grey, I'm freezing out here. We've now got nine minutes. Please. *Let's go.*'

'I just don't want to be draggin' Emily's name through the mud all over again. It's not right. When she can't defend her own self.'

'That's not what her parents think.'

'Aye – well, I never said we thought the same.'

'Yes, but they're right and you're wrong. She's *dead*. Look!' He pointed at her grave. 'You honestly think she's worrying about her reputation right now?'

Grey smiled.

'That's the whole bloody point of dying. You stop worrying about crap like that—'

'Oh, is that right?' said Grey dryly.

'Hm? . . . Look, Grey,' he added more quietly, 'maybe she is sitting up there somewhere, cursing herself for having been a bit of an old slapper. I don't know . . . Seems unlikely. But who knows? What I do know is that she's dead. And that you've been punishing yourself for it long enough. And that Messy *isn't* dead. And nor is Chloe. And you aren't either. Yet . . .'

Grey didn't move. Charlie stood waiting, bent against the wind and the rain. But Grey stayed where he was. 'The Deagles won't do it without you, you know. I told you they're going to throw everyone out. It's your last chance . . .'

But Grey said nothing. He stayed put. He pulled out another cigarette and started lighting it. With a sigh Charlie turned away, back into the blackness.

For a while he walked slowly between the gravestones, searching half-heartedly for the minicab headlights. But he didn't care anymore. There was no need to hurry . . . He imagined Jo and Messy and Mr and Mrs Deagle, waiting, pinning their hopes on him. He imagined their faces as he arrived, looking behind him for Grey, and then their disappointment when they realised he was on his own . . .

*Crack!*

He jumped. A twig snapping. A footstep.

'Grey?'

*Crack!*

It was coming towards him. Charlie walked faster. He started humming again.

*Crack!*

It was right behind him, and then so was the familiar laugh and then Grey— 'You're goin' the wrong way,

300

Charlie old man. Come on. It's this way. We'd better hurry.'

But by the time they reached the road, the minicab had left without them.

Ten minutes past five. The Deagles' sitting room was already full, Messy had slipped off to buy some crowd-mollifying alcohol and Jo was doing her best to keep everybody under control. 'They'll be here at any minute,' she kept saying. 'Any minute now . . .'

Eddie Deagle pulled Jo into the kitchen. 'He's not found him, has he?' he asked.

'He might have done,' Jo said stubbornly. 'He probably has, for all we know. We've just got to wait a tiny bit more.'

Mr Deagle wanted to believe her but it was becoming ridiculous. They both knew it. 'I'm givin' him ten minutes. Ten minutes,' he said, just as a man with a moustache pushed his head round the kitchen door. 'And then,' Mr Deagle continued, 'I'm throwin' the whole bloody lot of you out.'

'Is this a bloody wind-up or what?' said the moustache. 'Is he coming or isn't he, excuse my French . . . But where the fuck is this character?'

'I told you!' Jo cried, spinning around. 'He's on his way! He'll be here any minute.'

'So why do I get the impression this is a total fucking fuck-up? Why's Mrs – Whatsername telling me nobody knows where he is?'

'She's called Mrs Deagle,' said Jo. 'And I don't know why she's telling you that. You'll have to ask her—'

'She told me to ask you.'

301

A pasty-faced man in glasses barged up from behind, knocking the moustached one out of the way and straight into Jo's belly. 'Sorry,' he said vaguely, adjusting his glasses. 'But can someone just tell us what's going on?'

He was quickly followed by others, until there was hardly breathing space in the tiny kitchen. Within minutes they were all shouting and arguing with each other, shouting into their mobiles, shouting at Eddie, shouting at Corrine, shouting at Jo. Eddie Deagle stared out over the crowded room, through all the mayhem, and suddenly something snapped. He couldn't stand any more. 'Right then!' he roared. 'That's it! He's not comin'. Everyone out!'

'Oh no, please, wait . . .' begged Jo. But another contraction, the fiercest by far, made her cry out in pain. She grasped hold of the kitchen sink. Breathed . . . Breathed . . . Breathed . . . Breathed . . . Nobody seemed to notice. When she looked up most of the press had already spilled out into the hall and back onto the road again, and Mrs Deagle was standing over her.

'I'm so sorry,' Jo babbled. 'I am *so sorry*. I thought— Christ, I don't know what I thought. I wanted to help Grey . . . and Messy, and Chloe. You don't know Chloe but they've put her in a fucking home. And then there's poor little Colin. And I was so certain . . . You know, if you *want* something badly enough . . . I am so, so sorry.'

'I think you should sit down.'

She would have done, and very gladly, but outside they heard a car sound its horn, and people had all started yelling again. The two women stared at each other.

'Eddie?' Mrs Deagle shouted. 'What's going on?'

By the time Jo, Eddie and Corrine Deagle reached the

road, the disbanded press conference had re-formed itself into a tight cluster around a white van, and Charlie and Grey McShane, to the flash of many cameras, were both climbing out of the back of it.

They straightened up, surveyed what they could of the scene.

'Excuse me,' murmured Grey. He fought his way through the journalists towards the Deagles, who were waiting for him, arm in arm at the door of the house he had once known so well . . .

They looked at each other for a long time. A long time. Grey nodded uncertainly.

' . . . I'm sorry,' he whispered.

'And so we all are,' said Mrs Deagle at last, and two fat tears spilled out over her painted cheeks. 'Come on in.'

He followed the Deagles into the house. Jo, thinking after fifteen years they might welcome a few minutes alone, tried to close the door behind them. But the press pack had already waited long enough. They jostled her out of the way and hurriedly jammed themselves back into the hall behind them.

Which left Charlie, still bloodstained and bruised from the experience with Les, and now smeared in mud from the cemetery, and Jo, monstrously, grotesquely pregnant. On their own at last. And they looked at each other. Charlie started walking towards her. She took a single step towards him.

And her waters broke.

By the time Messy found her way back from the off-licence, which turned out to be quite a distance away, Charlie and Jo were already in the ambulance on their way back to Edinburgh and the nearest hospital. In the crammed front room Eddie and Corrine Deagle had positioned themselves (just as Jo had promised) on either side of Grey, and Mr Deagle had delivered a short and moving statement apologising to the police, the courts and especially to Grey, and finally admitting that he and his wife had lied.

'If Grey McShane had been anything more than a friend to our daughter,' said Corrine, 'I would have known about it . . . Eddie and me can never forget what he did, and nor can he, and now Emily's dead. But it was an accident. We've accepted that. He was never a bad man. And he loved her. Which is a lot more than I can say for most o' the young fellas she brought back here. Emily was a beautiful girl.' Mrs Deagle's brightly coloured face suddenly broke into a smile. '. . . But she liked her fun, didn't she, Alistair?'

'Yes, that's all very well,' came a nasal voice from the middle of the room, 'but if young Emily was having it away with all the lads, I don't see why we should be expected to believe that Grey McShane was an exception.'

'You can believe what you fuckin' like,' snapped Grey.

'Because,' Mrs Deagle said quietly, 'I've got her diaries.'

Grey paused. He hadn't known. Not that it mattered anymore. Not that it had ever mattered. It was just that he hadn't known. When they sent him to jail all those years ago he hadn't known that they'd *known*; that they'd had evidence to prove it. He turned back to the nasal journalist. 'I'm tellin' you the facts now because my girlfriend . . . The woman I love—' He glanced across at her. She had just come in, bringing cold air with her into the smoky room, and a carrier bag full of alcohol. 'Hey,' he said, gazing into her beautiful face, 'all right, Messy? You OK there?'

She nodded at him.

'Messy Monroe, over there, who you've all had a bit o' sport with in the past, of course, had her daughter removed from her, as you know, because of her association with me. And if we're to be together, she an' me an' young Chloe, I need to get this conviction overturned. And until then – LAMSBURY SOCIAL SERVICES, IF YOU'RE LISTENIN' – I shall be stayin' here in Scotland, far away from both o' them. So you can bloody well return the child straight away. OK? Right then. Are we finished?'

In the end she and Grey only had an hour on their own together before Messy needed to leave for Fiddleford again (with Mr and Mrs Deagle, it turned out. Charlie, during one of his previous telephone calls, had invited them both to stay.) The journalists took so long to leave, and then the Deagles took so long to stop talking about train times, and go upstairs and pack . . .

They left a silence when they had finally closed the door behind them, into which, after a small pause, Messy and Grey started laughing. Out of relief. Not because anything was funny. Out of the joy of being in the same room together. They trampled over the empty beer cans to get to each other.

'I *think*,' said Messy, squeezing him tight, 'I think it's going to be OK.'

'Aye,' said Grey, rubbing his cheek in her hair, breathing her in. 'It's going to be OK now . . . I'm sorry, Messy.'

'Nonsense! Could have happened to anybody!'

'Aye, very funny.'

'Well. Almost anybody.'

'. . . God, I love you, Messy. I love you so much.'

'Yes . . . Good,' she said vaguely.

'*Good?*'

'Look, we haven't got much time. Are you going to show me round your home town or . . . what?' She kissed him again, slowly and deliberately. 'We've got an hour, Grey. Any ideas?'

'Well . . .' he said. 'We could go and see how Jo's doing.'

'Or we could just telephone later.'

'Or I could show you the petrol station where I used to work.'

'Or I could just imagine it.'

He smirked. They both smirked. 'Or there's a bed and breakfast just around the corner . . .'

Jo was approaching the end of a long labour when, late the following morning, somebody from the council rang Messy at Fiddleford to inform her that in the light of recent developments (plastered as they were over that day's newspapers) they had decided she could come to pick up her daughter at any time. Messy and the General were standing outside the children's home about fifteen minutes later.

Most of the children (those who had agreed to attend that day) were already on their way to school by the time Messy and the General arrived, so the place was fairly empty. Set in a large converted town house on the expensive side of Lamsbury, it must once, beneath the lime-green paint, self-closing fire doors, and dismal hotpotch of institutional furniture, have been an elegant and pleasant place to live. No longer, of course. Though the pinboards were crammed with brightly coloured posters imploring residents to approach life more positively, there was, beneath its courageous, well-intentioned kindliness, an impersonality to the place which made Messy shiver, a core of lovelessness as poignant as it was, of course, inevitable. As they were led through the corridors to their appointment Messy had to fight the desire to just snatch what she had come for and run.

But first, in the carers' staff room (vacated but for Chloe's designated social worker and Paddy the care home duty officer) she was required to endure a long pep talk about parental responsibility. Various things were explained to her: that Social Services would be paying Chloe unannounced visits from now on; that until Grey's conviction was officially overturned he was never to be left alone with Chloe under any circumstances.

'OK. Fine. So where is she?' said Messy, standing up, unable to wait any longer. 'Can I go and fetch her now?'

But the social worker said she would fetch Chloe herself and bring her down. The reunion, she said, needed to be supervised.

'*Fine*. Whatever. *Anything* . . . But please, *please*, will you *supervise* it then?'

The General, by contrast, feeling quite rightly that he would be 'a bit *de trop*' at such a tender moment, told Paddy he would slip away before the social worker brought Chloe in. He asked if he could go and see Colin.

'Ah, Colin,' said Paddy regretfully. 'He's not been a happy lad, Colin hasn't. He's been back in town up to his old tricks again.'

'Well, what did you expect?' said the General.

Paddy shook his head. 'We've had the police out searching for him both nights. They found him halfway to

Fiddleford one night. And then back at his mum's the next. Sitting on the doorstep.'

'Where was the mother?'

'She won't have anything to do with him.' He looked from Messy to the General. 'I probably shouldn't say this, but that lad's been in and out of here since he wasn't much older than Chloe, and when he came in this time, he looked better than I've ever seen him. And that's the truth. When he's not screaming and yelling, all he's talking about is his ruddy chickens!'

'Yes, of course,' murmured the General, nodding thoughtfully and edging towards the door, 'the chickens. Right then. I shall leave you three to it – and Messy,' he winked at her, 'I shall be waiting for you and Chloe. In the car. On the corner of Kilbury and Knole Street. Left outside the door. All right? Got that?'

It wasn't hard for the General to find him. He followed the noise. As soon as he stepped out of the staff room he could hear it: Colin's voice, yelling out obscenities, and the sound of objects being smashed against walls. The General hurried down the corridor – almost, for the first time in twenty years, breaking into a run. Beyond what was the television lounge (except the telly had been stolen) and through yet more swinging fire doors, the General came upon a small ante-room. There were shards of glass all over the floor, a smashed window, an upside-down coffee table, a handful of angrily strewn plastic chairs and what looked like a mugful of coffee splattered against one wall. And in the middle of it all, Colin Fairwell. Still shouting, but now wrapped in the restraining embrace of Steve, one of Paddy's kindly colleagues.

'Good God!' said the General. 'What in Hell's name is going on?'

Colin snapped to attention. Blushed a deep purple. 'Oh,' he said sullenly. 'It's you, is it?'

'What *are* you doing, Colin?' The General turned to Steve. 'You can let go of him now.'

Steve hesitated.

'Let go of him,' the General snapped. 'Please. If you wouldn't mind . . . Your colleague, Paddy,' he added, 'knows who I am. He knows I'm here. I'm a friend of Colin's.'

Steve looked warily down at his ferocious little captive. 'I'm going to remove my arms now, Colin,' he said patiently. 'Are you ready?' . . . and released him. 'OK? Calm now? Are you going to clear up the mess you've made?'

'Fuck off,' snarled Colin.

'Colin, you're being vile,' said the General, scowling at him. 'I'm so sorry. The boy's got filthy manners sometimes, as you've obviously discovered. But from what I understand he's had a rough couple of days. Mr— Forgive me, I don't know your name?'

'Steve.'

'Mr Steve—'

'No—'

'I would be most awfully grateful, Mr Steve . . . Would you mind very much leaving us alone for a moment?'

He left them, reluctantly, and Colin and the General set to work straightening up the room. They didn't speak for a while. It was obvious that Colin was very angry and the General could understand why, but it didn't help him to know how to begin. They had almost finished tidying

309

when he burst out awkwardly, 'I had a meeting with Mrs Hooper, by the way. She said she'll sell the eggs on the nod, so to speak. *Under the counter*, until we get the paperwork done.'

'Not much use to me, though, is it? Stuck in this shit'ole.'

'Well!' The General was stung. 'And you'll settle in very nicely I dare say, using repulsive language like that.'

'I am settlin' in. *Very* nicely. Thank you.'

'Ha! Excuse me, but it certainly didn't look like that a moment ago.'

'Yeah, right. Like you fuckin' know. What do you know?'

'Nothing at all . . . I wouldn't pretend to.'

'So shut yer ugly cake'ole then,' Colin murmured.

The General pretended not to hear and together they picked up the pieces of broken mug in wounded silence, until Colin spoke again. '. . . Chloe'll say goodbye though, won't she?' he said. 'Before she goes.'

The General put the bits of crockery into a pile on the broken coffee table. He took a plastic chair and set it against the wall. He straightened it, adjusted the angle slightly. 'I was rather thinking,' he began, and adjusted the chair again, '. . . Colin, I gather your mother doesn't – didn't—'

'On one of her walkabouts,' he said defensively. 'She's a very busy woman.'

'Yes of course. Only I was thinking. Do you think – that is to say we are all going to miss you at Fiddleford – or wherever we may be. Dreadfully. But perhaps . . . You'll think it presumptuous. Only I know nothing about these sorts of things. I was thinking maybe of some sort of adoption—'

Colin looked coolly at the General. 'You're too old,' he said baldly.

'Ah well. Yes of course. I'm so sorry.' Colin's watchful eyes stayed on him. 'How silly of me – and you have a family of your own. And so on. Or not. What not. *Anyway*— I certainly didn't mean to— I hope you're not—'

'No, because what *I* was thinkin',' Colin interrupted, 'was if you went for one o' those resident's orders. Especially seeing as I've already been staying with you. An' the chickens are proba'ly missin' me. You can say that, you know. Even if they ain't. I reckon we stand a chance of a *resident's order*, General. Once all the fuss 'as died down.'

'Ha!' said the General in astonishment. '*Ha!* I say! *Ha! . . .* Well. Excellent. *Right then.* Let's finish this up and then you might need to fetch a pullover or something—'

Colin looked confused.

The General held a finger to the side of his nose. 'As an intermediary arrangement,' he muttered, sidling closer to him, 'I was thinking we might implement a somewhat covert system of unofficial *exeats*. Don't you think? Because it strikes me that so long as we get you back by tea time –' He cast an eye around the room, at the window that Colin had just smashed, at the pile of broken crockery sitting beside the broken table leg. '. . . I can't honestly imagine they're going to miss you much.'

'You what?' he yelled. 'You mean we're going to Fiddleford? *Today?'*

'*Shhh!'*

Colin threw his arms around the General's neck and kissed him.

'For Heaven's sake!' The General shook him off. 'I shall

be waiting for you in the car. On the corner of Kilbury Road and Knole Street. Do you know it?'

'O' course I do.'

'Right then! Time check?'

'I'll be twenty seconds.'

'*Excellent. I shall see you there.*' The General was humming as he left the room.

Way back in gestation week twenty-eight, when Jo Smiley still felt very much on top of her game, she had gone to the trouble of typing out a detailed Birth Plan which, if things had gone as they were meant to, she would have handed over to the midwife on arrival at the Lamsbury cottage hospital, three weeks hence. There were, it had stipulated, to be no painkillers; no monitors; where possible, no white coats. She wanted underwater labour; she wanted Mozart; she wanted Jo Malone Red Roses Bath essence . . .

Jo, her mind filled with New Age propaganda and, as always, desperate to do things perfectly, had been determined to embrace the whole ghastly birthing experience with wakeful, open-hearted enthusiasm. Because childbirth, so she had heard (and so the opening paragraph of her Birth Plan had explained), was meant to be 'a mystical thing, a magical apotheosis, a precious opportunity to connect with the cosmic self, a process where pain, in perfect synthesis with nature, metamorphoses into a life-giving, life-affirming orgasm of almost spiritual intensity'.

But the overnight bag she had so tenderly put together at Fiddleford all those weeks ago, which had included the bath essence, the Mozart and the Birth Plan, was a long way from the Royal Infirmary, Edinburgh. And Jo had never known such agony. Within two hours of arriving at the hospital she had demanded an epidural, and had promptly fallen asleep.

Fourteen hours later, having barely felt a thing, having made him swear never to breathe a word about the epidural drip still attached to the base of her spine, she and Charlie looked down on their brand-new, sleeping twins – a girl (called Georgina) and a boy, of course; both beautiful, of course, with a mass of dark hair each ... and all their worries faded away. There were the four of them, together, and nothing else mattered. Nothing in all the world.

At some point a little later, when they were idly envisaging their children's future, Charlie mentioned the offer he'd had on the house. And Jo had laughed.

'Are you mad?' she said. 'I love Fiddleford! We both love Fiddleford! Why on earth would we want to sell it?'

'Yes, but realistically—'

'These last few days, Charlie, I've actually missed Fiddleford almost as much as I've missed you. Not quite as much. Obviously. *But almost.*'

'No,' he laughed. 'That's appalling! Is that really true?'

'Anyway,' she said. 'What about everyone else we've got living there? We can't just turf them out! Where would they all go? And what about all the people in the future? They'll still need somewhere to hide. Where are *they* going to go?'

'Yes, but practically speaking—'

'Charlie, *fuck* practically speaking. Fuck the council! Fuck everybody who's trying to close us down!'

'That's disgusting language,' a woman in the neighbour-ing bed informed her amiably.

'Sorry.' But she was mid-stream. 'Seriously, Charlie,' she tried to whisper, 'fuck all the *petty* bloody law enforcers!

313

And fuck the media and its trivial fucking "moral" outrage! They're a bunch of lazy, smug, hypocritical, mealymouthed, mean-hearted sodding dictators and I hate the lot of them. Fuck them! Fuck their opinions! Fuck their pathetic little laws! It's *our* house. It's *our* refuge. Why the *fuck* should we submit?'

'My God,' he said appreciatively, and slowly the ward filled, first with his, and then her own astonished laughter. 'You're supposed to be exhausted!'

'Adrenaline,' she mumbled. 'Must be the adrenaline.'

'Ten months in the country and you've turned into a revolutionary! It's extraordinary!'

They drank to that, as well as to the twins. They drank champagne *even though Jo was breast-feeding*, and they realised as they drank that never in their lives had they ever felt more united, or happier, or more in love.

And for the next couple of days, while Jo recuperated and they began the long journey (by hire car) back to the South, they didn't mention the possibility of selling Fiddleford again. At first because they honestly didn't think about it. They were too happy, and still a long way from home. It wasn't until they had crossed the border into England that the anxiety began to gnaw, and after that, with each mile they left behind them, the reality of what lay ahead loomed gloomier. They didn't speak much. By the time they passed Taunton they hardly spoke at all; neither wanted to be the one to say it but they both knew, and they both knew the other knew: Fiddleford was going to have to go.

Messy and Grey's contribution for the cottage and walled garden, though very welcome, would hardly even cover the cost of the Fire Authority demands. And then there was the water, and the kitchen and, worst of all of course, the stables. Charlie and Jo hadn't a hope of raising £750,000. And the council, having taken possession, could do with them what they liked: sell them off for executive housing; open a conference centre, a Safe Injecting Zone, a public swimming baths . . . their refuge could not be a refuge if the world had access to it, too. The refuge could not function. It would have to close. And eventually – this year, next year – Maurice Morrison would be still lurking, waiting. And the house would have to be sold.

Fiddleford Manor was strangely silent when its current owners finally arrived home. In the hall they were confronted not by the expected welcoming party, who were all in the cottage still eating lunch, but by a mountain of depressing-looking post. They paused in front of it, exchanged glances.

'Come on,' sighed Charlie. 'While the babies are still asleep. Let's get the worst over and done with.'

'Crikey,' chuckled Jo, fingering the pile unenthusiastically, and then pulling out a coy peppermint green envelope. 'Look at this one!'

The letter she held was addressed to them both. In a neat, childish hand, above a smiling watermelon motif, both their names were spelt wrong.

In London Sue-Marie had spent the early part of the morning at Maurice's hairdresser and then later, at his tactful instigation, consulting with a cosmetic surgeon about her repulsive facial flaps. Maurice had assured her that though he personally thought the flaps were 'rather special', it was now incumbent on her, with the more public role she would henceforth be playing, to allow the world to read the expression in her eyes.

She loved her new hair, and the surgeon had assured her that her 'overlap', as he called it, could be removed with no trouble at all. And though the sex of her imagination (or sex of any description at all) had yet to materialise, Sue-Marie Gunston was feeling great. She was in love with London. She was in love with her new social whirl. Her new, metropolitan future, far away from boring Lamsbury and the dirty countryside, was looking very golden and in a week or two, thanks to Maurice's munificence, she would even be able to see it when she smiled.

Maurice, too, was feeling good. He had ridden the rocky patch of the last few miserable weeks with his usual deftness of touch, he thought, and his life was once more in control again. Sue-Marie had not mentioned Derek or his ludicrous Kenyan holiday again, and Maurice was confident that she never would. That dark Fiddleford night, a pact of silence had been forged between them – between two desperate people – and it had been sealed with the most revolting kiss of Maurice's life. It didn't matter. Nothing mattered anymore. His phantoms had evaporated the moment that Very Important commiseration call came through, and he knew he was back in the fold again.

'It's at difficult times like these,' said his benign absolver's most valued adviser, who had seen Mr Morrison sobbing on the evening's news, 'when we need our families around us, I think.'

'Ah hahahaha!' Maurice had laughed hysterically. 'My thoughts exactly! I'm so glad He agrees. *You* agree. We *all* so very much agree. I am a man, and I say it myself, who is *desperately* in need of a wife! In need of a woman.

A divine, delicious, devastating *woman!* Ha ha! But I'm working on it! Have no fear!'

And today was a very special day, because Maurice was giving a very special lunch. He had hired the city's best caterers, the city's best florists, a flautist, a magician, a contortion artist and a delightful duo of brooding Croatian boys to help with the parking.

Only sixteen guests were expected, and among them only two who signified. Perhaps they had taken pity after his terrible last few weeks; after the sterling performance he gave outside the London Central Hospital. Perhaps they wanted money off him. They could have it! Honestly – who gave a fuck? But sitting that very day at his very own dining table and for the very first time would be no less than the marvellous, utterly *marvellous*, marvellous, marvellous Mr and Mrs Tony B.

. . . *Ting ting ting.* In fact he'd *tinged* early because he glanced across the dining-room table and noticed Sue-Marie Gunston stuffing a meringue into her fat face, and he thought, with a flush of anger, that she might at least have had the decency to forego her pudding today. Under these circumstances. There were little globules of cream seeping out from either side of her mouth and she was smirking. No doubt boring Tony senseless about fucking thermometer probes . . .

. . . *Ting ting ting.* 'Prime Minister . . . Cherie . . . Tony . . . Mr Blair, Ms Booth . . . Ladies and gentlemen, ha ha! *All* of you . . . Perhaps I should begin, Cherie, by saying how stunning you're looking today, and what an honour it is to have you and your redoubtable husband at my humble abode.' A smattering of applause. 'And how grateful I am

for your unstinting support in recent, terrible weeks ...'
Maurice Morrison paused for effect. 'And now, if I may, I
would like to take this opportunity to introduce to you all
a lady without whose kindness and sheer ... *gumption* ...
I simply could not have survived them. She's a lady who
has dedicated herself to safety in the workplace – and that's
something which has always been very close to my heart –
and even more so as I stand before you now. A humbler
man ... *Even more so* ... Sue-Marie, God bless you, you
have been my tower of strength!' He smiled at her, and she
smirked back, almost believing every word. '... We met,'
Maurice continued, 'while I was staying in the West Country
at a beautiful house to which, fingers crossed, I hope soon
to be in a position to invite you all. As my guests! It was the
house we both fell in love with, wasn't it, Sue? And the house,
ladies and gentlemen, where we both fell in love ...'

'*Awww!*' said the Prime Minister.

'Ladies and gentlemen, Tony ... Cherie ... May I present
to you my future wife. Sue-Marie Gunston!'

*Dear Joe and Charles Maxwell-Macdonnald,*

> *As you will no doubt ever so shortly learn, my circumstances
> have diversified somewhat since I last encountered you. I am not
> in the employment of Lamsbury Council any longer, and do not
> envisage retrogressing to this location in the foreseeable future.*
>
> *As it is I am very happy at this moment in time, encountering
> all sorts of celebrities and other fascinating personalities, and
> frankly, Mr Maxwell, I do not know how much of the situation
> you are sentient of but suffice it to say – no way is Fiddleford
> Manor the house for me!*

*Unfortunately, for copious reasons with which it would certainly be unpolitic to encumber yourselves, I cannot offer any advice re reparation of stables, but you might find it serviceable to know that all other restrictions and costly alterations being imposed on the house at this time can be reversed with a simple un-registering of your location as a hotel. This can be achieved, I believe, since consumers are in actuality paying for the service of advice which is provided while they are in residence there, and therefore edibles, bibulations and all facilities and amenities provided at your private domicile are purveyed free of all or any charge.*

*I hope this is of help to you all, and that it may cause you to foresee a situation in which you could keep hold of the house, and not recommend it for external purchase! And I anticipate you will comprehend when I request you to demolish this communication, as I would not like 'certain persons' to know I had been assisting you in any way!*

*I wish you the best of luck in the future,*

*Yours sincerely,*
*Sue-Marie Gunston*

So when Messy, Chloe, Colin, the General, Mr and Mrs Deagle, Nigel and Anatollatia returned to the house they found Jo and Charlie, each carrying a mewling baby in one hand and joyously ripping down Sue-Marie's prohibition notices with the other. 'We have our house back!' shouted Charlie, passing the letter round.

The General rushed off to the cellar and returned holding the only bottle of champagne which had survived poor Caroline and Jasonette's final rampage. And after the first wave of twin worship and general celebration had died

319

down, and they were all seated around the old kitchen table, and they'd drunk to the babies, and to Jo, and to Charlie and Jo, and to Nigel and Anatollatia, and to Colin, and to the General, and to Messy and Grey, and even to Sue-Marie Gunston and Maurice Morrison, there was a tiny lull.

'We thought we'd call the boy after you, General,' Jo mumbled suddenly, looking unusually embarrassed. 'If you don't mind.'

'Oh! . . . Goodness.' He blushed with pleasure. 'Thank you, Jo.' He beamed at her, and she beamed back. 'Thank you. Both. Charlie. Joanna. Thank you. Well – To Georgina— To Georgie and James, then.'

'To Georgie and James,' they all shouted.

And then another lull. 'But the sad fact is,' Charlie said, 'none of this really solves the basic problem. We still can't run the refuge if they take the stables. We still need to find the money for the stables.'

Nigel cleared his throat. He nudged Anatollatia. '. . . Oh!' she screamed. 'The stables! I meant to say! God—' She slapped herself on the forehead. 'You guys will never guess what we found when we were mooching around down there yesterday. Didn't we, babe? Wait a moment. Wait there. I'm going to get it.'

As she left, they heard the gate buzzer sounding. It echoed through the hall, the dining room, the drawing room, library, kitchen, pantry, back hall, boot room . . . There wasn't a corner of the house where it couldn't be heard.

It buzzed once. It buzzed twice. Corrine and Eddie Deagle looked at each other in bemusement. 'Isn't that the front gate?' said Corrine. It buzzed a third time. Colin and Chloe quietly slunk out of the room. It buzzed a fourth time.

Charlie, Messy and the General all started talking at once.

'Oh my God, of course!' exclaimed Jo, grinning suddenly. 'How could I forget? I'm worse than Anatollatia!' Charlie was already holding one twin, so she handed hers to her father-in-law, who scowled about it but didn't quite dare to complain. 'I'll just be a second.'

. . . 'You see,' said Anatollatia, dodging round Jo as she made her way back in, 'it's virtually *exactly* the same as one my uncle left to me. And my father was in a terrific bate because Uncle Ernst had known for years he was leaving it to me, so he should have signed it over before. Because of the taxes. Anyway. Boring. *The point is*—' She laid a scroll on the kitchen table and very carefully unrolled it. It was a sketch, a small dirty sketch of an old rural scene, with what looked like Salisbury Cathedral in the background. 'You know it's times like this,' she said, enjoying the moment, 'people should be grateful I'm such a nosy parker . . . Because look, it's actually of the same churchy-thing as mine is, if you can believe it. Only from a slightly different angle. Plus I know it's the same artist because I did History of Art A level and you can sort of recognise his yokels and stuff . . . *plus* . . .' She bent closer to it. 'If you look down there—' they all craned forward to see, 'there's a teeny-tiny siggie. See? C-O-N-S-T-A-B . . . Guessed it yet?' She grinned. Never before had she been the recipient of such respectful, grateful attention. Never before had she felt so useful. 'Good news, hey, guys! And guess how much it's worth?' she said. 'I mean even *after* death tax?'

'Charlie?' Jo poked her head back round the kitchen door. 'Come out here a moment, will you? There's something I want to show you.'

'Jo! My darling Jo! You will never guess what Anatollatia has found in the stable! You will never ever, *ever* guess—'

'Hm?' She wasn't listening. 'Can you come out here a second, Charlie. *Please*. Just very quickly. There's something I want to show you—'

'Jo, she's discovered a fucking—'

'Quickly, quickly, come here!' She pulled him out into the hall and opened the front door. 'Go on,' she said, nudging him through. 'Go on! *Go on!*'

Parked up on the gravel was a truck, its back ramp down. Out of which . . .

'For the new generation,' said Jo triumphantly, 'for *our* twins . . .'

. . . tumbled two very small Highland calves.

'But then I felt so sorry for them,' she said. 'The poor things are so young. It seemed so cruel to separate them from her. And ten months in the country may have turned me *slightly* savage, but I'm still a sentimental townie at heart . . .'

The trailer shook. There was a loud scraping sound. And behind the calves, very slowly, with a hay net hanging haphazardly off one of her giant horns, emerged their big, fat, clumsy Highland mother.


The Soppy End

# The New You Survival Kit

## Daisy Waugh

**Is it time to break all the rules?**

**Jo Smiley** has got a desperately glamorous job, she's a member of all the right clubs, and her friends are the coolest and cruellest in London.

**Ed** is a TV producer famous for his gritty and important documentaries. He's also a liar, a cheat and a phoney. In other words, he's Mr Right.

And **Charlie's** a charmingly clueless pub singer in cowboy boots. Until he meets **Jo** who thinks she can make him a social success.

But who is really showing who the way to survive? Will **Charlie** learn to play by the rules? Or is it **Jo's** breathless life that needs the makeover? And is it too late for either of them?

From PR heaven to paparazzi hell, this wickedly funny novel has all the social tactics you need to survive the twenty-first century.

'A hilarious, witty comedy of modern manners.'

ADELE PARKS, author of *Playing Away*

ISBN 0 00 711906 2